The Author

Susan Duxbury was born in Shipley, West Yorkshire, England, and educated at Salt's Grammar School in the famous model village of Saltaire; then Leeds College of Technology where she gained a diploma in hotel management. After emigrating to New Zealand, she travelled to Australia and met her German-born husband. They lived and worked in the Australian outback, where she began writing her first book.

She is also a successful short-story writer and actively engaged in German/British relations; has two sons and lives with her husband in north Germany.

www.susan-duxbury.com

The Devil's Clown

Susan Duxbury

copyright Susan Duxbury 2014

All rights reserved

Children deserve a better world…

Herstellung und Verlag:
BoD - Books on Demand, Norderstedt
ISBN 978-3-7347-7009-8

Contents

Chapter 1 5

Chapter 2 32

Chapter 3 43

Chapter 4 58

Chapter 5 64

Chapter 6 72

Chapter 7 82

Chapter 8 98

Chapter 9 105

Chapter 10 114

Chapter 11 126

Chapter 12 154

Chapter 13 172

Chapter 14 188

Chapter 15 191

Chapter 16 217

Chapter 17 226

Chapter 1

The telephone rings and the chimes enter her room, breaking the silence and demanding immediate attention.

The girl hurries downstairs taking them two at a time. She must hurry; it is her duty to hurry; it is her duty to lift the receiver and wait for the caller to tell her his name, although she already knows it's a man. She has known it's a man since the time he had coughed. It had been a deep rasping cough; an unfamiliar cough. But the man hadn't spoken – he never does! It's always the same when she waits for the click, the ultimate click telling her the line has gone dead.

Mum will want to know and it's strangely important she gives a satisfactory answer to *all* of Mum's questions.

She remembers the cough

Telephones are monsters. They're no use to anyone, says the clown inside her. You won't find them in a field or in a tent, which is another good reason for Miss Flummi to stay with the circus.

The fanfare of trumpets, the rolling of drums and clashing of cymbals swell in rhythm, growing louder and louder and drowning the monster's penetrating chimes. The ringmaster, proud and magnificent in red with gold trimmings, waits for his cue behind the dining-room curtains. "Ladies and Gentlemen," he announces entering the ménage, flourishing his top hat with a ceremonious bow: "it is my very great pleasure to introduce the one and only…" here, another roll of drums to heighten the excitement, "Miss Flummi, the world's greatest clown!"

The applause is deafening when she enters the ring in the baggy trousers from Miss Dixon's Charity Shop, (who has a soft spot for clowns) and the plastic tomato over her nose, tightened with elastic to prevent it slipping down her chin and becoming entangled with the strings holding the collapsible top-hat (from the joke-shop) perched on her head at an angle.

Later, they'll say what a mighty show it has been – the hilarious clown running in circles and the rubber-doll turning somersaults on the invisible trampoline. She'd go on forever if it wasn't for the monster on the sideboard with its shiny black belly, which invariably puts a stop to it all.

The monster on the sideboard is the root of all evil, says Miss Flummi, the clown. It never speaks when she answers. All she can hear is the sizzling and crackling of sausages frying on an outer-space stove. Gloria says it's an alien who is calling. She'll find out the name if it's the last thing she does.

Beautiful Gloria knows all the answers. She is the friend with the almond-shaped eyes; red lips formed into the permanent smile and cheeks as smooth and rosy as freshly picked peaches. "Don't worry! (says Gloria). After the alien has finished cooking its dinner it will enter the house through the 'phone."

"Enter the house through the 'phone?"

"…inside a balloon," adds Gloria sweetly, like it's an everyday occurrence for the alien to enter the house through the 'phone and inside a balloon.

"Inside a balloon?"

This is all a bit much, Gloria telling lies again! She'll lock her up in the broom-cupboard under the stairs because she knows what it's like being locked inside a broom-cupboard, sitting in the dark and thinking about her lies.

"By the way, Gloria, do aliens cough?" she yells through the broom-cupboard door, but there's no answer. The cough still resounds through her head; a man's cough, not Dad's bark or old 'Biggsie' over the road spitting his lungs onto the pavement, but a hollow echo like it had come up a drainpipe. "Hey! Mr. Alien! – what an evil cough you have!" she'd yelled down the 'phone then squealed in disgust and dropped the receiver, which had jumped up and down like a black shiny fish on a hook. By the time she'd hauled it up again, the line had gone dead.

An alien who calls, day in and day out, but never speaks when she answers! How angry is she about that? – angry for having to leave the ménage to answer the 'phone; angry that the audience has walked out in disgust.

The lounge is now empty and the curtains are closed. The anger remains; it will come and go until she has punished them all. That's the good thing about accidents!

...

The imaginary audience has come alive. It is the artist's nourishment, watching the rapidly growing queue outside the Big Top; watching expectant faces awaiting admission. The acrid smell of animals mingles with fresh sawdust. Hoards of excited children are hushed along by their elders, intent upon finding their places on tiered circles of wooden benches surrounding the ring. When the band strikes up, the familiar sea of bright faces turns in one direction, waiting for the big moment; waiting for the fun. A clown survives on fun and merriment and it is Miss Flummi's job to make people laugh. There's nothing quite like it, wearing the ridiculous clothes, the oversized shoes she keeps in a pillowcase tied up with a bow; being chased around the ring by a horde of impish tiny clowns. She'll escape by leaping onto the trampoline, to the roll of drums and the clashing of cymbals. Up and down she'll go, higher and higher, twisting and twirling, as free as a bird and without a care in the world.

At least that's how it seems – but don't kid yourself! The demons will return, along with the anger. They'll be out for a fling, sooner or later; Gloria with the permanent smile in the white satin dress embroidered with flowers, and the mysterious man who never speaks when she answers; the alien who has stolen her mother.

...

She can't stop the demons and doesn't want to think about her mother; but memories return, bringing the pain.

"Been a good girl today, have you?"

Charmaine dashes about the kitchen having no time to dawdle, emptying the oversized bag of shopping she's collected on her way home.

"Yes Mummy, I answered the 'phone."

"Ah! Who was it?"

"The alien, Mummy!"

"The alien? Now behave yourself! Ten-year-old girls don't tell silly stories! I'll have to wash out your mouth!"

"It's Gloria who says he'll be entering the house through the telephone...says he'll be inside a bubble! But I don't believe everything Gloria says," she adds hurriedly, eager to please, eager to avoid the dreaded soap in her

7

mouth, "so I'll take her into the bathroom and wash out *her* mouth instead, if you like…"

The lopsided shopping-bag succumbs to gravity. A tin of peas crashes onto the tiles, followed by a tin of smoked salmon rolling in diminishing circles. With an impatient sigh, Charmaine grabs her coat from the back of the chair and makes for the door. It bangs behind her with an ear-splitting crash.

Oh Gloria! Beautiful Gloria is upstairs in the bedroom and such a pleasure to look at. She doesn't want to hurt her best friend; doesn't want to wash out her mouth or lock her in the broom-cupboard for telling lies. The girl buries her face in the soft and unbelievably shiny black hair. Together, they watch the car reverse down the drive; hear the screech of tires as it races down the hill and disappears around the corner.

"When mummy returns, she'll be as happy as a lark," says Gloria.

…

She would have stopped answering the 'phone a long time ago if it hadn't been for Carol, Queen of the Classroom. Her sudden friendship with Carol has been proving hard work.

"Pick" – it demands by way of its usual high-pitched chime – "me up!" in two outdrawn clangs; repeating itself with relentless vehemence; commanding the attention she hasn't given it for years, so it seems. She sits on the stairs next to the pile of ironed sheets, her head beneath a towel, hoping the dining-room monster will go away if ignored. That's what you get for swearing eternal friendship, for pricking your finger and mingling your blood with someone like Carol who demands to know why she never answers the 'phone. The familiar sadness alternating with anger descends upon her like a plunging dark cloud. Think hard, she tells herself, think hard! The last time – had it been the last time she'd been suffering from a cold and lost her voice? This time…? What shall she say this time? Will they believe that the bell isn't working? Yes! The bell isn't working. "It's a new system and they can't get the parts." She speaks with astounding sincerity, enough to convince a group of schoolgirls who are no longer kids, but fourteen-years-olds, with formidable auras seeping through their pores.

"What kind of a system?" Big Thora, the hockey-team goalkeeper whose wrath can be gigantic, looms up against her, with the thick orange braid hanging over her shoulder like a rope to be pulled, if one dares.

"It's an American system. We're trying it out for the company that invented it ... still in the experimental stages, so they're sending a technician who'll fix it ... complicated system ... top-secret."

The modest, self-disparaging expression in clear, frank eyes: who can help but believe her? At first, she'd been surprised at her ability to conjure up lies at an opportune moment; but now, she even believes them herself.

The monster is still on the sideboard. It is standing next to Auntie Lucy hugging a teddy-bear, and Dad wearing a blue-checked shirt, smiling their happy smiles from gilt-edged frames, reviving lost memories through sparkling dust that dances about them like pieces of magic. Her hand trembles as she lifts the receiver and listens to the silence. The dark cloud descends, but there's no fooling her now. Having discovered the trampoline, she can escape her demons by flying through the air like a bird.

...

She hasn't changed much! Her reflection is still pale and far too solemn. She tries a smile, like the woman pasted onto the pillar with the sparkling white teeth, perfectly formed and zipped into her mouth, which is something she'll never achieve.

Her eyes are those of a cherub on the church ceiling; big and blue with an innocent look. Light brown curls cover her forehead and a couple of corkscrews dangle around her ears. Twist a glamorous knot! Fix it with a pin at the top of your head and admire the sophisticated look. Admire the athletic figure, flexible limbs, slim, graceful hands and nicely formed boobs. Hey kid! You're not a bad-looker!

"Do you think I'm beautiful, Gloria?"

Gloria, enthroned on the bed, smiles her permanent smile.

But there's no escaping the oppressive silence; no reason for gaiety when nobody answers. Dark clouds herald discomforting thoughts and she shudders when she thinks about her 'birthday-party-fiasco'. The memory of it has been interfering with her sleep and the shame of it has been troubling her mind. There'd been no birthday party after all, because Mum had gone to a meeting and she'd hidden behind the curtains pretending no-one was home.

Memories of Grandma's chocolate cakes are like ghostly children coming out to play!

"Here's your magic wand, Gloria!" The girl props a pencil under Gloria's arm. "I'll tell you my wish. You must keep your promise and make it come true." She takes a deep breath and closes her eyes. "I wish they'd run a fish and chip shop like Mr. Darcy's up the road. Mr Darcy isn't a bit like Dad! Mr. Darcy is an amateur comedian. He calls himself Charlie Chippie and has a fat stomach that hangs over his trousers; wears funny hats and jokes with his customers while frying the chips. Mum has left me the money. I'll go and get some right now!"

People laugh when Charlie Chippie wraps the food in yesterday's newspaper and says he'll be buggered if he'll give them today's paper for nothing. "Yer just a skinny old bugger", someone yells from the back of the queue. Their laughter is contagious; it spreads down the queue and into the street. The girl in the queue thinks it must be a wonderful feeling, making people laugh.

"Skinny old sod – my old man!" agrees Holly Darcy, as thin as a rake and named 'the funny fat fish fryer'. "A pennyworth o' batter! Is that all yer wanting? Ha!"

That's what she'll do, make people laugh! When she has eaten the chips, she'll go to her room, dress up as a clown and make people laugh.

"Don't mope," says Gloria comfortingly. "What's a fish and chip-shop compared to Prince Charming? He'll whisk you away on a beautiful white stallion and you'll live happily ever after."

"Thanks Gloria! You've really cheered me up! Let's look at the album to see what the clown is wearing before I dress up. Let us step into the miraculous world of the incredible! That's what it says on the poster; colourful pageantry and magic which must be seen to be believed! You know that Mum grew up in the circus; don't you?" she reminds Gloria. "Let us imagine the white horses galloping into the ring, tossing their heads covered with bright red plumes. Meanwhile, I'll untie the red bow, open the checked pillowcase and change into Miss Flummi," she hurries to put on the baggy trousers. "Miss Flummi will run around in her oversized shoes and make you laugh 'til your sides ache."

There'll be hell let loose if they discover her in their bedroom with the rose-bud wallpaper and matching curtains; the bedspread in various stages of bloom. She'd rather die than have her bedroom walls covered with dead roses instead of clowns and circuses. In the dressing-table cupboard there's the small, leather-bound album along with the rest of Mum's secrets which she'll look into later before going through Dad's drawer. She removes the album and returns to her room.

"Hey Gloria, look at him! Look at the midget artist performing a handstand and juggling six balls with his feet at the same time." She turns another page to examine the faded photo of her grandmother dressed in a tutu, sparkling in the spotlight as she spins through the air, ready for the somersault before the split landing. One can almost hear the roll of drums, the frenzied applause of the audience.

"I'll let you into a secret, Gloria," she waits a moment to heighten the tension. "Grandma and Granddad Libella were circus-artists; true circus-artists, they were!"

Gloria smiles her permanent smile as the girl tells her story; the story she has told a hundred times before. Some have rolled their eyes in silent entreaty; others have smiled like Gloria, which is decidedly annoying and deserves to be punished because there's nothing to smile about one's grandmother dying in the circus ménage and leaving the ring rolled up in an elephant's trunk. She's heard about Mr. Loosely the plumber, putting his head in the gas oven for not paying his bills, which is a suitable punishment for people like Gloria.

Later, after Sally has switched on the oven and put Gloria inside, she wonders what life will be like without her best friend. She considers the question and then turns off the gas, because there'll be nobody to talk to if Gloria dies.

"Let's join the circus and travel the country with funny clowns and all kinds of artists. Do you feel the magic, Gloria? Look, I can do the splits! I'll clear away your doll's things to make room for the pirouette, and the elegant hand taking the call. Then I'll open up the pillow-case and turn into Miss Flummi again."

The applause has died down and it's time for bed. Tomorrow, Mrs Lightbone will allow her to use the harness and practise the 'Salto Mortale' for the Junior Championship in trampoline jumping. She has no fear of heights and her chances are good, says Mrs. Lightbone who is her trainer.

...

Her mother's steps are hardly audible on the carpeted staircase. They stop outside her door so she closes her eyes, feigning sleep. The sound of breathing draws closer and then fades away. The door closes quietly, ending the intrusion. She opens her eyes, switches on the torch hidden under her pillow and returns to the circus.

The tiger is balancing on a chair next to Grandfather. Grandfather is 'The Great Libella' and walks the tightrope. "Here's the clown, Gloria! Look at the water spouting out of his ears. Don't talk so loud," she whispers, "because Dad is coming upstairs. Don't worry! He never comes into my room!" They admire the pretty lady in a beautiful gown, in the centre of the ring with the horses, and then Grandma Libella once again, hanging single-footed from the trapeze like an open umbrella upside-down.

"Don't be frightened, Gloria!" she whispers as the shouting begins. "They only quarrel at night because they don't speak during the day." Gloria's nightdress needs rearranging but there's no time for trivialities. She hears the telephone ringing; listens to the hurried footsteps descending the stairs and then the soft laughter seeping through the floor, which makes her shiver with anger because there's nothing to laugh about when you're answering the 'phone. Later, footsteps ascend the stairs and enter the room across the landing. Low murmurs get excited; now they are urgent, developing into hectic whispers, swelling in volume, loud and ferocious, and she reckons if she had rose-pattern-paper on her wall, she'd be upset too. Now Mum is screaming and Dad is shouting but there's a remedy for that! Run a fish and chip shop and make people laugh! Don't they know there'll be no more quarrelling if they make people laugh? There's nothing quite like it! – making people laugh.

Such strange noises ...do men cry?

"Pull the blanket over your head Gloria, we'll return to the circus!"

...

There's a nude at the back of Dad's drawer, stretching her limbs on a leopard skin rug and displaying her parts, which is shocking and has been troubling her for weeks. But when she finds the courage for self-examination with the hand mirror wedged between her legs, she concludes it all looks the same, which is of little importance when she reckons the naked woman must have some kind of effect on her father, or he wouldn't be keeping her at the back of his drawer.

Aren't parents the sexless individuals she has thought them to be, whose job in life is to provide for their children?

The pin-up goes around the classroom and circles the yard. Big-eyed screechers yell 'wow' and 'huuuh'. The hardliners, who know a thing or two about sex, who have done the unmentionable deed, experienced the pleasure and excitement (and there's a four-lettered word to go with it), say, "Hey, just look at those boobs – what a couple of hooters! ...you can't shock me with a bit of 'porn' ... where has it come from? ... Sally Foss? I told you she's mad!"

There's a big fat ink-blot over the pink nipple and a corner of the page has been ripped off, which might go unnoticed if she returns the picture to where it belongs, and turns her attention to the photo-album instead. But the photo-album is nowhere to be found and she's in a hurry. What about that chocolate-box with the crinolined lady on the lid? A quick inspection of its contents reveals how much her mother has earned and what she has spent it on. The light blue costume – "exactly right for the office," Mum had said – from 'Le Chic' in the High Street – had cost half of her salary. Dad keeps complaining about money and that's another piece of the puzzle that doesn't fit!

She returns the chocolate box to the cupboard; sits on the bed and closes her eyes. Why is she delving into her parents' lives, considering their lack of interest in hers? How trivial are their secrets? What do they know about her achievements and the success she enjoys with Mrs Lightbone? They only listen with half an ear when she tells them about 'The Nissan Cup', held annually in Switzerland. It might as well be on the moon for all they care – the oldest trampoline competition in the world, for which her trainer has entered her name.

"You'll need to put in plenty of practise," says Mrs Lightbone. "What about weekends?"

…

Looking over the sea of grey berets worn at all conceivable angles according to the disposition of their wearers, she watches Mr. Samson's bent figure appear around the side of the solid granite building; the Victorian edifice of a school built by the far-sighted entrepreneur, set upon educating his mill-worker's children.

Amid a harrowing percussion of barks, groans and hisses, the caretaker selects the longest key from those around his waist, opens the wrought iron gates and jumps to one side as fast as his rheumatic legs will allow. Someone nudges Sally's arm as she enters the school and turns to face the girl behind her, whose eyes move like a preoccupied cat as she opens her blazer, displaying the cigarettes and lighter as proof of her adulthood.

Sally has an image to uphold. One must appear bored when seething within, due to her sudden and unexpected rise in status. A newspaper article covering the renowned 'International Trampoline Competition', has described the local girl taking part, as a dedicated athlete and 'an example to us all'.

Her brow rises condescendingly. "You know I don't smoke, it gives you bad breath."

The haughtiness of the reply hits the mark. Carol's pained tolerance of her is a thing of the past. One simply must keep one's cool, especially when someone like Carol is begging for her company; an unimaginable situation until now.

As they sidle out of the crowd and head across the freshly mown stretch of grass forming a borderline between the street and school grounds, there's a hint of pleading in Carol's voice. "You're still coming to my party next Saturday, aren't you? John Bridges is coming too!"

"Hey! You mean John Bridges the pole-vaulter?"

"And get this! He's been asking after you!" Carol heightens the drama by making her point with a well-manicured finger.

She'll have to pull herself together. Getting excited about John Bridges doesn't fit the image; a Mona Lisa smile is the thing. "I faintly recall him asking me how fast I can run the two hundred meters. Of course, I told him it was none of his business."

Another milk-curdling shriek cuts the air. "I don't believe it!" Carol doubles with laughter and shakes her head in mock disbelief. Then she suddenly has an idea. "You can stay the night. Lots of people stay the night when I throw a party and my people are off playing golf. Just say the word and I'll get Jenkins to organise a bed." She looks at Sally enquiringly. "Don't mind sleeping with Josie, do you? Her parents are going to Cannes for the film festival, so she'll be staying over too. By the way, did your people make a fuss about you skipping your training?"

"Mum made a fuss, but I managed to persuade her." Sally concentrates on keeping the haughty expression.

"I should think so! You're seventeen, honey, so don't take shit from your parents! If your mother gets narky, tell her to piss off!"

Tell Mum to piss off...? "Mum never interferes these days," she lies, recalling the latest outburst which had been the worst of them all. As usual, she had greatly despised herself for upsetting her mother, and as always, she had been at fault for messing things up. Somehow, she can't stop messing things up and wishes she wasn't so thick. Her stomach is squirming; the dull pain has returned and she can't make out where it comes from.

No! She hadn't thought they were spending money on extra coaching for nothing!

What will Mrs Lightbone say if she goes to a party, after all the hard work getting her fit for the competition? It doesn't bear thinking about!

You should be ashamed of yourself! Tell me you're ashamed of yourself before I wipe that silly expression off your face with the back of my hand!

"*I'm ashamed of myself!*"

"*Don't you ever dare to be ungrateful again, do you hear?*"

"*Yes Mummy, please don't get mad, Mummy!*"

"You're right Carol," says the girl. The tightness in her stomach has reached her throat. She can't cry now, despite tears waiting to be spilled. "If she gets narky, I'll tell her to shut her blower and keep it shut," she announces, trying to sound confident.

It works! Being bold and dynamic gets rid of the tears. She fingers the letter in her pocket, addressed to Mrs Lightbone. Copying Mum's signature, her slanting italics, had been like copying a Rembrandt.

"We can go back to school after break –think up some shit as an excuse!" says Carol as they walk past a building-site. She removes her light grey uniform beret, twirls it suggestively around her finger and then shakes an abundance of blonde tresses for the benefit of the bricklayers, who look around meaningfully and pose for the whistles.

The avenue bordering the playing fields, leads past the old church with the overgrown graveyard and up to the gently sloping lawns of the memorial park. There, the wealthy patriarch reigns from the granite pillar where thousands of workers, dead and forgotten, once put him. Propped against his weathered stone feet is a wreath wrapped in lanky lengths of faded yellow ribbon. The park is almost deserted at this time of the morning, apart from a distant dog-owner with two golden retrievers, chasing a ball and barking excitedly.

With an air of nonchalance, Carol removes a couple of cigarettes from her inside pocket: lights them, inhales deeply, then exhales meaningfully before handing one to Sally, who knows she must smoke it to the butt or her life won't be worth living despite the oncoming waves of nausea. But taking deep breaths doesn't do the trick and neither does swallowing (which had helped at the dentist). She can't afford to be weak, not even now that she's behind a nearby rhododendron bush, losing the battle to keep down her breakfast.

How can I keep my cool, when my skirt and shoes are covered with spew?

For God's sake! - do the best you can, with the tiny pool of brackish water from the defective fountain, the dehydrated Cupid surrendering his spout. Why don't these fountains work when they're needed?

"I'm going home!" she announces miserably. Hasn't she made a horrific fool of herself? Dare she beg Carol to keep it a secret? Oh Jesus! How she stinks! It's the mouldering stench of brackish water mingled with the sour odour of vomit and she'd rather make a run for it without further ado. "I'm going home!" she repeats. "Tell Mrs Lightbone I was sick on my way to the gym."

Carol remains seated on the memorial steps next to the wreath, calmly pulling at her butt. Her features are sharp; eyebrows plucked into permanent surprise. Her new best friend is a bore, but wait and see! There'll be enough opportunity to liven her up.

...

On a top-deck back-seat of an almost empty bus, the short journey home is uneventful, apart from the half-stoned tramp (is he a clown?) in a ragged coat and bowler hat, who has fallen asleep, now that the conductor has told him to behave himself or he'll be feeling his arse on the pavement.

There's no place like home when you're sick, even though the nausea has gone, walking down the road and in the fresh air. Enlightened by the pleasant relief of sudden recuperation, she steps onto the stone wall in front of a house. It is time for her entrée into the ménage; time for the artiste to return to the ring wearing a royal-blue robe dotted with sequins; to step gracefully along the (stone) wall dividing the ménage from the audience. Her feather-plumed headdress waves majestically as she spreads her arms, slowly and gracefully, to dance towards hyacinths and daffodils, around the silver Mercedes limousine parked at the side of the road. An imaginary roll of drums announces she'll mount the stone steps. The invisible audience holds its breath as she produces a key from the chain around her neck and unlocks the door. The well-worn satchel slips from her shoulders. The door closes with the twist of an elbow – a well-practiced trick – accomplished a thousand times already, with the exact amount of pressure. It clicks softly, avoiding the rattling of glass panes when she pushes too hard; nor will it re-open if caught in the wind. Perfect! The carpeted hallway is dark and cool, due to doors being closed to keep the rooms warm. The faint odour of Dad's 'take-away Bengali curried chicken' from the previous evening reminds her she's hungry.

I'll put my stinking clothes in the washing-machine and clean my shoes before going upstairs to see Gloria. She stops to listen. Is it the rustling of paper she can hear? *There's someone in the lounge, moving about in an extraordinary manner and making weird noises, like a marathon-runner...Johnston's house was burgled last week. Now it's our turn! Oh God! I'm on my own with a burglar in the house!*

She looks around wildly, thinking he must have seen her coming up the path; heard her unlocking the door.

He'll be out to kill me! I'd better get out as fast as I can!

Wait! Is it Mum's voice I can hear? Thank heaven it's only Mum! What a relief! Thank goodness you're here, Mum...! I need looking after! I've been sick!

She listens, intent upon regaining control over her breathing before calling her mother, who will open the door with a welcoming smile. She is ready to be spoilt, to be looked after and cared for because that's what happens when you're ill. How pleasant it will be, lying on the sofa, warm and safe beneath a blanket. Mum will run backwards and forwards with a pile of comics and chicken soup – Grandma Foss' remedy against bad colds and stomach-ache.

A sudden premonition prevents her from opening the door. Is it the long low wail ending in a high-pitched giggle or the crescendo of rustling paper? Definitely not Mum turning magazine pages. Is something wrong? She hears the man's voice... not Dad's voice! Dad isn't home – there's no bike propped against the garage wall – no take-away meal in the kitchen. Is Mum in the lounge with a strange man? What is she doing? Where are the answers?

The man coughs. She has heard that cough over the 'phone, and then a thousand times in her dreams. She has seen the alien, a face like a frog with pointed ears for catching signals, entering the house through the 'phone, inside a bubble, which is ridiculous and impossible.

Does he look like a frog? Is the frog puffing and panting like a long-distance runner? Why is Mum moaning? Is her stomach-upset too? Perhaps she has hurt herself and is helpless. Mum has never moaned like that. Should she get help? Dare she look through the keyhole?

An eye focuses on the head of light brown hair; long and straight, cut to the chin. A man...and naked...! She has never seen a naked man in such a position because Dad always covers his 'parts' with a towel. She'll have to find the reason; it is imperative that she finds out why the alien is on top of her mother, bending over her wide opened legs and putting his mouth on the most private of places. The nausea returns. Her stomach is empty. She retches silently.

Mum seems to be enjoying herself! Yes! Mum is definitely enjoying herself, like she's never enjoyed herself before! The noise is enough to awake the dead, like Grandma Foss used to say, whom she still hasn't forgiven for dying. She'll get down on her knees and ask Lord Jesus to put everything right. That's what she'll do! Like Grandma Foss said – no need for a mite like yourself to be worrying your head over the silly things that grown-ups do. *Before the Lord Jesus puts everything right, she'll take a last look.* The eye focuses on her mother lying on the couch, gazing at the ceiling like the naked lady at the back of Dad's drawer. The rhythmic rustling of the newspaper is gathering speed, indicating passion reaching its climax.

White bodies move in ecstasy on the brown velvet couch, up and down, up and down, rhythmically, faster and faster, groaning, panting. The screams! Terrible screams make her tremble with fear! The door is the flat brown monster; the impenetrable monster. It separates her from her mother. The alien has entered the house and he'll take her away.

Go on! Have another look and don't be a simpleton any longer!

They're doing it lying down. Carol says she did it with Jimmy Becks, standing up and propped against a wall. Until then, she had always thought they did it like dogs. Once more, the eye penetrating the morbid magnet of the keyhole focuses the woman on the couch and melting into the alien's kisses. The girl turns away, unaware of the warmth leaving her body. She stares at the carpet. The colours are ghastly and dingy. The vintage ship, the Christmas-present she'd painted, is hideous and tasteless; they hadn't thanked her as effusively as she'd expected and it's hanging lop-sided, almost begging to be removed. With the picture under her arm she leaves the house as silently as she had entered, thinking how contaminated and filthy the place is... *grey patterns and whirling images replace pale-skinned frogs on brown-velvet couches...*

The girl marches down the road to the canal, past neighbouring houses and the milkman pulling the trolley filled with empty bottles, clattering in crates as he returns from his round. He shouts something at her, and then shrugs indifferently at the uncharacteristic lack of response; raises his eyebrows at the uncanny gait; the mechanized robot-like strides. She crosses the ancient wooden swing-bridge at the bottom of the hill; a relic of a bygone era, when goods and mill produce were transported by barge. After a few yards along the embankment, the girl suddenly stops as though examining her reflection in the dark, murky water.

The long-distance runner rounds the grimy walls of the derelict factory and sees the girl. He is sure she is one of those freaks attracted to the canal embankment like flies around shit. He's seen them praying to the sun and dancing along the old towpath with enlightened expressions on their faces. This girl is standing like a statue and holding a framed picture over her head; disposing of rubbish in an unconventional manner no doubt, like the three-piece-suite that had been blocking the barges.

She throws the picture into the canal and he feels like applauding; couldn't have thrown it further himself! It won't be likely to sink for a while – floating on piles of debris hemmed in by a log. A stone from the dry-wall of the neighbouring field follows the picture with a splash. Aha! Another mad woman pulling down walls! Heavy ripples spread across murky water, forming a circle of miniature waves. By the time he reaches the girl, the picture has gone.

…

She's got the punishment she deserves for looking through keyholes. Strange, how the suffering stops when one's head has grown numb from the pain. Pain is an old friend. It comes and goes. Her steps are heavy and cumbersome. She is no longer the trampoline artist who flies through the air; neither is she the clown who'll make people laugh. Images fade, switched off by an invisible hand.

Now she has arrived at the bus station. *So many people, but no-one to help me! How can I explain the predicament I'm in? Should I ask queuing passengers if they've had sex with the alien? It's something to be considered! On second thoughts, they'll say I'm a creep asking provocative questions; call the police and have me locked up.*

The intense odour of snack-bar frying distracts her attention and she retches once more behind a wall. Before commencing her journey to the next lamp-post, she removes the newspaper from a bin, which will clean her as well as anything else. *Take a look at the headlines! And while reading the newspaper, enjoy the cosy smell of freshly baked bread, reminding me of happy evenings with Grandma Foss in her kitchen. It fills my stomach and makes me feel better. Mum says they use extract from beetles to colour pink icing, decorating these buns in the bakery window. Oh! I'd almost forgotten! But Mum can't be trusted for the truth, or anything else for that matter.*

"I'll have a sticky-bun please!"

The middle-aged woman behind the bakery-counter has almost finished serving the stiff-looking matron with the pillar-box hat, but there's still plenty of gossip to be spread; a detailed account of her daughter's wedding, who has married into money and thrown in her job. With half an ear she registers the girl's order, hands over the bag and holds out her hand, clicking her tongue impatiently while the girl searches her pockets and finally hands over the money.

Standing on the pavement outside the shop, Sally eats the bun and wipes her hands on the newspaper. Her fingers are still sticky, black and streaky from printer's ink and she wants to go home.

Tired workers with expressionless faces don't give the girl as much as a glance as she squeezes onto the bus, hangs onto the strap and alights outside the pseudo antique-shop where two rickety chairs on the pavement are meant to attract buyers.

Nothing has changed. The day has been uneventful, other than the rancid sticky-bun which has upset my stomach and caused me to vomit. It is definitely the bun and nothing else, which has made me feel ill!

The house is empty and silent, as always.

Go into the bathroom, clean yourself and come out again. Gloria is waiting!

She disposes of the clothes still soiled with vomit. She would have done it earlier but something prevented her from changing her clothes and she'll be darned if she can remember what it was. And her satchel is still in the hallway. Had she forgotten to take it to school? There she is! Gloria enthroned on the pillow waiting to ask the question – always the same question – day after day – week after week. "*Did you have a nice day at school?*"

"I didn't go to school!" She answers impatiently.

"You didn't go to school? Why not?"

Gloria's facial expression never changes and the lackadaisical attitude is getting on Sally's nerves. Does she detect a slight note of disinterest in her friend's voice? She could swear that Gloria is not the slightest bit interested in her well-being and besides, she has been a great disappointment just lately. She'll never forgive Gloria for allowing the alien inside the house. He had stolen her mother. Nobody should be allowed to steal someone's mother!

"Never mind, Gloria! Tell me what has happened today!"

Gloria is smiling but her eyes are empty. Traitor's eyes are always empty. "Gloria! Oh Gloria! Why did you remain on your throne while he contaminated the house? Why did you let him take Mum?" Now she is shouting, almost screaming. "You should have stopped him, Gloria. You'll have to be punished."

A sudden blow and there is a loud thud – such is the force of Gloria's removal from the throne which has been hers for a decade. The half-open mouth smiles at her from the carpet, but the row of white pearly teeth (which Sally has always admired) has disappeared somewhere inside, leaving a dark toothless gap. A heavy foot lands on her head and splits it open, revealing an eye. Another heavy foot transforms the eye into a bullet. It ricochets against the door and into a corner. The other cheek crumbles beneath a marble trinket-box and a second eye shoots out.

The executioner, having destroyed the demon, performs the tribal dance; stamping in circles and jumping about until the head is a mere pile of crumbs. She brushes them into a dustpan, together with the black shiny hair tied in a pink satin ribbon which has lost its hold on the decapitated doll's body, and hurries downstairs to the garden, complaining hysterically about unfaithful friends. A puzzled neighbour, attracted by the shouting and screaming, watches the bundle of rags catapulting through the air at great speed, watches it crash against the garage and fall into the open dustbin upon a bed of vacuum-cleaner dust.

"Hello my love, alright?"

She closes Gloria's coffin and stands at the gate on the back lawn, impassively observing her father's attempt at accessing the garage. He doesn't request help and she offers no assistance either, as he balances his take-away-supper on his bike, wrapped in the familiar maritime flair of 'Holly's Haddock and Charlie's Chippies'.

"Yes, Dad!"

"That's good!" he remarks absent-mindedly, having decided to leave the task of opening the garage until later. He props his bike against the wall next to the roll of chicken wire, which has been there as long as she can remember.

The smell of fish and chips causes another turn of her stomach.

"Got stuck behind a bloody manure carrier!" Matthew is mildly annoyed, which is as angry as he'll get. Running his bath is a ritual; the indispensable luxury of removing the strains of a factory floor always succeeds in lightening his mood. He sinks into the hot soapy suds. Tension leaves his body together with the profanities of being a shop-steward. Keeping peace among workers is a job he truly hates, but successfully conceals; his calmness being mistaken for the strength of character he doesn't possess.

The fumes of mid-city traffic ooze from his clothes, making her dizzy as she sits on the stairs, head between her knees; an often practiced remedy against fainting at school after standing too long during morning assembly. The hallway darkens in the evening light and her father emerges from the bathroom, freshly scrubbed. The clean white vest barely covers his large, pelty frame and his short cropped hair is wet and spiky.

He faces her questioningly. "Why are you sitting on the stairway alone in the dark?" Without waiting for an answer – hunger being stronger than curiosity – his features relax as he remembers his supper and makes for the kitchen. "Mmmm! Want some?" He grabs a tea-towel from the back of the chair and reaches into the oven.

"No thanks, Dad!" The familiar smell of fish and chips spread through the house, mingling with the filthy aura of invisible contamination. Either she'll purify her room, or kill herself. She decides on cleaning her room.

"Go on! Have a few chippies then!"

"No thanks, Dad!"

The telephone rings. She can hardly bear the sound of it ringing, covers her ears and flees up the stairs to her room.

"Answer the phone, will you?"

"No, Dad!" she yells from the top of the stairs.

What the hell is the matter with the girl? His chippies'll get cold. He'll have to put them back in the oven if she doesn't answer that 'phone. And who could be ringing at this time of evening? Charmaine? Might she need him for a change? No such bloody luck! You'd think he'd got the pest! That posh book-keeping-job isn't doing her any good; no good at all... and after all that night-school studying! A bloody waste of time – that's what it was – bloody waste of time! Still grumbling under his breath he leaves the kitchen to answer the 'phone and returns five minutes later. "That was your Uncle Mike, wanting to know if I'll give them a hand when they move up to Dale Road," he yells up the stairs, trying to sound cheerful and adds, "You can come down again! The 'phone won't bite!"

She couldn't care less if Uncle Mike moves into Buckingham Palace! Uncle Mike, who'll put his fist in a face at the shake of a leg, with Auntie Lily and three gregarious cousins in Buckingham Palace...now that *is* something to think about! For a while, it even succeeds in distracting her attention.

Matthew opens the newspaper, but closes it again. "When was the last time we ate together?" he looks at his daughter questioningly. "It's not healthy to stuff yourself with junk food!" His bushy eyebrows draw into the frown of sudden revelation and a row of deepening rifts reach his cropped hair, giving him the air of a chastising monk.

"Don't know, Dad!"

"Well, it's not healthy...!" his voice trails off as his mind delves into faded memories. "When I was a kid, we took our meals together – all ten of us! I'll tell yer something! Nobody was allowed to start eating until we were all sitting, freshly combed an' scrubbed, after your Granddad Foss had said grace, bless his soul. Now then! What d'ya think about that?"

"Don't know, Dad!"

"Ah well! That was a long time ago! Nowadays, women don't cook like they used to. Mind you, she's a hard working woman, is your mother; very hard working indeed!"

The brown velvet couch enters the corner of her eye and ghastly visions appear. For a moment, she is tempted to believe she has imagined the rhythmic rustle of newspaper, the deep rasping cough, the alien's body on her mother...in the lounge...on the brown velvet settee...legs open wide...oh my God!

She'll never sit on that brown velvet settee again; not for all the money in the world!

"Put on the telly lass, will ya!"

"I'm not going into the lounge, Dad!"

There is a short, pregnant silence and newspaper rustles as he peers over the edge. The sound of rustling paper reminds her of something ... she doesn't want to think about it...please God, not again...!

"Why not?"

Her voice is almost panicking. "You should get rid of that pile of newspapers, Dad! At least you shouldn't be keeping them next to your chair."

"Why should I do a thing like that?" Matthew's voice projects the incredibility of the request. "I haven't read them all yet."

"They're contaminated, Dad!"

"I beg your pardon!"

"Filthy! They're filthy and I hate them...do you understand, Dad? I hate them!"

Now she has burst into tears, leaving him bewildered; thinking the girl must be under some kind of stress! Too much training – these gymnastics and competitions are going to her head! He has lost count of the competitions she has won, although there are plenty of trophies in the cabinet to show for it! Charmaine says they take up too much space! But it *does* keep her occupied and she obviously enjoys it. What's the name of her trainer? Mrs Lightbone? Now that's the right name for a gymnastic teacher. She seems to think our daughter has talent, or she wouldn't be ferrying her about the country to all these events!

"Anything good on the telly tonight?" he asks, eager to change the subject, yearning for a moment of peace. He's had enough unpleasantness to cope with just recently, since they've cut the tea break at work. And now, to crown it all, his daughter is grinding him down. That's adolescents for you! Get too damned big for their boots and start thinking selfishly. If there's any more trouble he'll hand in his notice – that's what he'll do! – hand in his bloody notice, and Willy Armsley can call the men off on a half-hour strike for the sake of three hours of non-permitted overtime, right up 'til doomsday if he feels like it. Jesus Christ and Holy Mary Mother of God! Too much for a man who wants nothing but a bit of peace and quiet and gets a hysterical daughter instead! He examines the television-programme. 'The Morecambe and Wise Show' at nine fifteen! That's what a man needs – a good laugh and a bit of slapstick!

"Don't know Dad! I have a lot of work to do."

Thank God her voice sounds normal again. Best to ignore these occasional tantrums, he thinks, and remarks absentmindedly, "Homework, eh?"

"Sort of! I need to do some washing and clean my room."

"That's my girl!" He closes the newspaper and takes it into the lounge, to the armchair in which he'll fall asleep within the hour. There's the sound of water running into a bucket; the squeaking of the cupboard door beneath the stairs. It needs oiling but he hasn't had time! Who bloody cares...?

It is vital her room be kept clean! There's no time to be wasted, although one can't actually see the alien's filth, which is spreading through the house like an invisible shroud. Her eagerness to clean has released surplus energy; it enlightens her mood and generates excitement. Could that be the solution? Cleaning her surroundings; getting rid of dark thoughts and troublesome visions?

"Alright my love?" Her father's voice and the click of the gas fire; spurts of laughter and applause, suggest he'll be otherwise occupied before falling asleep.

Isn't this relieving... so exhilarating! Why haven't I done this before? Washing, wiping and dusting – cleaning the paintwork; polishing my dressing table...self-purification...exciting! It's going right through my body...aaah!

How could she guess that chasing the vacuum cleaner could bring such joy? It cracks explosively as Gloria's eye sucks into the tube. Gloria – gone forever!

Don't forget the striped bed-cover and matching curtains! Take them downstairs to the machine! Ah – the joy of it all! Is this like sex? Sit on the bed and keep calm!

But she can't sit for long! Dressing-table trinkets, the bracelet and necklace from Auntie Joan drop into the bucket of hot soapy suds. They are clean and shining when polished with a towel. She returns them to the shell-covered trinket-box; admires them gleaming in the light. Her gaze wanders towards a flimsy hammock of cobweb stretching across a corner of the room and stirring in the draught. Soon, it will be sucked into the cleaner and gone forever.

Further examination of the ceiling makes her feel dizzy. Get on with the job! There's no time for dizziness!

The tumbler is signalling – the washing is dry! Hurry downstairs, two at a time if you please! It's a gas, gas, gas! I'm a witch, witch, witch! - smoothing my bed with my broomstick!

Someone is climbing the stairs, bringing more filth and invading her purity. Nobody can enter her room and destroy the perfection; the perfection of decontamination, with the exception of a few minor blemishes still to be dealt with.

"Hello, love! Have you been busy?"

"Yes, Mum!" The girl remains motionless.

"Have you been cleaning your room?"

"Yes, Mum!"

"...at this time of night?" Her mother steps over the broom, carefully keeping her balance in the elegant black-suede stilettos she wears at the office.

"Stay where you are, Mum!" The tone of voice, the unexpected sharpness of command, directed at the glamorous figure wearing a royal blue angora pullover and black pencil-skirt, matching the shoes, shocks for a moment.

"Why can't I come in, dear?"

"I've just dropped one of those mother-of-pearl earrings you bought me for Christmas. Perhaps you might tread on it."

"Oh! I see!" Charmaine fixes her gaze on the floor. "I've been attending a meeting. The bank requested a preliminary balance from one of my clients, which is why I'm late." Words gush into an awkward silence. "Are you coming down for a cup of tea?"

"As soon as I've found my earring, Mum."

...

Charmaine bangs the heavy tray onto the tiled coffee-table. Matthew snorts and his head jolts from the threadbare cushion which immediately slips down his back. She finds a morbid source of enjoyment, watching him wake with a jerk, although has never succeeded in making him angry, however much she tries. His lack of aggression has deepened her loathing. She twitches her lips, posing the question she has repeatedly asked herself over the years.

Why on earth had she married him? Couldn't she have escaped from the circus and the father she still loathes, on her own?

The sound of a door sliding open still makes her shudder. She hates sliding doors! They remind her of her childhood, and the dividing door in the caravan, slowly opening. She remembers looking through half-open eyes at the dark silhouette watching her; then soft footsteps approaching her bed and she'd felt his breath on her cheek. Why had he knelt at her bedside? Why had he spoken to her in this unfamiliar tone, telling her she was his beautiful princess and must do what her mother once did, bless her soul and may she rest in peace. She can still hear the voice she'd once hated; strange and alarmingly heavy with passion.

"That's how things have to be done to make your daddy happy, both at home and in the ménage. Give me a kiss and leave your hands where I'm guiding them. Now move them ever so slightly like I've taught you."

The silence had been broken by the gasping and shaking. Would it soon stop? Please God, let it stop! She'd put her dirty hand beneath the bedclothes and pretended it had never happened because 'The High and Mighty Don Libella' had a reputation to keep. There's no safety-net for Don Libella! Only a run-of-the-mill performer uses a safety net, he used to say, that bullying father of hers who'd forced her limbs into unnatural positions. Such a shame she hadn't inherited her mother's suppleness.

She'd hated her father; hated the circus!

Mouth-corners droop in an expression of distaste as she watches Matthew rub his eyes and peer through the dust which permanently clogs them. Why doesn't he get them tested? Such a coward! Hasn't he put off the ultimate deed, a thousand times already?

"Had a good day, love?"

Strange – she reflects – that he craves peaceful conversation despite being woken with a jolt, guaranteed to enrage the most placid of characters. "Yes, thanks!" she replies; rids herself of the tray and with an exasperated sigh, turns down the television volume and pours two mugs of tea. Her daughter tiptoes into the room and she thinks how irritating the girl can be, standing in the middle of the room, sipping her tea as though she doesn't belong. Why can't she sit down?

Charmaine, addressing no-one in particular, announces she'll be taking the car to the garage.

"What's the matter with it?" Matthew is suddenly attentive.

"There's something wrong with the cooling system – needs a new radiator!"

Matthew thinks, of course they'll tell her she needs a new radiator! Soon, they'll tell her she needs a new car, and that's where the money will go! What he doesn't know about car radiators isn't worth knowing. He subdues his growing frustration. "Why don't you let me have a look at it?" he suggests almost too calmly, "might be just a simple welding job."

"The last time you looked at *my* car," she emphasises – "it stood outside the garage for a whole month! Sorry, Matthew! I just can't bear to go through that again," answers his wife and sighs, looking pained. There's an uncomfortable silence as she examines her nails, turning her hands up to the light. She considers a wash and set as well as a hairdresser's manicure, to be grooming essentials for keeping competition at bay – and there's plenty of competition at the office! Pretty young typists, but shallow, of course, chosen for their beauty rather than efficiency, no doubt! She searches the back of her hands for the unsightly blemishes of coming age, and is suddenly aware of her daughter. "Come on, dear! Sit next to me!" She pats the brown velvet cushion.

Sit there, next to this obnoxious woman who happens to be my mother and does dirty things with strange men, on this very same brown velvet settee, in a room void of cleanliness and purity, polluted beyond redemption? I'd rather die! The girl moves her weight from one foot to the other, stares at her mother like she's staring at a stranger. "I haven't finished my homework," she whispers, backing out of the room.

Charmaine shrugs and idly contemplates her husband; head thrown back and mouth wide open; an empty beer can in one hand and the racing results in the other. Day for day, ten long years, she has been leaving her lover (the love of her life) in their camping-site hideaway to return to this mausoleum. Her eyes wander over the yellowing wallpaper loosening in the corner; the floral carpet, threadbare at the door. Who cares? When Sally leaves home, she'll leave too! The 'phone rings and Matthew opens an eye. "Don't bother, I'll answer it!" Charmaine announces hurriedly.

Now her face is no longer tense. Her cheeks are flushed and the sparkle in her eyes reveals she is a woman in love. She closes the dining-room door and sits cross-legged on the carpet. The telephone receiver is wedged between shoulder and cheek because she needs her hands for the excitement...

Chapter 2

On second thoughts and after a final, furtive inspection in the full-length mirror, Sally chooses the sexy off-the-shoulder dress. There'll be no hiding *her* light under a bushel this time! Those guys will flutter around her like moths around a flame, when she makes her entrance in Mum's Caribbean-style see-through beach dress over the pink bikini. Clandestine cupboard and drawer rummaging-sessions have revealed these sexy and no doubt expensive beach-clothes in the corner of Mum's wardrobe, which won't be missed for a couple of days because as far as she knows, Mum's going nowhere, at least not yet! Attempting to subdue her excitement, she folds them into her bag and hurries downstairs.

"Isn't Mrs Lightbone picking you up?" Her mother, still wearing the lilac cashmere twin-set, looks unusually concerned, standing to attention like a sentry in the hallway beneath the square of white wallpaper, which makes the girl wonder if they haven't noticed the picture is missing and what they would say if they knew it was at the bottom of the canal among a pile of debris and she'll never give them a present again, not if they get down on their knees and beg her to paint one, which they never would anyhow!

"She's picking me up at the top of the road."

Charmaine relaxes, convinced she has made the right decision by keeping her daughter away from temptation. Sally isn't cut out for parties. If anyone should be going to rich people's houses, it should be herself. One must stake the priorities according to one's achievements. What could be better for Sally, than long hours of training and weekend competitions with a trainer who'll pick her up and drive her home?

But...! ...and here she raises the imaginary finger – one must be consistent. The silly girl is still sulking, but that can't be helped! She pecks a kiss on an impassive cheek.

"Bye love!" Her father has turned down the television; his voice comes from the depths of his chair. It follows her as she leaves the house and is still with her as she makes her way to the bus-stop at the top of the road. She doesn't want to think about her father: doesn't want to think about having deceived her trainer, either. Occasionally, she has considered sharing her secret with Mrs Lightbone and wonders what her trainer would say about the alien stealing her mother. It's all very well telling your secrets to someone you can trust, if you're sure they won't tell you to stop telling lies (which she is sure Mrs Lightbone would never do, but one can never tell). She has tried to get herself talking; opened her mouth but nothing has come out. Perhaps she should retrace her steps and go home; or better still, return to the circus. She'll soon feel better if she returns to the circus.

She returns to the circus on the top deck of the bus, where the imaginary audience frenetically applauds the fantasy trampoline performance: the jumps, swirls, backdrops and somersaults, still going on in her mind when Thora's father stops the car outside the bus-station.

There's a sense of achievement, climbing into a car and squeezing into the back with her friends. It hasn't been easy, gaining admission to the group with whom she has been attempting to form friendships but without much success, until becoming 'junior champion in trampoline jumping'.

"What's your present?" enquires Thora, the giant no-nonsense princess who'll get to the point without waiting. A Cilla Black bob has replaced the red plait, suitably back-combed in the form of a knight's helmet; shiny and lacquered into place. Sally, intent upon remaining cool, takes the David Bowie LP out of her bag which has cost the best part of two-week's pocket-money because Carol says that life is a bore without Bowie.

The car brakes at the traffic-lights and Thora's dad yells he's sorry because Joan is wailing, having got herself into a drama. Applying lipstick is a hazardous job in a braking car and her mouth has turned into a letter-box slit. Sally opens her bag for a tissue. The bright pink, pool-party bikini comes to light and causes a minor sensation.

"I'm too fat for a bikini," Thora moans despondently, but soon has second thoughts and her face lightens up. "Hey! Chris Mackie and Norm Walton are bringing the other guys from the band, so at least we'll be having decent music. Chris is an absolute genius on the drums. Joan fancies him!"

"Don't let on!" Joan yells hysterically, pushing aside her 'mouth' problems.

The car turns off the main road and heads towards the part of town where shady trees and well-placed shrubs conceal luxurious homes. Thora's father has his misgivings. Who can compete with a set-up like this? 'Upper class' parties are out of a working-class man's depth, he reflects, watching their hesitant steps up the tree-lined drive towards gothic-styled pillars, into the wondrous world of the wealthy.

An elderly uniformed maid opens the heavy oak door and utters a professional greeting. What might have been a smile flits across her smug features. "Would the ladies please leave their luggage in the hall, all you need are your bathers!" She speaks in the distant tone of the long-suffering; being the 'remote-control system' and 'inconspicuous eye' in cases of irregularities. "Phone the golf club!" they've told her.

It's a fine way of keeping an eye on one's teenage daughters' nocturnal comings and goings, she complains to her niece, who invites her for Sunday lunch, once a week after church.

The maid gestures half-heartedly towards the oak-panelled alcove, indicating where they should leave their bags. "Plenty of towels around the pool; no need to start rummaging in your bags!" she informs them, economical in word, unwilling to bother with teenage trivialities.

Three girls follow the maid along the thickly carpeted hallway and down a flight of white marble steps covered by a length of crimson carpet, lending the palatial touch to an otherwise conservative interior. Each cabin has a white marble toilet, shower and sink; a treasure-trove of golden fixtures, porcelain dishes, matching tissue holders and expensive lotions. Who has seen anything like it? Who has seen such luxury before? Forget your tarnished taps; cracked bathtubs, chipped tiles and permanently clogged flow-pipes!

Fluffy white towels are an ideal requisite for the 'nonchalant look' when one is unaccustomed to exposing one's body. Decently wrapped and in suitable pose, they stand in a group, wondering how to deal with such illustrious surroundings. Have they ever seen anything like it before, intricate tiled patterns on the wall, and a pool surrounded by marble columns? A Donny Osmond-double chases a squealing beauty, sporting the flowing mane of a Farrah Fawcett hairdo. Others lounge on striped deck-chairs, or move to the sound of reggae music which dominates the scene through a couple of loudspeakers placed on the walls at each end of the pool.

"Want some grass?" A young guy, suspiciously thin and suffering from acne, lights up a joint and passes it around. Sally is reminded, with an unpleasant jolt, of her faux-pas with the cigarette and hopes Carol won't yell about her spewing behind a rhododendron-bush in the park. Thora takes a drag and looks like she's climbing an imaginary mountain while Sally, eager to avoid repetition of previous dramas, dives head first into the pool. It is soothing and silent beneath the commotion.

The perfect dive, with hardly a splash, has aroused competition. Who can catch the girl in the bright pink bikini? The champion pole-vaulter watches her surface and crawls down the pool after his prey.

"Come on, you guys; eat your ice-cream!" There's nothing like ice-cream tortes and dishes of fruit for getting them out of the water. Carol strikes a casual pose against a white clothed table. Things are going to plan, but competition is tough. There's no denying that Sally looks gorgeous in that bright pink bikini and admiring glances haven't escaped her attention. An athletic champion as one's best-friend is losing its charms and keeping oneself in the centre of things is proving hard work. Roll on the 'Bloody Mary's', the 'Manhattan Coolers' - that's when the *real* fun begins! The pole-vaulter has a reputation to keep. Bets have been placed as to how long it will take after Sally has drunk those treacherous cocktails. They've got it all arranged; the lights; the music, slow and romantic. He'll begin with the compliments. She'll behave like a lamb. John Bridges has screwed them all, until now.

...

At last, the 'phone! The sound of it ringing is music in her ears. There's nothing more exhilarating than ironing while Jeff whispers things in her ear over the 'phone. He drives her mad, telling her which parts of her body he'll be examining with his tongue. Oh God! She can hardly bear it.

She'll have to pull herself together. The last time he went on like that, the room had filled with smoke and there'd been a hole in the pillowcase. She'd almost panicked, opened the window and closed the door less Matthew should awake and yell for the fire-brigade.

Darling Jeff! He has no sexual inhibitions! Tucked away in a corner of their long-lease caravan, there's an unashamed variety of erotic techniques which have induced her to overcome her prudery and got her well and truly hooked. Now her life centres on their meetings; she yearns for the excitement, the exotic pleasure of his hands slowly moving over her body and the mind-busting sensation of sweet helplessness.

Her lover is her employer, but who cares? There's been no talk of marriage, although circumstances are changing and she wonders how he'll react when the inevitable happens and her marriage breaks up. Will he take her in his arms? Will he comfort her for the miserable life she has led until now? Does he know about the suffering caused by this uncaring and neglectful husband of hers? Will he leave no stone unturned to make her happy? She can't live without him. Unyielding bliss is engraved upon her soul. In her fantasy, she breathes, eats and sleeps with her lover as she lies next to Matthew, tossing and turning, suppressing her passion, dreaming of a new life with Jeff.

But there's an annoying cloud on her romantic horizon and she has come to realize there'll be no compromises regarding Jeff's time-wasting hobby. "Your active sponsorship of the cycling scene is spoiling our relationship," she'd told him quite plainly. "All this stupid cycling – chasing up and down hills in the pouring rain – it's a waste of the valuable time we could be spending together!"

The vehemence of his reply had shocked her. "If you can't accept me how I am, we'll have to finish the relationship!"

For Christ's sake! She hadn't meant it like that, she'd assured him. Later, she'd needed her 'little helper' behind the self-raising flour, which had immediately lightened her mood.

The telephone is ringing at last! Although her fantasies have led her to the brink of desperation and Matthew is asleep in the armchair, she'll allow it to ring a third time before picking it up. Today, it's her turn to make the excitement; disclose her wildest dreams in a low whisper which causes him to relieve himself right away – at least she suspects he is relieving himself, judging by the ecstatic noises she registers with great satisfaction, thriving on the promise of things to come. These are the dreams that come true on Saturday afternoons, when Matthew is doing overtime and Sally is somewhere else, taking part in another competition or doing extra training with Mrs Lightbone.

In sweet anticipation, she wedges the receiver between shoulder and ear.

"Sorry to be disturbing you Mrs Foss! Patricia Lightbone speaking! I have some very good news for Sally. Is she home?"

"Oh! Oh! I beg your pardon!" Charmaine leaves her ecstatic cloud and bangs down the iron, her mind in a flurry. "Surely you know that Sally is at Mount Lodge!" Haven't you just driven her there yourself?" Her voice rises notably; hectic blotches appear on her face and slowly spread over her neck.

Until now, Patricia Lightbone's ability to recognize bogus excuse letters has filled a whole drawer full of blatantly forged letters with the weirdest excuses, from nursing Auntie Penelope's sick dog, to being locked in a bank safe and playing midwife to the cat. Now she has exposed the girl's deception – although unwillingly – and the mother is still yelling down the 'phone.

"I just wanted to let Sally know, those who couldn't make it, there'll be another meeting on the 15th of next month. Don't be upset with your daughter, Mrs Foss. She's been training hard and a little amusement will do her no harm; besides, it's important she makes friends."

Charmaine is unable to speak, dismayed at the over-tolerant attitude. She slams down the 'phone and suppresses a desire to send the empty glass vase on the sideboard hurdling through the window. *Clench your fists and breathe deeply to a slow count of six,* said the doctor. *Keep going; ignore the trembling, hot flushes and chest pains. There's nothing wrong with your heart! You are living under stress, Mrs Foss! Push out your stomach and breathe... slow and deep...slow and deep...*

The address! What's the name? Horn? For God's sake! There's a whole page of 'Horns' in the telephone-book! What's the name of that television-producer?

"Hey Matthew, wake up! Where does that television-producer live – the one whose daughter goes to school with our Sally?"

"Huh, eh?"

"Pull yourself together, Matthew, this is an emergency! Our Sally has gone to a party at his house, when she's supposed to be at Mount Lodge with her trainer. I'm going to get her back!" She taps a foot impatiently, waiting for her husband to get his wits together and answer a straightforward question.

He clears his throat. "Oh aye? Well, you can't really blame her for wanting a bit of fun after all that training, can you? Besides, she's turning into a real 'good-looker' is our Sally. Might get herself onto one of them television shows." Matthew chuckles.

"Don't you *dare* laugh, Matthew!" The menace in her voice, the daggers in her eyes might easily intimidate the bravest of men. "If you'd taken more interest in the girl, this wouldn't have happened; so tell me where Carol Horn lives and I'll be off right away." Her voice trembles with subdued anger, and the craving for 'her little helper' behind the self-raising flour.

The whisky is taking effect, when she parks the car alongside the high stone wall, concealing floodlit flowerbeds and white marble statues from prying and envious eyes. The gates are still open; suppressed fury sets her in motion and she strides up the drive and pounds the knocker on a heavily carved oak door, with the intention of waking the dead.

The maid, who opens the door, wonders what the wild-eyed woman could be wanting at this time of the evening.

"I've come to collect my daughter, Sally Foss."

"Indeed? Please wait here and I'll go and get her."

The impatient tapping of high-heels on mosaic tiles echoes through the house. The distant strain of music and a woman laughing reaches her ears, interrupted by loud whistles and fading applause. What are they up to at this time of night? She smothers the urge to go in search of the music, reminding herself that in a private house one can't go where one pleases. Why are they taking so long?

The uniformed maid reappears, followed by Sally on unsteady legs, a glass in her hand and still in the embrace of a tall blond body-builder-type guy. Charmaine can see he'll get what he wants, this sex-oozing Adonis, but not from *her* daughter! Her daughter? This beautiful young woman with blonde wavy hair hanging loosely over her shoulders – is she her daughter? Her eyes run over the transparent flowered beach dress; over the bright pink bikini, and her anger explodes. These were the clothes she'd been planning to wear, on the holiday with Jeff, which he'd cancelled, for Christ's sake! And to make the situation unbearable, he'd cancelled it for another frigging cycling rally.

"Take your filthy hands from my daughter!" she commands in a voice still trembling with emotion. "And you come with me!"

The girl's tongue refuses to follow her mind. Since flirting with John words haven't been coming too easily, especially after taking a drag at the joint someone had given her, and John had refilled her glass with that beautiful mind-bursting punch. She is still thinking about his hand in her bikini, very slowly pressing his way down, softly massaging her clitoris which had nearly blown her mind. She hadn't even cared if others had been watching! She'd like to tell them about the wonderful excitement. She'd like to tell them how beautiful she feels; if only the words would come out of her mouth.

The walls are moving. Hallelujah! The whole house is moving! What a gag! She can't help laughing while it's circling around her, faster and faster, making her even more dizzy. Her legs are a little weak and she'd rather be making love to her new boyfriend, than standing around with her mother like some kind of geek. Faces are taking on catastrophic dimensions. *Oh how funny it is! If only Mum could see herself through my eyes – her long face and sagging chin.* She giggles at inanimate objects suddenly springing to life. The country cottage on the wall is rocking backwards and forwards. Christ Almighty! This is amazing…!

John opens his arms and she immediately loses her balance. "You sod, you've let me go!" she mumbles against her mother's breast. Somewhere behind her – she can't look around – she hears Carol's shrill voice. "What's going on?"

"Mrs Foss is fighting the good fight, against the Devil and Damnation," John explains between outbursts of laughter as Carol observes the scene, hands on hips and a provoking smile on her face. Charmaine notes the bikini-bra supporting more than it covers; the ridiculous yellow ribbon on the Josephine Baker banana skirt; the matching flower behind the left ear. The Hawaiian flair is of place between oak panelled walls and Axminster carpets.

"Welcome to the Missionary Circle, Mrs Foss! Come and join us for a Bloody Mary, a gin and tonic, or perhaps you might prefer a nice cool beer? We've got some hip musicians and loads of records, still fairly popular among your generation. How about Vera Lynn and the 'White Cliffs of Dover'? You can fight the good fight right down to the cellar."

Sally's mouth moves in silence. They don't understand what she is trying to tell them. They don't understand anything – her new circle of friends – her new handsome boyfriend, exactly how she has dreamed him to be. His name is John Bridges. He'll be picking her up outside school and carrying her satchel before very long. The others will go green with envy – those who've jibed and gossiped about her not having a boy-friend. She can't wait to see their faces when she enters Loopy's Coffee Bar holding John's hand. Later, she'll invite him home for Sunday tea, but not before Dad has decorated the place. He's says he'll do it, but keeps putting it off.

Mum doesn't fit in! She's spoiling all the fun! I would rather stay here, but no-one will listen. John offers Charmaine a joint. Sally suppresses a giggle which ends in a choke. There are daggers in her mother's eyes. She knows all about these daggers – they scare her to death! She can see them quite plainly which is strange, because she can't see much else. *Oh God, please tell them to stop all this madness. I would rather tell them myself, but the words won't come out.*

John lifts a casual hand, unable to express himself because things have taken a turn and are now weird and funny. The joint is taking effect. The old hag of a maid is regarding him suspiciously so he'd better make himself scarce. He doesn't want trouble; he wants sex – and sex he'll get. "Goodbye you fucking cruel world!" He lifts a limp hand and wanders off.

The maid, a staunch Methodist, gives Carol the look that transmits enough is enough of the capricious behaviour. If Miss Carol doesn't watch out, she'll be onto her parents because her patience is running out and she's had enough of the rich. One never knows what they'll do next. "It's the result of having too much money," she tells her niece later; and proof that evil comes to those who reject the God-fearing life. It's time to get rid of these troublesome people, whoever they might be, even though the weather has taken a turn for the worse and is now raining heavily. She watches the mother supporting the girl as they stagger down the drive. *There's nothing better than a cold shower for bringing people to their senses followed by the odd prayer to get them home in one piece.* The maid closes the door, still muttering to herself.

...

Approaching headlights zoom like oncoming meteorites, flashing through space and disappearing into the night. Lonely lampposts fade away one by one, replaced by beautiful faces and flashing white teeth which jeer at her from the bill-boards. *Wait until Monday;* they seem to be saying. *The word will have got around before you enter the classroom, about your crap mother turning up at Carol's party and dragging you away! So don't give us those airs and graces about having your name in the newspaper. Who cares about trampoline-jumping? You're real scum, with a mother like that!*

The clown in the bright green bowler-hat races towards her and she wishes her mother would stop the car so she can get a closer look. The clown with the big red nose, the painted nostrils and the enormous white mouth, is trying to tell her that Circus Poppi is coming to town.

Chapter 3

The clown runs down the line blowing the oversized whistle in his painted mouth, stumbling under the weight of his heavy load. "Programmes, programmes!" he yells at smiling mothers and laughing fathers whose children can't decide whether to laugh or cry until he attempts the sidekick and loses his balance, setting off squeals of delight. He strides around in his ludicrous clown's shoes, shouts, whistles and distributes programmes from the shrinking pile as they enter the gaudy world of Circus Poppi.

Who can resist the mysterious invitation of the circus? The all-consuming tent, a white canvas outer shell with soaring peaks, is securely grounded by invisible stakes and an intricate assortment of ropes; a windowless structure with the promise of adventure; the doorway to a magical world.

A giant wave moves slowly towards her and carries her away. The old photo album springs to life, enticing her into the brilliant world of the impossible; the deafening applause of the magnetized audience. This is the world of the clown! This is where she belongs! Ignore the acrid odour of animal dung; the lines of washing refusing to dry in the aftermath of a shower, transforming the field into a mire. There's a hand-written ''Staff Wanted'' notice outside the red and blue ticket-office cabin. A dark-skinned woman of indefinable age, laughing eyes and glittering combs in her black hair, sells tickets through a sliding window.

"You can apply for a job after the performance," says the woman offhandedly, but not in an unfriendly manner, her concentration fixed on the growing queue. She sells her tickets with an unwavering smile, showing various shades of oversized teeth, to enter a strange and vibrant world dominated by the 'Big Top'. The huge tent is surrounded by smaller tents that serve as animal paddocks. A long trailer is the lion's den, connected to the 'Big Top' by a strong wire tunnel. Caravans, new and luxurious or old and shabby, stand next to the heavy vehicles and colourful trailers.

If Mum had been with her she wouldn't be standing here, on her own, imagining people are giving her the eye because she's lonely. *Everybody belongs to someone! I am the only exception!* Belonging to nobody is making her angry and the longer she stands the more intense is her anger, until she fears she might burst if she doesn't examine her watch like she's waiting for someone. Aha, waiting for friends is she? That explains it! Not alone after all, eh? – must be a popular girl if she's waiting for friends, (they might think). Adopting a casual look, she fingers the note in her pocket, left on the table by her mother, under the vinegar and next to the money.

Gone to another crap bogus meeting, have you Mum?

The crowd carries her inside the 'Big Top', past a dark-skinned girl selling candy-floss from a tiny hut which looks like wood, but is nothing more than a card-house. Two usherettes in royal blue uniforms with gold trimmings check tickets and seat numbers among tiered rows of planks surrounding the ménage.

Where is the clown who entertains the waiting audience? There he is, running around the outskirts of the ring, waving an oversized red balloon. Now he's chasing along the rapidly-filling rows of spectators, getting tangled among stragglers in search of their seats. The balloon bursts and ear-drums vibrate. Lightning fingers produce another balloon from the rest. Ceremoniously, he presents it to a small boy. Ungrateful child! The boy hits the clown on the head with the balloon. Sprays of tears spout from his white-rimmed eyes. There's no shelter from the tears as the clown runs amok. Excited screams fade to the roll of drums and the ringmaster enters the ménage.

The weeping clown sprays the ringmaster with tears and is sent off in disgrace, but no matter! He'll appear again, to distract the audience's attention from three helpers in dark red uniforms, moving at great speed, erecting ropes and ladders in the background. Meanwhile, the ringmaster's voice echoes around the tent and can't be ignored. With a flourish of the hand fit for royalty, he is proud to announce the world-famous breath-taking, daredevil performance of the one and only – Flying Santinos.

Small and lithe is the rule of the air. Grandfather and two sons dressed in the sparkling leotards of a family high-flying act, chase up the rope like it's the easiest thing in the world. From the platform they hurl through the air at a speed of 60 miles an hour, watched anxiously by the Spanish mother who'll throw up the balance poles before they cross the ménage on a tightrope, precariously balancing on each other's shoulders.

Her eyes are bright and the anger has left her. Here is the metamorphosis to the world she desires, the fun and excitement, the clouds of dust dancing in the spotlight behind six liberty horses, proudly tossing the plumes on their heads. They leave the ring and the ever-present odour of animal dung mingled with horse sweat. The thrilled audience can hardly imagine the endless hours of training before perfection is achieved, when the juggler enters the ring. Balls fly through the air as he circles, two-meters high on a unicycle. And not enough! Coloured rings swirl around his arms and neck. In the darkness, luminous balls trip the light fantastic through the air between twirling rings, a fire of iridescent blues, greens and yellows, inducing gasps of astonishment out of the blackness. Lights are switched on and there is a thunder of applause. The juggler bows graciously and takes a call, then another, before reversing into the background of heavy curtained folds.

The spotlight moves towards the ringmaster, who watches the clown in fake horror. Why is he in the ring again when he has no business to be there? And why is he carrying a large wooden box? A dialogue of arrogance and buffoonery ends with a boot to the backside, underlined by an orchestral drum, sparking-off tumult and the clashing of cymbals. The ringmaster has had enough! The clown is a nuisance and will have to go! Put him inside the box and take him away, orders the ringmaster. Will he fit inside? Of course he won't. His arms and legs can't be bent and he won't be ordered about. The ringmaster closes the lid; two pallbearers appear to carry him out, but the clown won't be beaten. Unnoticed by his adversaries, accompanied by a prolonged roll of drums closing with a thud, he falls out of the bottom and lands on his feet. Children shriek with excitement. The audience applauds. The clown bows and finishes his performance with the vaudeville flourish, before being chased from the ménage by the ringmaster.

Now it is our most famous Western hero, Lucky Luke, who throws his knives into the revolving wall, around the living body of the one and only Annie Oakley, fresh from 'Annie Get your Gun' and spinning in all directions. The audience holds its breath; children dare not look; knives whiz through the air and land where they should. There is an audible sigh as Annie steps down, still in one piece and ready to take a call towards precisely thrown knives displaying the outline of her body.

Later, the crowd wanders around the field. Children form a lively queue to have their photo taken in wild-west manner, on the back of a horse. The clown puts his arm around an elderly lady and leaves the imprint of his mouth on her cheek as she giggles, due to the unaccustomed attention she is receiving. Near the entrance, a group of rough-looking men stand around holding their papers, outside the ticket-cum-employment office. The black-haired woman's earrings jingle disruptively as she beckons the girl inside. "Take a seat, my dear. You're looking for a job? What can you do?"

The door flings open and the ring-master, still wearing his bright red coat and carrying his top hat to complete the redoubtable presence, enters the office. His moustache quivers as he picks up the telephone. The girl watches fearfully as he dials a number because she doesn't want to be reminded of the monster on the sideboard, or the alien who had entered the house and stolen her mother, which is ridiculous. She must change her thoughts! Nobody can enter a house through a telephone and steal someone's mother. The ringmaster replaces the receiver with a sigh of exasperation and speaks to the woman in a foreign language. "We'll wait another ten minutes," she replies in English. Her jewellery rattles like a suit of armour as she turns to speak to the girl, but holds her breath because the girl is acting strangely; looking desperately between the door and the telephone as if planning an escape. "Is there anything wrong?" she asks the girl.

"I hate telephones!"

The woman laughs, thinking the girl must be joking. "Do you? That's very unusual. I've never met anyone scared of telephones before."

"I hate the sound of them ringing. I thought there were no telephones in a circus."

The woman speaks soothingly, sensing the girl's desperation. "This is a battery-operated field telephone, honey! It's essential in cases of emergencies. Accidents often happen in a circus! So are you going to run away from my telephone, or tell me what kind of a job you are looking for?"

There's a moment of silence before Sally answers. "My greatest wish is to be a circus performer," she announces shyly.

"Ah yes!" The woman's head goes to one side. She'll give the girl her full attention – if only for a while.

"I'm Junior Champion in trampoline gymnastics," says the girl proudly, with a suspicious eye still on the telephone. "My grandparents were famous circus performers, The High and Mighty Don Libella's – you might have heard of them," she adds lamely. Her confidence has left her and there's an uncomfortable silence.

The ringmaster avoids the question; mops his brow and loosens his collar instead. He is accustomed to pseudo-talented artistes with rabbits in top hats who'll play trumpets through their noses. His broad, good-natured face remains impassive. "We're a circus, my dear, and not the local gym. We are part of a Spanish circus dynasty," he adds proudly, pushing himself up to greater height. "We left our country when it was being run by a bunch of horse-thieves. These days, we return home when the north European winters get too cold for working in tents and living in fields. Now we have expanded throughout the world because we love to entertain people. We engage our artistes through agents and rarely engage permanent acts, apart from the clown." There's another pause as he braces himself. "How old are you, and what else can you do?"

"I'm seventeen – almost eighteen – and can do anything," she replies nervously because the woman's face has signalled she isn't impressed.

"If you're under-age, your parents must give their consent by signing this form. At first, we'll take you on for feeding the animals and cleaning out stalls. We also need a reliable person to look after the children while their parents are performing. Do you like animals? Do you like children?"

"Oh yes, I adore them, all of them – everything!"

The ringmaster hesitates, trying in vain to recall 'The High and Mighty Don Libellas, concluding them to be one of these long-forgotten pre-war acts that keep cropping up among circus workers' reminiscences of 'the good old days'. He'll make enquiries – but later! If the girl wants to join the circus and her parents are willing – why not? He sighs audibly. Many an over-exuberant emotion has been quenched by the manifold discomforts of life on the road.

The telephone rings. The girl jumps up, breathes deeply and returns to her seat. "I'm very good on the trampoline ..." her voice trails off as she watches the woman lift the receiver, thinking that telephones are hideous and she would rather stand outside for an hour than sit next to one.

"Alright, alright, my darling, we'll take you on!" assures the ringmaster, glancing at his wife who has set about a lengthy conversation with some nameless caller. "If your parents agree, they should fill out this form and sign it. Be here at seven on the dot tomorrow evening and you'll be proud to belong to the famous Circus Poppi, owned by yours truly Alfonso Poppi and my wife, Clementina." He makes a sweeping gesture towards the colourful figure wildly gesticulating into the 'phone.

...

Charmaine empties the groceries onto the kitchen table. Matthew is in the lounge, consuming his 'take-away' in front of the telly, judging by the live horse-racing commentary. And where is Sally? Upstairs, no doubt; doing God-knows-what in her room.

She checks her watch and suddenly feels tired. It's been a hard day in the office and she has hardly seen Jeff. What's a day without Jeff? Nothing! The emptiness is makes her depressed. Perhaps a pill might help, or better still, her 'little helper'. She takes a swig from the bottle behind the self-raising flour. She needs a kick before facing her husband.

He looks up from the newspaper as she enters the lounge, thinking how self-confident she seems; and so glamorous – as glamorous as a Hollywood star. "Hello!"

"Hello!" she replies, without the trace of a smile.

"Had a good day, then?" He tries to sound cheerful.

"Yes thanks!" she answers abruptly, avoiding his puppy-dog gaze. Should she eat something before going to bed? A salad sandwich, perhaps, with low-calorie mayonnaise and a cup of tea to follow? She examines her nails: the varnish is chipping already, and then looks around for her manicure-set.

He watches from behind the newspaper, knowing he has lost her, but never giving up hope of regaining her love. They can't keep going on like this, existing in parallel worlds and under the same roof. Something beyond his control is about to happen; he senses the impending change. Should he take the initiative? Reconciliation is the word! Or should he wait and see how things develop? Problems have a habit of sorting themselves out.

He doesn't need a career woman, but a wife, for God's sake – despite the amount of money she earns; at least that's what she claims, but he's never seen any of it and they haven't had a holiday for years. Those were the days! Those were the days, when they'd been happy! Those were the days when he'd earned enough for the three of them; for the mortgage and a good holiday on top! But had they been happy? He wasn't so sure. What the hell does she do with the money she earns? She'd refused to tell him when he broached the subject, perhaps a little too timidly. Jesus, how his stomach had turned when she'd said it was none of his business. Christ, what a mess! Instead of the suffering, these late night quarrels, he should be threatening her with divorce. That might shock her; might bring her into line, but there again, it might not! What if she agrees? What will he do without her? Ride his bike into the back of a bus? Kill himself, like Frank what's-his-name down the road, after his missus had left with the kids. He'd hung himself in the garage using a length of rope from the sledge. What a bloody stupid way to die! Frank had always been a tight-fisted bugger – could have treated himself to some decent twine for the very last act – it's not every day you'll be hanging yourself.

"We're working-class, salt of the earth an' proud of it," his Dad used to say. Aye, there was no messing about with his Dad. He could still hear his voice; that broad, no-nonsense Yorkshire- dialect. "Don't get yourself one of them career women, lad," he'd warned. "Ambitious women are difficult to manage – 'ave yer balls before y'can say Jack Robinson!"

I need a woman like my mother. I need a woman who'll make a good meal out of nothing – who'll look after the kids without complaining. Even thinking about it turns me over, but I'll have to put my foot down; show her the limits. These quarrels are hell. I'll do it tomorrow! His stomach turns when he thinks about tomorrow – and then their previous quarrel when he'd lost control of his emotions.

Bloody embarrassing, breaking down like that! A man shouldn't weep in front of a woman – they lose respect! No wonder she fled out of the bedroom, rushed downstairs and spent an hour on the bloody 'phone. Who the hell was she talking to at that time of night? It doesn't bear thinking about! I'll steer my bike into the back of a bus, I bloody well will! But I'll have a bit of fun before I do it!

He turns his mind to more pleasurable thoughts; Friday night fun-sessions at 'The Angel', Jimmy Leach's birthday party, and 'Blondie', who'd jumped out of the cake. The strip-tease that followed had caused havoc in his pants. It still doesn't fail when 'the need' comes upon him; when he examines the naked woman at the back of his drawer and thinks about Blondie.

Leaving her husband to his silent reminiscences, Charmaine finishes her nails and discards the shoes she has been wearing all day, the sexy high-heels which are now killing her. She'll have to straighten things out if she wants peace and quietness while eating her supper; explain to Sally why she'd opted out of the promised treat, of accompanying her to the circus. Sighing wearily, she climbs the stairs and knocks on the door, which the girl promptly opens as though she's been waiting.

"Hello love! Did you enjoy the circus? Sorry I couldn't come with you but I had to go to an important meeting, so I'll just say goodnight. I'm knackered and off to bed!"

"Goodnight Mum! I had a lovely time at the circus." The girl speaks softly. "Sign this form, please. No need to read it, Mum, it's nothing important! Just to give permission for another Sunday training session with Mrs Lightbone up at Mount Lodge. I'm feeling much better now!"

Thank God the girl is behaving sensibly at last! A working mother can't tolerate a daughter going wild and getting drunk. Adolescent issues must be nipped in the bud before they get out of hand. She turns her attention to the paper thrust under her nose. Another form to be signed? Certainly! Extra training might be expensive, but it keeps the girl occupied. "Are you going with Mrs Lightbone tomorrow?"

"Yes Mum! I'll be leaving early – about six in the morning. I'll take some sandwiches."

"Well, there can't be anything wrong in that! Why do I have to sign it, then?"

"Because tomorrow is Sunday, and we're not supposed to train on Sundays without parent's permission. It's one of these silly new rules! Here's a book to rest it on, Mum. I'll hold it while you sign."

Charmaine finds it ridiculously uncomfortable signing one's name on a dotted line and standing barefoot on the landing. Why isn't the girl allowing her inside? If she wasn't so tired, she'd be putting her straight!

"Goodnight Mum and take care. Say goodbye to Dad for me, will you?"

Sally closes the door, clenches her fists and stifles a shriek of triumphal-pleasure. The bizarre experience of 'hating one's parents' has finally hit her. They can't fool her, she knows their secrets. Hasn't she watched them closely, reduced them to a colony of ants hurrying backwards and forwards, transporting objects important only to themselves and oblivious of scrutiny? Hasn't she developed this strange feeling of power; this growing feeling of indifference to protect her from unloving parents? Now she is certain, Dad wouldn't turn a hair if her life was in danger, and what does she think about her mother? Disappointment has grown into hate. Hating one's mother is like swimming alone in the middle of an ocean. How can one love a mother who doesn't love her daughter?

It had been another chance to rummage. Having examined her mother's bedroom cupboards, it was time for the brown leather bag on the table since Charmaine had locked herself in the bathroom to get ready for her lover and was unlikely to come out for a while. She'd stifled a cry of triumph on discovering the receipt, neatly zipped away in a tiny compartment, to confirm Mr. Jeffrey Nelson's payment of two hundred pounds for the 6-month lease of a caravan on Holly Hill Camping Park.

Mr. Jeffrey Nelson is Mum's boss and Mum is having an affair with her boss! I can't believe it! And get a load of this! He is the alien! He is the one who entered the house through the telephone! He is the one I watched through the keyhole, making love to my mother on the sitting-room couch. Now they screw in a yukky caravan in Holly-Hill Park. Mum, I hate you! Oh! How I hate and despise you!

She remembers how impatient she'd been for her mother to finish her bath and leave the house, oblivious that her daughter had known where she was going. After Charmaine had sped off in the car, she'd sprinted up the road in a flurry of excitement and caught the next bus. The rumbling monstrosity had calmed her nerves with its stopping and starting, until reaching the banner advertising holiday cabins and caravans at reasonable prices. In the far corner of the parking lot had been her mother's green Ford next to a silver-grey Mercedes.

Here's the checked pillow-case containing Miss Flummi's clothes; the striped braces to hold up her pants; the big red nose and the ridiculous shoes with the cardboard soles to make them even bigger, covered with window leathers tied up with red ribbon. She has fixed the braces so the pants will fall down when she dances, having practiced the routine in front of the mirror a hundred times already. It's time to go to the circus and make people laugh. There's nothing quite like it, making people laugh!

But before leaving home to make people laugh, she'll be collecting the debt. Oh yes! She'll be collecting the debt. There's a heavy price to pay for stealing someone's mother.

...

The chorus of birdsong is an early-morning celebration over busy town roads. The air is cool and hazy with the promise of a perfect Sunday. Today is 'Grand Finale Day'. It is the ultimate end of one life and the beginning of another.

The girl pulls the hood of the dark jacket over her face as she enters the bus. She has already deposited the rucksack containing the few personal belongings she'll need for a new life, together with Miss Flummi's pillowcase tied up with a ribbon, in a bus-station baggage locker. The bus is almost empty, apart from a couple of old men on the back seat, locked in a passionate discussion on racing-pigeons. The bus rambles up the hill towards the moors; past rows of cottages and an empty shopping-centre, into the village square which is the end of the line. Sally leaves the bus and walks up the road towards the old church with the silent bell, unnoticed by the sleepy bus-driver who fumbles in his pockets in search of cigarettes, to bridge the time while waiting for return passengers.

The stone mansion, which has housed three generations of Jeffrey Nelson's forbearers, comes into view. It is beautifully placed among well-kept gardens overlooking the wooded valley, with a stream running over the ancient stepping-stones people have used as long as they can remember. The place is vivid in her memory, where they'd picnicked a long time ago and in a different life. She tastes the potted-meat sandwiches; sees them in her mind's eye – Auntie and Uncle, cousins and grandparents; the scene is still with her, as clear as spring water.

She zips up the collar of her jacket. Her watch tells her it will be another hour before the race begins, according to information in the *'Herald'*. She knows he will reach the starting point in good time, which is why she is here to meet him. It's a stroke of luck she has read the article about the well-known local businessman and hobby racing-cyclist who is sponsoring the race.

Pine trees form an alley to the mansion at the top of the hill. Camouflaged by low branches, she stands behind a tree and waits. A thrush keeps a safe distance and picks between gnarled roots. It flees to safety when she moves her head to watch the stooping figure of a man, hoping he won't come in her direction as he crosses the road further down the valley, some distance away. The figure disappears into a side road and she sighs with relief.

Her heart skips a beat when she sees him standing at the top of the hill, framed in the gateway like some motionless hero. The girl watches the cyclist lean his bike against the gatepost as he fixes the reflective straps on both arms. Slowly, almost thoughtfully, he pulls on his gloves, tests the handlebars with short sharp shakes before throwing a leg over the bar. She sees him rest his foot on the pedal and turn it slowly, before starting the ride along the crest of the hill.

Now he has reached the road and is coming towards her, gathering speed, body thrust forward, dynamic and shocking; pedalling as if in rhythm with her mother's body. She imagines herself triggering his excitement when she picks up the 'phone; hears him laughing with unbounded pleasure as he plunges towards her like some strange kind of missile, whooping with glee. Is it the thrill of speed that is sending his spirits soaring or is he shouting in the wind, telling the world that racing downhill at top speed is like having sex with her mother?

The cyclist sees the dark hooded figure emerge from the shadows and swerves to avoid a collision. "What the hell...!" he yells. But there's no escaping the onslaught; no way of avoiding the figure as it leaps towards him like black lightening.

The moment he loses his balance he senses the fall will be fatal; sees the picture of the man fleeing from the girl, down the road leading to hell. He catapults over the handlebars. His head smashes against the pavement-corner and his body remains there, inanimate and strangely crumpled, alongside the road.

...

It hasn't occurred to them that she has left. It is late evening, when they finally notice she hasn't returned.

Together – and it has been a long time since they have done anything together – they enter her room. The wardrobe is empty. Her suitcase is missing. Her savings-book has gone too, with the five thousand pounds transferred into her account from the grandfather in Spain.

Charmaine picks up the envelope propped against the dressing table mirror and Matthew stands open-mouthed as she reads that his daughter has left home – forever. She'll soon be eighteen, she points out in the letter which Charmaine is now reading again. She has joined the circus. The circus is in her blood. Mrs Lightbone will understand.

"In her blood?" Charmaine crumples the letter in disgust. "What a selfish little bitch she is, expecting me to tell Mrs Lightbone that I'm very sorry, but my daughter has joined the circus and she can stuff all that extra training, stuff all that collecting and driving around the country; stuff all those endless competitions, making her into a star." She raises her voice, face red with fury. "I'll give her the trophies! Empty that cabinet and give her trophies for all the trouble she's been, or throw them away! I'm not keeping the damned things!" She emphasizes the fact with the menacing finger. "Say something, for God's sake!"

"What can I say?" he shrugs helplessly. Should he worry about an eighteen-year old girl? She's still pure! No damaged goods in that girl. He hopes it'll stay that way for a while. "Our Sally's a big girl now, my love!"

Ignoring the daggers in her eyes, he turns to camouflage his disappointment; returns to the comfort of his armchair in the hope his wife will overcome the gigantic passion she habitually develops when something goes wrong. Best to leave her alone 'til she's blown herself out, he decides. In the meantime he'll barricade himself behind the newspaper and wait. On second thoughts – he throws himself into the armchair with a sigh of relief – it's a pity she has forfeited a promising career for the likes of a travelling circus.

He can hear her shouting in the dining-room, telling Mrs Lightbone there'll be no more training for Sally because the ungrateful bitch has left home. He doesn't approve of the strong language she's using when referring to their daughter, but what's the use of complaining? "Yes! I have to call her that, Mrs Lightbone," he hears her say, "…and

I'll say it again! She's an ungrateful bitch. After all the time and money we've invested in her training, she steals away without saying a word!"

There's still plenty of scorn in her voice. "Yes, Mrs Lightbone," he hears her continue and fears she won't calm down for a while. "I can understand how disappointed you are, but she'll soon be 'of age', so there's not much we can do. You'd like me to keep you informed? Of course!"

Thank God she has put down that damned 'phone. Aw Jesus, it's ringing again! Who the hell can it be this time? He hears her answer and wonders about the ensuing silence.

"It's not true!" she almost whispers. "No, no, no!" Her voice has reached screaming pitch. "It's not true! There's been some mistake!" She sobs and stutters. "I saw him yesterday and he was p-perfectly f-fine!"

Him? Matthew closes the newspaper. Who is she talking about? Who the hell is 'him'? At least she's not referring to their daughter. Nasty things can happen to young girls when they leave home, even to sensible girls like Sally.

The scream echoes throughout the house, shrill and painful.

What is the matter? Why is she wailing like that? It's agonizing! He throws down the newspaper and listens.

"No, no!" she repeats, "It can't be true! Please tell me it's not true."

God Almighty, she must have lost her balance and knocked something over. He rushes into the dining-room and watches her in dismay, kneeling on the carpet, pounding the wall with her fist, the telephone receiver dangling beside her. He picks it up and his face darkens as he listens to the woman at the other end – a colleague, she explains – with some very sad news, very sad indeed!

Now she is rolling on the carpet. He has witnessed her tantrums, but never like this. This is something serious.

"Somebody very dear to your wife has been killed," the voice over the 'phone continues.

"Ah yes, how unfortunate," he replies. He doesn't want to hear; he has known all along.

"Actually..." there's a long pregnant silence, perhaps they've been disconnected.

"Hello?"

"Actually," the voice repeats, "I'm afraid it was Jeff Nelson, our boss."

He covers the mouthpiece with a shaking hand because he doesn't want them to hear the noise in the background; the wailing and crying of a heartbroken woman; he has no intention of feeding their gossip.

"Like I said, Jeff and Charmaine have been very close. To put it frankly, they've been having a relationship for almost ten years. I'm sorry to be talking like this, Mr. Foss – terribly sorry – I'm not one for gossiping…"

After slamming down the receiver he remains staring at the 'phone as though fearing it might spring back to life with more painful truths. Of course he has known, but chosen to ignore it. What a fool he has been. He should have driven himself into the back of that bus.

"Come on my love, try to get up and don't worry. I'll look after you!" He speaks soothingly; helps her to her feet, her legs weak and body trembling. As a first-aid helper on the factory floor and trained to recognize the symptoms of shock, he knows what to do.

…

Chapter 4

Patricia Lightbone sighs as she replaces the receiver. Shotgun weddings, adolescent crises, moving house or failing standards, are the customary reasons for premature school-leavers. She knows them all, but has never lost a student to the circus before.

A girl who writes fake sick notes and leaves home? What does she make of that? She shakes her head and returns to the kitchen. The crap parents who could never keep an appointment have been a running joke among colleagues. "You'll have to bind, gag and drag them into the school if you want them to listen," they'd told her.

"But there's another problem besides the fake note," she'd informed them at the teacher's conference.

"And what's the other problem?" they'd asked.

"Carol Horn!"

"Bah! If I had a friend like Carol Horn, I'd also run off to the circus."

Patricia Lightbone puts the meal in the oven. Her husband will be late again, no doubt. She can't remember the last time he was punctual. It went with the job.

Detective Chief Inspector Nicholas Lightbone – 'Nickbone' to his colleagues and members of the 'Bowling Green Amateur Dramatic Society' of which he is a member – hangs up his coat and runs his hands through the thick grey hair still clinging to his head beneath the hat he always wears when working outdoors.

"Did you have a good day?" He kisses his wife on the cheek.

"Yes darling, apart from some surprising news I've just received, which I'll tell you in a minute." She disappears into the kitchen and reappears with the fish gratin, two thirds of which she serves to her husband.

"Sally Foss, the most talented student I've had for years, has run away to the circus – the one on Black's Field – Circus Poppi I think was the name. Mind you, there's not much her parents can do about it. The girl will be eighteen next month. Her mother works as an accountant with Nelson and Sons."

Now that *is* a coincidence! Detective Chief Inspector Nicholas Lightbone has his theories about coincidences. One might read about them in thrillers, but you seldom experience them in reality, although they're worth investigating if connected with a crime – and Jeff Nelson had died just a few hours ago. After coming from the morgue, he always goes through the symbolic routine of washing his hands; this time to rid himself of the vision of the poor fellow's head, the skull smashed open to reveal part of his brain; an uncertain case of accidental death. And now, while transferring the last piece of fish from his plate to his mouth, he wonders if it's going to be one of those tricky 'accidents' where there's more to it than meets the eye. Nickbone wipes his mouth with the serviette, trying to ignore the growing premonition that his last month of service might not be as straightforward as he's been hoping – dammit all! Just as he's beginning to study the role of Edward 1V in Shakespeare's King Richard III. Jack Finch, the producer, says it will be a challenge, but there's still plenty of time before the winter season begins – and why shouldn't they try one of the classics for a change? If all goes well, they'll follow up with Oscar Wilde's 'The Important of Being Earnest'. Roll on retirement!

He looks at his watch. It's time to leave, for yet another rehearsal.

...

Walking to work, with the script in the pocket of his Harris-Tweed jacket, is an excellent method of learning one's lines. Passing the park gates, he is proud to note that he hasn't found it necessary to refer even once to the scene rolled up in his pocket, in comparison to yesterday, when he'd wondered if he'd ever learn his lines. King Edward has his entrée in the first scene of the second act and announces (quite appropriately) – 'Now I have done a good day's work'.

Nickbone contemplates the importance of emphasizing the spoken word with the use of suitable gesticulations and intonations. Wrapped in his deliberations, he fails to notice the woman walking towards him until the last minute, wheezing and panting with the heavy load of shopping. He steps to one side and apologises profusely in best cavalier manner. Having passed the supermarket, he strides with the lightness of a man fit for his age towards the central police-station in the town centre and through the heavily carved double-wooden-doors which, over the past century, have seen every type of criminal. After checking through the barrier he almost chases light-heartedly up the well-worn dark green linoleum stairs to his office, which is neither comfortable nor pleasantly decorated. If dark yellow walls are good enough for him, they're good enough for anybody else, is his usual comment regarding the despondent décor of his workplace.

The young constable takes his place behind the typewriter while Nickbone squeezes through the narrow space between wall and desk and into the wooden armchair, to prepare the interview with the man he calls 'The Old Soldier', true to his habit of categorizing witnesses. 'The Old Soldier, who claims Jeff Nelson was pushed off his bike, has left the stringent path of military discipline, judging from the state of his clothes as he enters the office wearing a polo-necked sweater in an advanced state of dilapidation with long woolly fronds dangling from the hem. Strands of hair, plastered over his head in a feeble attempt at camouflaging baldness, now hang about his ears. Watery eyes and trembling hands betray the craving for the restorative needed to keep him going while Nickbone sits back and folds his arms to contemplate, with obvious misgiving, the perfect specimen of an unreliable witness.

Tommy Thistleton (known as Tommy Tipple), takes a seat and recites his name and address like the text of a sermon. The young constable begins typing, but the witness stops to fumble in his pocket. Not having found what he's looking for, he takes a deep breath and commences to tell Nickbone what he knows about the chap racing downhill on his bike.

"Which chap do you mean?"

"The fellow who was killed."

"Good! You say you saw the fellow who was killed coming down the hill…?"

"Goin' like a rocket!" Tommy, now the rag and bone man and no longer the 'old soldier' according to Nickbone's sudden change of category, nods his head and screws his face into a look of agonizing pain.

"Go on, Mr. Thistleton!"

"I think I saw somebody come onto the road from behind the trees and push him off his bike."

"Thy word in God's ear!"

Mr. Thistleton seems suddenly confused.

"You think, or you know?" Nickbone twirls the pen between his fingers looking every bit the severe policeman. The typewriter is silent; the silence is broken by the heating blubbering through pipes and the faint roar of traffic entering the room through a half-open window.

"It was very early in the morning," Tommy Thistleton stops to think and scratches the bald part of his head. "It was like seeing a shadow."

"Was it a man or a woman?"

"I'm not sure. It was just a dark figure."

"Did anybody else see the figure?"

"I don't know!"

Nickbone is aware that a defence-attorney will make mincemeat of Mr. Thistleton in the witness-box, and it is time to take the bull by the horns. "How many beers did you have, Mr. Thistleton, *before* you saw the figure?"

Tommy Thistleton's facial expression changes into painful dignity. "I beg your pardon! I'm not a boozer, if that's what you mean. An' besides, what's wrong with taking a bit of something on pension day, eh? Anyhow, my daughter makes the hell of a fuss if I come home..." he takes a deep breath, "...intoxicated. So I didn't bother going home last night – stayed at my mate's place up near the moors, and did a bit of celebrating – nothing wrong with that ….." His voice trails off.

"Thank-you very much, Mr. Thistleton. I think that'll be enough for the time being." Nickbone nods to the young constable, who shows Tommy Thistleton the statement and where to sign his name. Nothing will come of it, is his silent prediction as the constable accompanies the witness to the door. A decent cup of tea, that's what he needs! A small indulgence, before visiting the offices of Nelson & Son.

...

"I'm terribly sorry, sir." The receptionist at Nelson & Son is tall and strikingly attractive, dressed in a smart black costume, fitting the occasion. "Because of Mister Jeffrey's tragic death, most members of staff are attending a conference. But you can take a seat and wait if you wish. Perhaps you might like some coffee!" She dabs away a tear with a lace handkerchief, smiles politely at Nickbone and waves an inviting hand towards the studded brown leather suite; the style of furniture his wife much admires but can't afford. "It would really have been better had you made an appointment under the circumstances," she adds, excusing herself as she answers the 'phone.

Nickbone avoids making appointments whenever he can and politely refuses the coffee. It's no use giving people time to prepare themselves for what they should say and how they should behave. He needs spontaneous answers – that's his strategy. Body language can reveal much information when someone is bombarded with questions, given no time to think.

The receptionist replaces the receiver and Nickbone continues. "Mr. Nelson's death must have been a terrible shock to employees as well as clients. Might I ask you a rather premature question? Have you any idea who might replace him?" he enquires, intent upon maintaining the respectful tone.

She sniffs away another tear and reminds herself to enquire after the gentleman's business as soon as she has calmed herself down. "Mr. Nelson Senior was here when I arrived this morning," she answers, still half-sobbing. "He requested our clients be referred to Mr. Gideon. Would you like an appointment with Mr. Gideon?"

"Mr. Gideon?"

"Mr. Gideon Nelson is Mr. Jeff's younger brother."

Nickbone declines with firm politeness, insisting his business can wait; turns to leave but changes his mind on noticing the equally attractive young clerk; blond hair carefully styled in a 'throwback look', wearing a light-grey trouser-suit and carrying a file under her arm. "Here are the tax returns for Benson & Woodward. Would you please give them to Charmaine?" she whispers, placing a folder on the desk.

"She hasn't come today!" The receptionist almost mouths the words, hardly audible as she takes hold of the folder.

"Oh! Hasn't she now!" whispers the clerk with a noticeable hint of sarcasm in her voice. Nickbone turns to examine the Gauguin print of a Polonaise beauty. *Do I detect a slight trace of disdain in her voice,* he wonders, straining his ears, proud that his hearing is as keen as when he'd joined the force twenty-three years ago. *Do I register a sigh of annoyance: a flustered statement about 'getting what one deserves and the higher one climbs, the deeper one falls'?* Hatred and jealousy can loosen the tongue. Dissatisfied personnel are a hive of information. He turns from the wall and politely observes how difficult it must be, working under such tragic circumstances.

"It would be much easier if people didn't get so emotionally involved," remarks the clerk snappishly, underlining the statement with a meaningful glance in her colleague's direction.

Nickbone raises an eyebrow. "I beg your pardon!"

"There are two ways a woman can work her way to the top," she announces haughtily, before opening the door and slamming it behind her.

...

"Jeff Nelson might have been pushed from his bike by some unknown person, although it will be difficult to prove."

Nickbone informs his superior officer that he has finished the report and contacted the local newspaper who will write a half-page account on the tragic death of a highly respected business man and supporter of the local cycling scene.

...

Chapter 5

Where are they going? Nobody will tell her. They say it brings bad luck. Circus people are superstitious. "We don't talk about future performances," explains Annie, Lucky Luke's wife and knife-throwing target. Annie sits on the caravan step to pull on her Wellington boots. Being a strong woman, she hooks the caravan and fixes the cables onto the Jeep. "See you later and have a good trip!"

Sally watches them exit the field and head for the main road. Her mind is empty as she continues stacking the planks into the trailer. Work is hard. Circus life is hard. She hasn't found anything comfortable in her new life, as yet. To make things worse, the director is still peacocking about in his red uniform and will cure the girl's circus dreams by having her muck out the stalls.

"She'll never recover!" he remarks to his wife. She glares at him disapprovingly; considers the 'hard-hand' treatment unnecessary; 'testing their stamina', he calls it! "She'll never get over shovelling shit onto a wheelbarrow and transporting it from one side of the field to the other," Alfonso predicts smugly, "Marek and Adam can be relied upon. They'll keep her working 'til she falls asleep on her feet."

Later, after she has finished stacking the planks onto the trailer, he tells her to help with the animals.

"Haven't I done enough?" she wails.

"Respect, respect! You've made a good job of stacking those planks." The circus director regards the pile appreciatively. "Now lend Marek a hand with the cleaning, will you, my darling. The sooner you've finished, the sooner we'll be off!"

Marek hands over a shovel: she regards it indignantly as though seeing a shovel for the first time. The horse-groom with the weather-beaten face lights a cigarette and inhales deeply, savouring the blend of nicotine and manure. "Mmmm, delicious!" he concludes with a sly grin.

Do they know who she is? Do they expect a Junior Champion in trampoline jumping and the granddaughter of famous trapeze artists, to be cleaning animal stalls?

"Don't fall asleep standing up! D'ya intend to spend the night here?" says Marek teasingly.

"But I can't be shovelling more manure!"

"Suit yourself! Either you work, or go home and forget about the circus." Marek shrugs offhandedly. "Don't worry, honey! You're not the first to change your mind – won't be the last, either! I'm sure Alfonso will take you home in his car, before he leaves." He squashes the butt with the heel of his boot and throws it outside, ignoring the trembling lips and tear-filled eyes because there's no turning back. Adam, his brother, who'll have his hair cut for family reunification, to please his long-suffering wife in Poland having worked out what she'll be spending the money on, appears with a wheelbarrow and ready to go off for another. "If you can't shovel, at least you can get rid of it – over there!" he lifts his shovel and beckons towards a rapidly growing heap of manure before refilling the barrow.

The smell of it enters her lungs; *better stop breathing! Hold your breath to avoid contamination!* She knows all about contamination!

"We are the night-shite shovellers, shovelling shit by night".

If she wants to join in the singing she'll have to start breathing.

They pitch two piles of elephant turds. "Hey!" calls Adam kicking a nicely formed turd towards her. "Have you ever seen shit like a rugby ball?"

She'll never get over the shock of having to transport such a disgusting load across a field. "I'll need a whole week to get myself clean," she moans to Adam when they meet on their journey. Adam rests his steaming wheelbarrow and tells her to keep it up because she's doing a good job. Then he pats her shoulder, causing further contamination and making her more than desperate to clean herself.

Alfonso Poppi says she can sleep in the back of the equestrian lorry during the journey. The circus director is an excitable man who underlines his words with wild gesticulations. "These Polish lads are respectable boys – and good Catholics!" he bawls. Being a good Catholic is a strong criterion in the mind of one who'll swear and blaspheme when he's angry and then seek redemption by kissing the gold cross on a thick gold chain around his neck.

The girl is homesick. In the darkness of the lorry, tears prick her eyes and then flow in full force. It is a doubtful achievement, leaving home without saying goodbye and stinking of animal dung, with six white liberty horses in a trailer behind, and two strange men in the front. Dying must be a wonderful feeling.

"There is never a day without a performance," Marek explains lightly without noticing her tears as he climbs into the lorry and lights another cigarette before turning the ignition. "The circus-route is planned one year in advance. Tomorrow afternoon, two-hundred miles north and God willing," he crosses himself and appeals to the darkening sky, "there'll be another long queue at the ticket office."

Who cares about long queues at ticket offices when you've just been through hell and come out at the other end, contaminated and filthy without washing facilities? With the help of a handkerchief and bottle of water she attempts to wash, which is all she can do before falling asleep in the back of the lorry.

...

The circus has arrived! In the early hours of the morning, the lorry jolts over the ruptured surface of a communal field in the insignificant industrial town; her home for a fortnight.

Everything is done at top speed; it is a perpetual race against time, re-erecting what has been previously dismantled. Those who gleam in the spotlight have now lost their glamour for a short while, teeming with rough hired hands, working with precision at tasks set to time.

Half awake, she soaks another tissue in the remaining water and wipes her face, pressing the cold dampness against her eyes, subduing fresh tears of sadness and disappointment; discoloured fingers and broken nails.

Who cares about 'The Great Don Libella' and the junior champion in trampoline jumping when six white horses are waiting for freedom next to piles of equipment that must be unloaded? Marek waits for Alfonso, who has raced up the motorway in his Chevrolet, and ignores her wailings about the filth and the dirt. Remaining unwashed is unthinkable! Don't they understand that cleanliness is vital?

She is surrounded by coloured vehicles that will soon be a circus, brightening the misty outlines of distant buildings. Adam shouts at her to keep an eye on the horses, so they don't get loose and make a bolt for it.

"Have some breakfast!" Marek sniffs loudly and points to a paper-bag, uncomfortably near horse's droppings and a resulting swarm of flies. Is there no escaping this filth? How can she eat in such surroundings? She'd rather roll up in a corner and die of starvation. That would be suicide! Suicide? Relieving herself of insurmountable problems is still a tempting solution.

"Good grub, very special grub!" Adam rolls his eyes in gourmet fashion. With horse-grained fingers, he tears off a hunk of bread, solemnly covers it with a thick slice of salami and forces it upon her, ignoring her refusal. Too tired and hungry to put up a fight, she eats it slowly, agreeing with Marek, as he attends to his teeth with a penknife, that Polish salami is the best in the world.

Tractors and a forklift move wagons and tents into position, and set animal paddocks next to the stalls. Children move purposefully, carrying equipment. And she, the misfit, watches them with envy; enviously because they know what they're doing, where and to whom they belong.

By midday, they have erected the Big Top and secured all the ropes. Animals have been given fresh hay; lions growl against the cage bars while local council officials with serious faces, check rigging, poles and cables.

Killing herself would be the perfect escape. Alone, in the shadow of the trailer, she meditates upon various methods of carrying out the deed and concludes it must be a painless death. Rolling around in agony and retching, doesn't appeal and she racks her brains for some method of escape in a more elegant manner. She must look her best, with a calm facial expression, clean clothes and a perfectly groomed body. Can she do it? No she can't! What will they think about a corpse that stinks before decay has set in?

Is the newspaper, bought by Marek for the football results, still clean? Can she sit on it? Is there anything worth reading – perhaps the local news on the back page? She turns it over and reads the caption; words swim in front of her eyes and she can hardly breathe.

'Tragic death in cycling accident.'

Don't read, for God's sake! Don't read it! Look away! Like a statue perched on the edge of the trailer, she dares herself to read it – just this once – she can't ignore it – but can she endure it? *Go on, don't be a coward! What harm can it do?*

'Mr. Jeffrey Nelson, the managing director of a renowned company of chartered accountants, has been fatally injured in a cycling accident'.

Will they find out? Is anybody watching? – hidden eyes, suspecting her secret? Hadn't it been just another sad case of accidental death? Did anybody recognize the mysterious person – the dark figure appearing out of the shadows? A figment of lively imagination as the article suggests?

Thoughts and images chase through her mind, interrupted by her mother. She doesn't want to see her mother; the looming shadow over her.

"Now why are you looking so startled? And what kind of a place is this, for a girl to be resting her head?" Annie, the knife-throwing-target, towers over her, speaking loudly and forcefully with a strong Irish accent. "…and where would you *normally* be sleeping, might I ask?"

"Don't know!"

"Has Alfonso not given you your accommodation?"

"Not yet!"

"'Tis a wonder anyone works for a circus director who doesn't give a monkey's fart about where people sleep. Come with me! " Annie grabs her by the arm and steers her across the field, dodging between piles of equipment, towards the half-erected 'Big Top' – a chaos of pavilion roofs and wooden planks where Alfonso is waving his arms and shouting orders to the tent manager, who conveys them to his workers.

Annie has no inclination towards social courtesies and immediately talks herself into a rage. "You are a circus director? Ha! Don't make me laugh. You're a bloody slave-driver are you not? Having this girl work like ten men and not giving her a decent bed."

Annie, tall and blonde with the chiselled features of the warrior, commands respect. A spade is a spade and she is the circus mediator who will smooth outraged spirits using the simple credo of attack being the best method of defence.

Alfonso Poppi – not the man to avoid an argument – screws his face into an agonising look, opens his arms in defiant helplessness and in a growling bass befitting his corpulence, lets forth a torrent of words.

"Hey, listen now! This girl tells me plenty of things about herself, and her mother who is the daughter of the High and Mighty Don Libella, signs the form and gives her permission to work with the circus. But all of a sudden, she can't talk!" Alfonso gesticulated excitedly, mixing his words with Spanish, or could it be Italian? One never knew with these circus people. "Wassamatta with the girl? Crucifixi! Why don't she come and say, Hey Alfonso, I need somewhere to sleep, huh? Am I supposed to think of everything? Am I some kind of a clairvoyant? Is this not the land of the free and home of the brave, where everybody can say what they think and ask whatever goddam question they like?" Alfonso's arms rotate like a windmill. "If she can't open her mouth, she don't belong to the circus!"

He turns and yells at the men who'll listen to any excitement, threatening to wrap his shovel around their heads if they don't to get back to work. Then he takes a deep breath, crosses himself and opens his arms. The tight hug embarrasses and surprises her, almost squeezes the air from her lungs.

"Now you promise to tell me what you need and in future, you speak your mind, huh?" He holds her at arm's length. "Forget your 'Psycho Assessment' stuff and don't wait for someone to ask if you need anything." She observes the fat finger in front of her nose. "You're not in a five star hotel, you're in the circus, *señorita* – it means you go around an' make people happy and if you're not happy, you're out of place, here. OK? If you feel like suffering, get yourself into a cloister and be a nun!"

"Okay! What are you going to do, then?" Annie enquires. Having worked herself into a suitable rage, she's determined to reap the benefits; tell Lucky Luke and anyone else how she gave the boss a piece of her mind.

Alfonso steers them towards a group of caravans at the far end of the field and an old-fashioned wooden trailer painted light blue, with white lace curtains covering three latticed windows. Comforting curls of smoke ascend from a tiny chimney into the early morning air. The three wooden steps of the converted mobile-library, creak under Alfonso's weight, as he climbs them to knock on the door. "Hello my darling!" he greets a dark-haired girl in a bright pink dressing-gown, who stands in the open doorway and rubs her wet hair with a towel; the usherette who'd checked Sally's ticket, sold ice-cream from the vendor's box and played a decorative part in the elephant show.

Reduced in height but not in presence, Alfonso descends the wooden steps and returns to firm ground. "Doreen, my darling, you've got a new room-mate," he announces without further question, then turns to Sally and scratches his head absent-mindedly. "What's your name darling – Sally? Ah yes! Forgive me, I'd forgotten but don't worry, I won't forget it again now it seems you'll be staying with the circus. Sally, this is Doreen! – and where's Nadja?"

"Nadja is setting up the kitchen," replies Doreen, still rubbing her dark brown tresses with the matching pink towel. Turning back to Sally, he says, "OK! Nadja is also your room-mate. They work in the kitchen, sell tickets and ice cream, sit on the back of elephants and are very nice girls." His head moves backwards and forwards as he speaks. Being eager to return to matters of importance, he suggests to Doreen she be a good girl and show Sally her bed in one of the three screened-off compartments.

"*Gracias a Dios!*" he mutters under his breath. Another problem solved! Alfonso turns his attention to the entrance gravelling, which is way behind schedule. Does the girl look happy? No! She doesn't look happy, he considers, thinking it's about time she brightens her mood.

"I'm extremely dirty," she says, ignoring her surroundings. "I've been cleaning out the stalls and need a bath."

Hacer de tripas corazon – what can't be cured must be endured. Didn't she tell him she's from a circus family? What kind of family? Does he have time to investigate people's backgrounds? *Mi Dios*! You'd think she has the pest. Now she stinks! So what?

The girl blows her nose. "I stink like hell. My clothes are filthy and I can't come inside until I've cleaned myself up."

"All circus people stink at some time or other, don't they Doreen?" says Annie. Doreen stops rubbing her hair and confirms that people who work with animals stink most of the time and a bit of horse shit never killed anyone.

"Take a shower!" says Alfonso, his patience running out. "We're a modern circus with a water-supply. All living-quarters have showers and most of them have cooking facilities. You can either take your meals in the circus canteen, or cook your own. So get inside and clean yourself up then I'll take you to the Santinos family, 'cos you're gonna look after their kids!"

…

Chapter 6

The system is based on rumour and gossip and occasional quarrels, especially when Jack Iski is around. He is bawling at Madam Pinkie again, that her dogs must be kept clear of Wanda and Loftus – his two Indian elephants – or there'll be all hell let loose. "I'll see to it personally that these worthless mongrels of yours will be squashed flat and you can scrape them up and feed them to the lions," he threatens and turns to walk off in a huff.

Madam Pinkie stands her ground and looks after him with her hands on her hips, knowing that the rest of the circus is behind her, because nobody likes the elephant-trainer, who often mistreats his animals and is suspected of having purchased them through dark channels. "You should be sent to prison and the key thrown away," she yells after the retreating figure who turns and gives her a threatening look which doesn't intimidate her in the least. "You have no right to keep them chained to metal bolts, forcing them to sway their trunks day in and day out in a far-corner tent." Madam Pinkie, whose hair is dyed to match her name, hasn't finished yet. "I've seen you hitting your animals with an iron hook! That's what makes them scream, and not my darling doggies!"

Having put Jack Iski in his place, Madam Pinkie makes for her caravan to get ready for the show. Doreen and Nadja have already finished checking the tickets and will be selling ice-cream during the interval. They change their blue usherette uniforms for the transparent harem robes, because they are also part of the elephant show. Soon, they will climb onto the elephant's heads while the animals raise a front leg. After the change of position, the elephants, having been trained to sit, ridiculously uncharacteristic, on their hind legs, keep a sad eye on Jack in the background and armed with the hook, while Doreen and Nadja take the call.

The quarrel between Madam Pinkie and Jack Iski has been the cause of some gossip but is beginning to lose its shine, now that the news is spreading about Doreen and

Nadja not having a decent night's sleep since the new girl moved in.

Annie, the knife-throwing-target, informs a tight-rope artiste about what Doreen has told her.

"I don't believe it!" Marta, easily aroused to indignation, belongs to the famous Santinos family. "Who would want to spend the night cleaning?"

"It's true! She spends the whole night cleaning, and seems to find plenty to clean in that little corner of hers, but don't ask me what!" Nadja confirms to various members of the Santinos family, who have come to check on the story.

Doreen says to Annie, "When Sally's not cleaning her room, it's her clothes or her hands; and when she's not cleaning her corner, her clothes or her hands, she's jumping around on the trampoline and playing at clowns with the children."

The problem of the strange new girl's cleaning tic is still a topic of discussion in the kitchen. A short sharp shriek comes from Nadja in the kitchen trailer where she is peeling potatoes for a communal shepherd's pie. "Cleanitis! I've heard of that before! Isn't it some kind of disease?"

"It's not just the cleaning, it's the lies she tells," says Doreen. "Ask Andrea about the episode with her mother-in-law!"

News spreads around a circus like wildfire. Now it has reached Annie and Luke.

"Hey now, just listen to this!" says Annie to Lucky Luke as he enters the caravan after knife-throwing practise. "Andrea said it all started when her 'in-laws' began thinking about retiring from the circus."

"Aw, for Christ's sake..!"

"Mind you, Andrea agrees it's about time they retire, instead of just talking about it. Know what I mean? Thirty years in the ring and time is beginning to tell."

Lucky Luke prefers to remain unbiased and replies that Gerti and Charlie have never been top liners, in contrast to their son Ron who is a first-class performer.

"Yes, but Gerti has got it into her head they should retire to a cottage in the country; had enough of throwing rings to Charlie, she says. Besides, the routine has developed into a comic number over the years." Annie bursts into laughter, almost allowing the milk to boil over. "I'm just thinking about Charlie in the ring, 6-feet tall and thinner than a rake in his top-hat, peddling with his stork-like legs on his high bike. It's enough to get any audience roaring."

Lucky Luke laughs and swallows his milk almost in one go. His wife continues, "Since they've changed the act into ''Charlie and Ron, the Jolly Jugglers'', Ron claims his Dad is the best mobile prop he's ever had. Andrea says she doesn't mind Charlie, as lean as a stick and all knees and elbows, sitting in a corner and hardly speaking a word, which she can't say for Gerti, who'll beat eggs with her tongue! Mind you, Gerti has never got over fleeing from the Russians at the end of the war, seeing people freeze to death and bodies lying all over the place."

Lucky Luke puts down his mug and groans with exaggerated boredom because there's no stopping Gerti from telling her stories once she gets going.

"Andrea says it's time somebody else takes over the job of listening to the 'sorry tales' – and there's plenty of listening-potential in that new girl!"

"Look outside! What's she doing now?"

Annie pulls back the curtain. "Working on a trampoline-number with the Santinos kids."

"So that's what all the noise is about!"

"And what is Gerti getting up to while Charlie and Ron are practising in the ring?" asks Annie, eager to deliver the answer. "She's inviting Sally in for a cup of tea, isn't she? Telling her about fleeing from the Russians and leaving the corpses where they've dropped down to die, because you can't bury the dead in frozen earth, which is how it was in the winter of '45."

"Well then! Gerti has finally found someone who'll listen."

"Yes, but get this!" Annie takes her place at the table. "Gerti has finally met her match. She sits and listens to Sally talking about her miserable childhood and has even given her money. The girl is as poor as a church mouse, she says."

"Well, I never..!" remarks Lucky Luke.

"I'll just go over to the kitchen and check up on that!" says Annie.

"Tell us another!" says Doreen to Annie, who has entered the kitchen trailer while they're washing the dishes. "Hey Nadja!" Doreen screeches to her friend who is stacking pans on a shelf. "Heard the latest? Our roommate doesn't have a penny to her name, ha, ha! Didn't we take just a teeny weeny peek at her bankbook while she was outside, banging the rugs?"

"Aye, we did!" answers Nadja, looking slightly ashamed.

"Good old Gerti! She's found herself the right one this time! Met her match, she has!" replies Annie, who can't wait to tell them what she knows – about the money Gerti has given to Sally and the small dark cloud developing on Gerti's retirement horizon. "Parting from the rest of the family is bad enough," Nadja butts in, "but now there's the problem of Sally. She can't deny the girl a helping hand, knowing what it's like not having two pennies to rub together. The girl needs a motherly friend and Gerti needs somebody who'll listen. It's a perfect set-up, Sally telling the poor tale, while Gerti takes the biscuit-tin from the kitchen cupboard and gives her the money. At least that's what Andrea says!"

"Watch her when she goes to town," Doreen wipes down the sink, addressing nobody in particular. "She's even been seen in the bank. Nobody goes into a bank, unless they've got money. Who needs a bank with your wages in cash?"

"You're right there!" agrees Nadja.

Annie poses the far-reaching question, "Does anybody know where she comes from?"

"Nadja knows," says Doreen. "She read the postcard!"

"Well, I didn't really read it," Nadja interrupts. I just happened to throw a glance at the bedside table and there it was, stamped and ready."

"Go on, tell us, Nadja!"

"It was addressed to Mr and Mrs Matthew Foss, somewhere in West Yorkshire..."

"Aha!" they chorus.

"…just telling them she's enjoying being with the circus and is travelling the country. She can't ring them up because there's no 'phone."

"That's not true either!" says Annie. "She could have used the 'phone in Clementina's office."

"That's what she wrote!" says Nadja looking offended.

"Weird!"

"You c'n say that again!"

Annie looks at her watch. Luke is eager to start practising their new routine. She makes for the door. "There are no secrets in this circus, so watch your purse, kiddo!"

...

When Annie returns to the caravan to prepare for the evening performance, her husband is already wearing the fringed western gear and looking out of the window, where Sally's new mini-circus trampoline-show is practising outside.

Little Paco is rubbing his leg and bawling his eyes out as the two older girls shout at their cousins to leave him alone and stop calling him a sissy! "It's not your ball! It belongs to Zasto – and he said we could play with it!"

"What a commotion!" says Lucky Luke, closing the curtains and leaning back on the settee. "Give me a moment of peace between performances, and I'll be the happiest man alive."

But Sally's enthusiasm is infectious and the children are quieting down, so he looks out of the window once more to enjoy the childish burlesque of jumps, loops and slap-stick chases. "Hey Annie!" he yells to his wife who is putting on her petticoats. "Look at this! Even the Moroccan women are coming outside."

"Keep your head up, Manuel and Concha. Pull yourself up on that imaginary rope – like this!" Sally shows them.
Paco and Maribel turn the long skipping rope for Pepe to jump; then Manuel and Concha join the hilarity of the small madcap clowns. Paco has lost his clown's nose and Concha, the cheeky one, picks it up. Now it's his turn to wear it. Paco howls again, but not for long as they chase each other around the ring with giant plastic sunflowers on their heads, fixed to their swimming caps and swaying as

they move. Manuel takes the watering can and climbs on the trampoline, to water the garden as it circles below.

Paco shouts, "Hey Sally, put on your costume! You're much nicer when you're a clown!"

Hurriedly, she opens the clown's bag which saves her soul against desperation; pulls the baggy trousers over her jeans and fixes the coloured braces, transforming herself into Miss Flummi. The children screech with delight at Miss Flummi's cardboard-soled giant shoes covered with window-leathers and a big red bow matching the nose. She runs around the trampoline. The braces come loose and the oversize trousers flap around her ankles.

Lucky Luke, still watching through the window, throws himself onto the settee and wipes his eyes. "Hey Annie, you wouldn't read about it! What d'you think that clown has under her pants? Bloomers! Bloomers, with a pink arse on the back!"

The noisy revelry has attracted a crowd and Alfonso's laughter booms over the field, watching Miss Flummi's fruitless attempts at sweeping up the tiny clowns with a gigantic yard brush. Until now, there has only been room for one clown in the circus. Is Zasto's position beginning to crumble?

Clementina has heard the gossip. She pulls up the bed-sheet but has no intention of falling asleep until the problem has been thoroughly discussed. "For Christ's sakes, Alfonso, I worry about you letting Zasto have his own way because he'll tolerate no rivalry. One of these days he'll get ill or have an accident and we won't have a clown in this circus!"

"I'm worried about the next time he gets shacked up with a woman!"Alfonso admits.

"He'll be off, just like that!" Clementina sits up in bed and clicks her fingers. "Imagine the headlines! Circus Poppi – the circus with no clown!"

"I know, I know, the girl has talent!" he admits. "Tomorrow, I'll have her in the ménage together with Zasto, to see if we can fix up a side-act routine – an' I won't take no bull-shit this time!"

...

Zasto's clown face is painted with a big white smile, but his forehead exposes the rivets of deliberation, having informed Alfonso for the hundredth time that he has no intention of working with a side-kick.

But Alfonso grabs his opportunity when the children have finished their tumbling and been called inside by their mothers. He waves his arms in admiration of another spontaneous performance. "I always say", he announces keeping an eye on Zasto, "that's what distinguishes the true artist from the amateur performer."

They observe Zasto from the corners of their eyes. The clown is mysterious and demands respect. With hands in his pockets he regards his surroundings, feigning indifference when Alfonso leads Sally into the 'Big Top'.

Infatuated by her immediate surroundings; the aroma of fresh sawdust mingled with the pungent trace of animals, the girl is aware of having arrived where she belongs. She has entered an Aladdin's Cave of safety nets, trapezes, trampolines, bars and beams, brightly coloured props, blowing whistles and shouted commands. It is a world of glittering performances that disappear like burnt-out sparklers when the audience leaves, forcing the artiste into habitual seclusion beyond that of normal life, reducing the ménage to an arena for human bodies performing unimaginable feats, together with wild animals, trained to perform against nature.

Adam and Marek nod politely as they lead the horses out of the tent, their harnesses reflecting in the light, and brightly coloured feathers dancing to the rhythmic movements of their heads. Miko, their trainer and the eldest of the three brothers, carries the long 'chambarrier' ring whip, already dressed in his white silken suit for the evening performance.

The five Santinos children are now subdued and disciplined, readily harnessed for a training session on the trapeze under the critical eye of Juan and his brother Mejandro. Their wives, Marta and Maria, are dressed in bright red leotards and patiently wait on the horizontal bar. Juan shouts instructions in Spanish and Mejandro stands directly beneath the safety net watching anxiously as Pepe, followed by Paco and Manuel, begin the rope-walk. Pepe is ambitious; has recently achieved his first successful somersault on the rope and proudly announces he'll be a top-class artiste and appear on television at Christmas.

Later, he'll climb into the circus cupola, swing from one trapeze to another and land without a tremor inside the frame and the hands of Uncle Juan. Paco or Manuel will replace Juan; Concha and Maribel will perform in other circuses, or replace Aunt Marta who has problems with her back.

Alfonso Poppi puts on his red jacket with gold braiding and regards himself in the mirror propped against the tent wall, smiling with satisfaction at the coup he has landed. A neat bit of diplomacy has persuaded Zasto to work with the girl – and there's plenty of potential in her. His nose for talent has never failed him yet - and his sharp business sense tells him he can engage a good performer at a cheap price. Moreover, it will silence the clown, who has recently been grumbling about being underpaid for a high-quality performance.

When Zasto gets rid of his clown's face, his natural looks are striking – a young Errol Flynn in his swashbuckling days, with that gleaming wayward smile; a mixture of sex and mischief that can't be resisted. He follows them inside the Big Top and stands next to Alfonso. His eyes glitter over the girl in the ring, telling her he'll get what he wants. They fluster behind his back, the pretty ones, who've already been in his arms and safely reached the other side. Either you sink or swim! This one will sink! Just you watch, kiddo!

Alfonso, with the dramatic gesture of the eternal showman, beckons towards her. "Come here my darling, come here!" He continues beckoning, ignoring her obvious discomfort at his impulsive embraces, coupled with Zasto's eyes running over her body. "I need a replacement for the Russian Illusionist. His agent has 'phoned me to say he's been taken ill and offered a contract with some second-class magician who'll jump in for the season. Circus Poppi doesn't work with second-class performers, so now we've got a problem – a big tent with a weak show. I need a highlight! Give me a highlight!" he adds theatrically.

Zasto takes the cue and throws back his head, displaying a row of white teeth. He removes an imaginary hat and bows deeply. Finally, he clicks his heels and stands to attention. What on earth is he up to? Is he about to salute? When he twists his right ear, there's a screwing noise from the depth of his throat. Suddenly, a ball appears in the palm of his hand. More ear screwing brings forth another ball, and then another. Soon, he is juggling with five balls and once more, Alfonso's laughter echoes around the tent.

Sally stands open-mouthed. She has never seen anything like it! What is happening? Something enters her mouth, propped between her teeth. She spits out the ball and turns her attention to the trampoline, determined not to be sidetracked from her big moment.

From the centre, no longer encumbered by her clumsy clown's shoes, she performs a series of back flips and triple twists, followed by the familiar routine practised to perfection in a previous life. Then she opens the checked pillowcase and is suddenly transformed into Miss Flummi the clown. Miss Flummi is sitting on an imaginary chair, reading an invisible newspaper. Now she is jumping about in the chair, going higher and higher. And oh, horror! What is she reading? Arms and legs shoot in the air, protruding in all directions.

Turn the page! Oh! The next page brings sadness. Where is the bright red handkerchief for mopping her eyes? She puts a hand to an ear. What are they telling her? The handkerchief is hanging from her back pocket.

Circus people watch the performance and applaud. Alfonso shouts "Bravo! Take a compliment! Take a compliment!"

A compliment? Nothing easier than that!

Zasto, the eternal performer and not to be outdone, puts on his red nose, turns up his face and howls like a dog. Who cares if he is in or out of the ring? The eternal performer is strutting about, his bright red nose in the air. He takes the giant comb from a back pocket, removes the tiny green hat and proceeds to rake through his hair, but in vain. The comb is entwined. How will he get it out of that mess?

"Your new partner says, welcome to the circus!" Alfonso shakes her hand and wonders about her eyes. Why are they always brimming with tears?

…

Chapter 7

On one wall of his study where he spends most of his spare time – and since retiring, he has plenty of spare time – are thirty-five wooden spoons. Some of them remind him of the cases he's worked on.

The centrepiece is an oversize jam-spoon with a strong broom-stick handle. The lower half, with a shovel-like scoop, is stained dark-red, due to the bubbling masses of blackcurrant-jelly it has stirred over the years; a harmless implement before becoming a weapon. Molly Braeburn had used it to strangle the pit-bull threatening her daughter, confirming Nickbone's theory about great strength being derived in critical situations. At least that's how Nickbone explains the incident to a visitor eager to hear more about an untrained and overweight woman of doubtful ability who had shot out of the kitchen like a rocket, slipped the spoon through the dog's collar, pinned it down with the full weight of her body, turned the handle and didn't get up until the animal was dead.

"Where is the other half of that spoon, over there?" asks the young policeman who has dropped by for a visit. They had worked together in a team and Nickbone is eager to remain in contact with his previous colleagues.

"Ah! Now we're delving into the dungeons of humanity – beaten away on little James Redburn." Nickbone shudders, remembering the bruises and streaks which had taken him to his limits. How the surreptitious Puritan inside him had cheered when the notorious bully – the aggressive boyfriend of a weak and passive mother – was sent to prison and the mercy of fellow convicts – child abuse being the lowest of crimes.

The young policeman takes a closer look at the old-fashioned wooden ladle; a strange apparition covered with indefinable lumps of unknown consistency which are, in fact, particles of dried and decomposed food.

"Ah! Now we're going back into the Middle Ages, when people stood behind castle walls and catapulted flaming oil rags into the enemy beneath. That's how Angelo Brizzerio protected his snack-bar from the gangster collecting 'protection money' – with the wooden ladle and lumps of red-hot bolognaise sauce catapulted into the thug's face," explains Nickbone who'll tell a good tale if he's in the mood. The young policeman nods his head understandingly.

"Down there, that tiny thing on the bottom row; you wouldn't connect it to the most spectacular robbery since Lady Turnball's jewellery, now would you?"

"The Rembrandt...?"

"Owned by none other than Peter McNee Junior and on loan to the Municipal Museum."

"Embarrassing..! Before my time, though!"

"A bloody catastrophe it was – just as he was about to invest in 'Beeper's Electrical Appliances' and generate a thousand new jobs."

"Oh aye! I was still at school, but remember reading about it in the newspapers. They were full of it!"

"Putting us under insurmountable pressure..." adds Nickbone dramatically, recalling the negative publicity which had almost cost him his job.

"I'll bet!"

"...to find the painting, which we finally did, thanks to this little wooden spoon taken from another exhibit, a Victorian doll's house, to prop open the window, wide enough for a painting to be pushed through. Ah well!" Nickbone said, reminiscing with a sigh. "The tongue grows loose when the mouth is dry and the glass is empty, with a wallet to match. An informant gave us the tip – a museum guard – lover of art. Six hours later, London colleagues unearthed the painting from the back of a Hampstead garage."

"Interesting! I didn't know the police had done such a good job!

...

Nickbone, having spent the best part of his life with the 'force', has grown old listening to stories – some true, others false – eye-witness accounts and figments of imagination. He has conducted countless interviews with all types of human-beings – bourgeois and proletarian, alcoholics and wife-beaters. He has lost count of those he has questioned and arrested – thieves and murderers, erring juveniles and drug addicts. Bible thumpers have amused him and schizophrenics have bothered him. There have been times when he has wondered if the world has gone mad!

So what now, besides collecting snuff-boxes and wooden spoons? Should he try his hand at gardening? It can be a pleasant occupation when the weather is good, but a miserable drudge when it is raining! Nickbone is at a loose end, once more. His wife is at work and his visitor has left. He goes outside and almost faces George whom he would rather avoid but now it's too late!

"It's the right time of the year to do something about those roses," remarks George from the other side of the hedge. His neighbour, who as senior manager of 'Greenwood's Gardening Centre' and honorary chairman of the local Horticultural Society, finds fulfilment in his immaculate garden. A hidden arm points a trowel in the direction of some lupines and then moves across the lawn like the barrel of a shotgun, while George mutters something about pruning the apple tree if he wants a decent crop, which we all want, or we wouldn't have an apple tree, would we? After the gardener has finished laughing at his own joke, he fastens the strings of his green apron and takes the deep breath of a man wanting something off his chest.

"Have you ever thought about adding a pond to the bottom of your garden?" he asks in the quiet and confidential manner of someone on the verge of asking a well-considered question.

Nickbone stares at the trowel pointing towards the firs.

"Chop them down," George continues, "and you'll have more light. We'll make a nice little pond – or better still, how about a waterfall running over a rocky stream-bed into a larger pond stretching across both gardens. You and I and a bit of spit," he gleefully rubs his hands together. "No trouble! Eh?"

Nickbone stares into the distance thinking his neighbour might be a nice chap, but they have little in common. *George has no interest in amateur dramatics, nor is he a collector of unusual objects. Has he ever asked about my work on the 'force? No! Never! On the other hand, I am no gardener. All I need is a nice green lawn to sit on, and nothing else!*

So what about travel?

Patricia says she'll be scratching the travelling itch when she retires and fancies doing a backpacker's round-the-world trip.

"Whatever route we take, there'll have to be some compromises about back-packing," Nickbone had said, favouring the luxury of a comfortable hotel bed, the enjoyment of fine cooking and excellent wine. And how would the necessary gear, the evening suit, fit into a rucksack?

Or join the 'pensioner colony' in Spain?

Ouch, for God's sake! He might be getting old, but still thrives on the stimulation of youth. Besides, his success in the role of Edward 1V has gone to his head, and he's fancying himself as Merryman the Butler in 'The Importance of being Earnest' which the amateur-dramatics society are planning for the next season. Being an Oscar Wilde fan, he wouldn't mind reading for the part and imagines his name at the top of the bill like many a budding actor before him. He collects the newspaper from the front lawn and goes inside to read it, leaving George at the other side of the fence to his horticultural dreams.

Announcing the arrival of the famous - 'Circus Poppi!'
The world's most exciting circus..."

His attention is caught by the gaudy advertisement, just as his wife arrives home still wearing the black tights and loose t-shirt of her 'musical-movement-working-clothes'. Nickbone thinks she still looks good for her age and makes a mental note to tell her so, but shows her the advertisement instead. "Does that ring a bell?"

"Without my reading-glasses it looks like Circus Poppi. Isn't that the one Sally Foss joined?" There's a moment of silence before the logical, follow-up question. "We could go to the circus, couldn't we? I haven't been to one for years! Besides, it'll be a great opportunity to see Sally and find out what she's doing. Do circuses have trampolines? I suppose they do..!" Her voice fades away as she put on her glasses. "Tomorrow is Thursday and it says here that the circus opens on Friday."

Nickbone nods.

"It'll be a pleasant drive! Does that café still exist? What was the name? 'Molly's Coffee Shop'! They served the best lemon-meringue-pie I've ever eaten. We can look around the castle gardens."

He smiles indulgently, having little inclination towards sightseeing.

Is he on the wrong track? There'd been more to Jeffrey Nelson's death than had met the eye, but his senior officer had taken a different point of view. The case had been closed and Nickbone had gone into retirement. Has he become obsessed? Is he trying to make a murderess out of an eighteen-year-old girl? Is he in his right mind for making tentative enquiries among former colleagues about further developments? He always asks, when they meet at the 'Malt Shovel' for old time's sake, and hears the same reply; "No further developments, old boy. Nothing that would justify re-opening the case!" But there had been too many coincidences! Too many hints of truth in the gossip! There had definitely been a love affair between Charmaine Foss and Jeffrey Nelson which might have caused the daughter to suffer and people have killed for less than that. One thing's for sure; if he hadn't gone into retirement he'd have investigated further, especially regarding the mysterious figure on the road.

Hey now, you know better than to put a fellow like Tommy Thistleton, a notorious drunkard, in the witness box. And besides, why the hell should you be bothering your grey masses when you have better things to do?

But his perceptive sixth-sense is nagging him again. In his youth, he'd considered himself freakish, unable to drop the habit of continually assessing people he hardly knew – and correctly, so it had proved. After joining the force, his analytical talents had developed in such an extraordinary manner, that he found himself able to predict people's actions; he could almost read their minds.

"I love circuses!" His wife breaks into his thoughts. Staying home for more than a couple of days invariably gives her the fidgets.

...

Patricia, in the passenger seat of the Ford, scrutinizes his profile. He has hardly said a word during the past hour, apart from absent-minded responses about the countryside looking nice at this time of the year. There's a suspicious furrow between his eyebrows and his lips, although firmly closed, are pursed in higher thought.

"Hey you...," she nudges him playfully,"...what are you thinking about?"

A typical woman's question! What should he tell her? Perhaps he's forgotten to clean his teeth and is thinking about turning the car and going back home to do the job. What a ridiculous question!

"Are we visiting the circus for some other reason?"

He glances sideways, ignoring her bluntness. "I am also looking forward to meeting Sally Foss," he admits tenaciously and concentrates on entering the round-about, heavy with traffic, before turning south. "Why did she leave school during mid-term, to join the circus, of all things?"

"If I'd had a mother like Charmaine Foss, I'd have run off sooner or later. You'll hardly believe it, but I haven't actually *seen* Mrs Foss, since her daughter played the white rabbit in 'Alice in Wonderland', six years ago!"

Nickbone makes a surprised noise.

"They were never home when I picked the girl up. It's a wonder she achieved the Junior Championship. I'd almost got her into the International Stream – and then she started hanging around with Carol Horn of all people! You know, Hank Horn, the television producer's daughter."

"But kids don't leave school in the middle of term without good reason."

Patricia lowers her voice. "Rumour has it that her mother went to Carol's house and dragged her away from a party. Then the school got a sick note and nobody saw her again. The last thing we heard, she'd got a job with Circus Poppi, and being almost eighteen, nobody stopped her!"

"Well then, under the circumstances, she's probably better off with the circus," her husband replies as red and green striped flags fluttering at the entrance come into view. At each side of the banner Circus Poppi is advertised in gaudy red letters. The fence continues behind the 'Big Top'; the huge white tent supported by two ship-like masts presiding over the circus like a protective mushroom, separating equipment and living space from the stalls. Children chase each other between ropes, piles of planks and stacks of empty crates, until it's time to take up their duties.

Patricia and Nicholas Lightbone join the queue in front of the ticket office, superstitiously placed in the directions where the money flows. Those in the growing queue wait patiently between lines of posters displaying gaudy circus scenes; a clown balancing on a ladder, a glamorous tight-rope-walker with the customary opened umbrella and a fearless animal trainer raising his whip at the lions. At each side of the entrance, two olive-skinned girls in blue and gold uniforms, check tickets and rip off the corners.

Nickbone purchases two tickets and enquires about Sally.

"Oh yes! Sally is still with the circus, sir!" The middle-aged woman with a bright red ribbon holding long black hair raises her eyebrows as though anything else might be an atrocity. "Today is the premier of their act. You'll be sure to enjoy it sir," she gives him a knowing look and then keeping a satisfied eye on the queue behind him, pushes two tickets under the glass.

"And where are her living quarters?"

"Sorry, sir! We don't encourage visitors inside the living-quarter areas!"

Nickbone nods understandingly. "My wife used to be Sally's trainer and we have brought her the mascot she left in the car." He holds up the bag containing the lucky teddy-bear Sally had sworn, she couldn't win a competition without.

"In that case, you can leave it outside her wagon door," says the dark-haired woman whose name is Clementina. Visitors holding up the ticket-queue with trifling questions are distinctly annoying. She is impatient to get it moving again.

"Manuel! Go and accompany this gentleman to Sally's wagon will you!" she calls the boy over and then takes the microphone. "Roll up! Roll up! Get your tickets for the show of a lifetime!"

A dark-haired boy of about nine or ten and wearing a blue satin shirt, points out the living-quarters at the rear side of the tent. His hand turns an invisible key and he suddenly springs to life with a succession of somersaults, effortlessly directed towards an old-fashioned trailer.

"That was very clever," Patricia is genuinely impressed and Nickbone feels obliged to reward the boy for this extraordinary performance.

The boy accepts the offered coin, doffs an imaginary hat, bows deeply and shouts through the half-open window, "Hey Sally! You've got visitors!" Then he retraces his cartwheels towards the 'Big Top' to take charge of the newly acquired popcorn machine.

...

Visitors? She raises her head and peers through the white lace curtain into an earlier life, locked away and forgotten, and instantly recognises the familiar figure; the woman standing outside, for whom she'd once felt great affection. And where had it got her? Now, all she feels is sadness and anger! Who is the elderly man staring at the door of the cabin? Who has given them the right to enter her new life? "Go away and leave me alone! Let me attend to my face!" she mutters. "The person you're looking for no longer exists."

She watches them hang the bag on the door-handle before walking away. After remaining motionless for a while, she opens the door and disposes of the bag in the rubbish-bin without looking inside. It's time to return to the mirror and the selection of bottles; the wet-white and boxes of eye-black, and complete the face created by Zasto.

Miss Flummi, the clowness, has a new face; white-ringed eyes pointed with black dots; bright pink cheeks highlighted with commas and black stripes, stretching from the big red nose to the thick painted lips. The chin is almost as red as the nose.

"Welcome to the circus, Miss Flummi!" She examines herself in the mirror and addresses the face. "How will you behave today, Miss Flummi? Will you be disobedient, cheeky, and disrespectful? Kids love a clown to do the things they are not allowed to – it sends them into raptures. You'll make a fool of Zasto, the simple-minded carpet clown with the oversize shoes and the baggy trousers with a backside patch. Kids love clowns to make fools of themselves in everyday situations and if you tear off that patch, a bunch of flowers will suddenly spring from his backside."

They've been practising it for a month and almost achieved perfection; exactly the routine which Zasto had performed as a child with his father, in the Hungarian circus. But the act had died with the father; now, it is being brought back to life by the son.

Will you sleep with me tonight, Miss Flummi? She can still hear his voice whispering in her ear; feel the constriction in her throat, wondering how she should react. It had been useless, pretending she knew all about everything, including men, of whom she still knows very little but is learning fast. A woman of the world might have produced some clever reply; but nothing had entered her head other than the intense longing somewhere inside her, when Zasto had looked at her with fierce eyes, breathing heavily and muttering things she shouldn't be hearing. Should she concede to his advances?

Try it out and see what it's like, this 'sex' you almost once had. She shudders at memories of shame and humiliation. They are locked away in the back of her mind and she won't let them out.

Zasto had stood watching her, waiting for an answer. "I'll be waiting, Miss Flummi!" he'd said in a seductive, foreign, yet familiar voice, addressing her new self. It had been a strange and wonderful feeling when they'd made love for the very first time; wild and intense, leaving her emotionally drained. Since then, it has become the drug she readily accepts without restraint, knowing she can return to the trailer with the beautiful feeling; the wonderful sensation of cleaning her environment and all her possessions.

...

Miss Flummi is wearing a bright orange wig beneath the miniature black bowler, a present from Zasto. She slips into the mud-caked clogs standing outside the door, worn for crossing the field. In the Big Top, artists are already waiting for their cues, standing in line, watching the ménage through peep-holes in the canvas.

The orchestra strikes up the fanfare and the audience applauds as the ringmaster strides into the ring accompanied by Zasto, the clown.

"Go away! Go away, you annoying clown," the ringmaster orders Zasto who is running in circles, clutching a bunch of huge, brightly coloured balloons. Ignoring the ringmaster's commands, the clown fixes the helium-filled balloons to his trousers to prevent them from slipping. The ringmaster puts his hands on his hips, having no intention of tolerating such behaviour. He removes his top hat and scratches his head, wondering what to do, ignoring the children's demands that he leave the clown alone. He has made his decision; takes hold of the pistol and fires, which echoes throughout the tent as he chases the clown. Balloons burst; children scream with glee, baggy trousers hang around the clown's ankles exposing the voluminous red and green striped underpants.

"Ladies and Gentlemen!" The Ringmaster takes a deep breath, having regained composure and control of the proceedings. He holds the microphone in one hand; makes sweeping gestures with the other. With great importance he announces the animal show, ignoring the clown, who walks off in a huff. "It gives me very great pleasure to announce a double sensation. Circus Poppi is proud to present the most intelligent dogs ever to appear in a circus ménage, together with the smallest horse in the world." His voice rises triumphantly. "Here is the one and only ..." another roll of drums..." Madam Pinkie's Horse and Dog School," he roars, stepping back into the folds of the curtain as the pack enters the ménage, yelping and panting with excitement.

But the severe Madam Pinkie, glaring over rimless spectacles, will have discipline in her schoolroom. A supply of biscuits from a hidden pocket persuades the dogs that their places are on a row of chairs in front of the blackboard. Madam Pinkie writes, with great flourish, the sum on the blackboard and the brown and white Jack Russell barks the result. Four and three are summed up in appropriate barks and a collie of mixed origin proves that mathematical geniuses don't have two legs. A prop man provides a skipping rope and the bright orange poodle jumps backward and forward over it, wagging it's tale at the thunderous applause and the prospect of a biscuit.

Time for a tune! The blood-curling howls of 'Greensleeves' spread through the tent, sending the audience into fits of laughter, only to be subdued when a prop-man reappears with the bridled dog, claimed to be the smallest horse in the world. The animal circulates the ring proudly tossing its head before springing through the hoops exactly placed by Madam Pinkie. Drums roll and the excitement of the audience is almost audible as the tiny horse reaches the climax. Brave and daring, the plucky animal jumps through the burning ring and immediately receives the frenzied applause of a relieved audience before leaving the ménage unscathed. Madam Pinkie takes the last compliment followed by her school of animals, strutting out of the ring on hind legs.

"Ladies and gentlemen! It is an honour and my very great pleasure to introduce one of the greatest pioneering juggling acts ever shown. Give a warm welcome to…" The voice climbs two octaves, "The Jolly Jugglers."

Gerti, ornate and unrecognisable in a glittering lilac gown, with matching headdress of dyed ostrich plumes, circles the ménage with sweeping gestures; a fine entrée for Charlie on his unicycle, suitably heralded by the trumpet fanfare. Dressed up to the nines in top hat and tails, he whizzes around the ring all arms and legs, like a big black spider catching the rings. Over the years, Gerti has cultivated the art of throwing rings onto protruding black limbs and Charlie's eyes bulge with feigned surprised as the circling rings reach his neck. Meanwhile, Gerti tosses the pole and takes a compliment on behalf of her husband who is transferring the ever-moving rings to the pole for a neat finish. Another compliment is underlined by an orchestral fanfare, and a roar of applause.

Ron appears, following spectacularly in his father's footsteps, introduced by Gerti, whose figure is no longer slim, but sparkles like a Christmas tree in the ménage. The fanfare induces another round of applause for Ron's mother, who disappears behind the curtain leaving an audience in breathless anticipation as the lights are dimmed. One hears the sound of tyres circling on sawdust. Anxious children fear ghostly shadows flitting across the ménage. Why are they sitting in the darkness? What will happen next?

The orchestra strikes up the soft chords of a Viennese waltz. Iridescent forms fly through the air – red, blue and green, through fine clouds of sawdust; bright circles of light changing shape in mid-air.

Somewhere in the audience, Nickbone is aware of Patricia's hand on his arm, enchanted by the abundance of shining objects – brightly coloured cones and spirals, rings and triangles, tiny shooting stars that appear from nowhere and fly over their heads.

Alfonso Poppi watches his artists through the peep-hole, congratulating himself on the long-term engagement of Gerti and Charlie. Over the years, he has kept a watchful eye on their son's progress – once a promising twelve-year-old – now a top number for a middle-class fee, and another three-year contract. The circus director rubs his hands. There's another promising candidate in the shadows behind the curtain, excitedly waiting her cue. In a few moments she'll have her premier, without his introduction.

Where is Zasto? Alfonso stands in the ménage, as rigid as a sentry. There must be no superfluous movements in the ring and he won't be turning around to search for his clown. He watches The Jolly Jugglers take their bows. Lights are dimmed and the spotlight fixes the red velvet curtain. All is well!

Zasto is a good carpet clown. His job is to make people laugh and distract their attention from background activities while the ring boys fix up the trampoline in a dark corner. The clown storms into the ring shouldering a large wooden box, parading around, laughing and indicating how proud he is of it. Without effort, he lowers it to the ground and opens the lid.

Miss Flummi, the rubber doll with the mass of bright orange hair and dressed in a black and white striped shirt, matching tights and long black vest with a large hole in the back, pops up like a jack-in-the-box and surprises the audience. She unfolds her arms and they hang over the sides. The clash of cymbals underline her movements as Zasto coos over his new doll; carefully removes her from the box and carries her to a chair.

But the rubber doll won't sit straight and flops from one side to the other. When the clown pushes her into place, an arm lashes out and hits him on the head, underlined once more by the cymbals! He staggers about the ring. This will not do! Things are out of control! Triumphantly, he demonstrates what he will to do with the giant hammer, but the children won't have him hitting his doll and there are strong cries of protest. The shameful clown cups an ear in disbelief, raises his thick painted eyebrows, removes his ridiculous tiny hat, and sprinkles the audience with sorrowful tears.

But everybody knows that Zasto is a loveable clown. He doesn't intend to hurt his doll, and loud cheers accompany his change of mind. He bends down to attend to his enormous shoe and Miss Flummi kicks his backside trouser-patch. A bright yellow flower slowly appears, accompanied by the strains of a violin. Now it is Miss Flummi's big moment!

The chase begins – around the ménage and onto the trampoline. But Zasto, with the flower sticking out of his backside patch, is far too clumsy and there's no chance he'll catch her as she flies through the air, rubber limbs moving in all directions. What can he do?

"Leave her alone!" yells the audience and there are hilarious screams when he notices the flower on his backside and chases it like a dog chasing its tail. Then, like a shy lover, he plucks the flower and presents it to his doll, accompanied by the wavering strains of the background violin. The audience is now satisfied when she pins the flower to her mop of bright orange hair before returning to the depths of the box. Zasto closes the lid, heaves it onto his shoulder and leaves the ring.

"Not bad for a start," whispers Alfonso Poppi, hardly audible due to the deafening applause. He reappears from behind the red velvet curtain, flourishes his microphone and introduces The World Famous, one and only, 'Flying Santinos'.

Patricia Lightbone squeezes her husband's arm: He smiles indulgently as her words melt into the music. At last, she can reap the fruits of her efforts.

...

As the Big Top empties, there's a queue outside the zoo-compound where a serious boy collects entrance-money. A couple of llamas stand patiently waiting to be stroked, ignoring the delighted shrieks of the children. A middle aged matron dressed in tweeds, who might be their grandmother, reminds the excited children to be careful because the animals might spit. A lonely white goat on a tether is permanently in search of the chewable; it sniffs at the tweed skirt but loses interest when the serious-faced young groom appears with an armful of hay.

Patricia isn't interested in the zoo. She can hardly wait to speak to Sally again – at last and after all this time! She nurtures some notion about renewing their relationship. What a career! Junior champion in Trampoline Jumping and now a circus clown – and what a clown she is!

She leaves Nickbone watching the good humoured attempts of a uniformed attendant at squeezing a coin from people around, for a 'photo with Wanda the elephant. The long-suffering animal still bears the colourful braiding of her Indian birthplace and her chained legs move restlessly, ignoring the commotion below. Nickbone senses the animal's misery and decides to watch the lions instead, growling and snarling over clumps of meat at the end of a rod. The old male prowls ferociously backwards and forwards – the typical movements of wild animals behind bars.

As Nickbone turns away feeling vaguely uncomfortable, his wife walks towards him looking equally gloomy.

"So you didn't see her!" He tries to avoid looking smug.

"No I didn't! She wasn't in her trailer before the performance and nobody knows where she is now."

"She was home before – just didn't open the door, did she?"

"What makes you say that?" she asks, disbelievingly.

"Because of the clogs!

"The clogs?"

"Artistes wear them to keep their feet clean when crossing muddy fields before performing. I noticed the trapeze artistes wear them. Sally's clogs – with the 'S' across the front – were on the steps outside the door of the cabin while we were waiting outside like a couple of idiots. I'll bet a hundred quid, the person whose name begins with an 'S' was still inside when we knocked on that door, or my name isn't Nicholas Lightbone!"

"Oh no! She wouldn't hide herself away, would she? It's not the normal thing to do, is it? We were a good team, and got on so well!" Patricia begins an intensive search for something in her bag, then blows her nose nervously before turning her attention to a couple of boys and a dog chasing a ball.

Nickbone's attention, however, is suddenly drawn by a crowd at the entrance and, for a moment, he ignores his wife's misery. 'STOP CIRCUS ANIMAL SUFFERING' is posted in huge black letters across a white banner, blocking the entrance and attracting a crowd. An elderly doorman is attempting in vain to assert his authority, but his dark red uniform can have no effect on the chorus of whistles and chanting of slogans. The two attendants, who rush to join him, realize the hopelessness of their efforts and turn their attention to the first priority – animal compounds in need of protection. Nobody will argue against pitchforks and clubs.

The demonstrators shout and chant to the bang of a drum. Wanda, the elephant, tired of having her photograph taken, raises her trunk, and the noise of her trumpets override the commotion until Jack Iski, armed with a threatening fork, leads her away. Suddenly, six circus musicians appear armed with violin, trumpet, percussions and horn. They stand in line until the Circus Director raises his baton. *'Oh when the saints come marching in'* spreads across the field. Cymbals crash and trumpets scream into 'The New Orleans Stomp'. The protesting crowd admits defeat and roll up the banner, having made their point. Another circus will appear in the region sooner or later, and they'll gather anew to carry out their mission.

"Come on, let's leave!" Nickbone steers his wife across the road between slow-moving traffic towards the car parked in the neighbouring field.

Chapter 8

Alfonso says he has half a mind to sack his agent for booking them up north at the end of the season, and move the circus, lock stock and barrel, to Spain for the winter.

"There's no sense in freezing our arses at our age," he complains to Clementina, busy with the flying crocheting-needle. She has almost completed another office curtain. Their luxurious caravan displays an assorted artistry, from crocheted cushions and toilet-roll covers, to a series of pin-point embroidered animal motives. There's hardly a wall which has escaped the embroidery, or an object that isn't decorated with some hand-crocheted covering.

Antonio, her son, says he hates the stuff. Just recently, he has pulled out his beautiful wooden caravan furnishings and replaced them with black and grey plastic. Clementina (getting her own back for the embroidery) says she wouldn't be seen dead in the middle of it; although proud of their individualistic son who has set his sights on Las Vegas, where wild animal shows are popular, and a couple of German animal-trainers are earning a fortune with white tigers.

She straightens one of her crocheted mats – pink, bordered with rosebuds – a pretty table centrepiece. Crocheting is good for the nerves. When Antonio is working with the lions, she must soothe her nerves. He loves the lions. "One mustn't think about what might happen," he keeps telling her, "but under no circumstances be careless or mistreat the animals, because they'll never be wholly tame."

Clementina, born into a family of balancing artistes, has learnt to keep her fears to herself. Sometimes, her thoughts return to Marvin – poor Uncle Marvin – the black sheep of the family, 'the master of the balancing-plates'. People used to say "he's a walking catastrophe! One of these days, he'll dig his grave with the bottle of whisky he is emptying."

She still remembers the screams; the men shouting into the night as they hurried outside, too late to save Uncle Marvin, in a drunken stupor against the bars of the cage and half of his head gone missing. The lions had gnawed at him. With their great claws, they had pulled at his body to get him inside. Mother of Jesus! Remember the clothes! Torn and bloody ... the bones and the hair!

Her fingers fly with the crocheting needle, speeding on unpleasant memories. At this rate, she'll complete the curtain before returning to the office. A window isn't a window without a crocheted curtain to protect against inquisitive eyes.

She unbuttons her cardigan; another hot flush is approaching. Alfonso's disposition is making things worse and she has a good mind to escape to the office and finish the wages. Now he's ranting on about the money they'll lose through heating the tent and keeping the water from freezing. "That agent must be bloody mad for booking us up north at the end of the season", he complains, generating excitement like a phosphorescent glow; excitement for the circus, the family and their daughter's impending marriage into the Petronella family. The wedding will take place in Spain, when they return home for winter. Clementina's admiration for the English custom of dressing up for weddings has conjured visions of an elegant bride's mother. It is the bright blue hat and matching coat in the bridal magazine on the table, which she is planning to wear.

A newspaper article has refuelled Alfonso's outrage. "Read this!" he commands, banging it onto the table with a bejewelled fist. "These 'CAP' people are causing big trouble! We can't ignore the negative publicity any longer!" A plump finger points out the article 'DO CIRCUSES MISTREAT ANIMALS?' , captioned, *The Captive Animals' Protection Society claim widespread cruelty to circus animals.* There's the 'photo of a sad-looking lion staring at the onlooker through the bars of a cage, and the female animal trainer who has allegedly whipped a chimpanzee to death.

Once more, Clementina is reminded of her childhood, and the dancing bear dolefully staring at her through the bars of a cage. The bear had been a big attraction in the parade when they had come into town. She can still hear it howling with pain, after her father's beatings to prove he was the boss. "One never argues with a bear," he would say.

"You should get Jack to stop maltreating his elephants," Clementina demands of her irate husband. He returns to the newspaper with a weary sigh. Jack Iski has a lousy reputation. It's about time Alfonso gets rid of him, she mutters to herself.

Alfonso puts down the newspaper, unable to concentrate on the national news when there are more pressing problems needing his attention. "The Arabian sheiks with the camels are behaving unprofessionally. They say they won't sign a contract with Circus Poppi before Circus Krone – the famous German circus – has made them an offer. If I'd had the clown number earlier, I wouldn't have signed another contract with Iski. At that time, I needed his elephants to fill in the gap. It was a bloody big gap, I can tell you!"

"The clown number? You mean Zasto and the girl?"

"They've worked out a damned good show! I can hardly believe my luck!"

"Professional as well as private, I hear."

Alfonso grins for the first time that morning and she notes her hot flushes are over.

"None of our business! The girl is eighteen!"

"But somebody should give her the whisper about Zasto being an addicted womaniser. He can't leave 'em alone, can he?"

"Wouldn't make much difference," answers Alfonso, taking a last sip of coffee.

Clementina knows; there's an unwritten law about circus people not interfering with each other's lives which, for the very first time, she contemplates breaking. Should she – or should she not? It might be tricky finding the right moment – taking the girl to one side and then broaching the subject diplomatically. She'll have to consider it carefully!

Alfonso puts on his coat and wonders if Zasto has finished rigging up the trampoline. Until the coming season when the new safety-net arrives, the trampoline is being shared with the Santinos, much to Sally's frustration, which means she'll have to stop cleaning her corner of the trailer, and at such short notice, if she wants to grab the opportunity of practising her routine.

Wanda and Loftus stamp their elephant feet as Alfonso strides across the field to the rhythm of their chains. Six white liberty horses romp around the paddock with the joy of regained freedom, tossing their manes, snorting over the fencing as he strides towards the cages, where Pasha, the ancient male, watches over his lionesses, asserting his authority with rumbling growls. Llamas, goats, mini-pigs and dogs, open their ears, snouts and muzzles to the early morning air and the aroma of food entering their cages.

The Big Top is standing for the twelfth time this season, and it will see fifteen locations before they pack their equipment for the winter and the troupe of artistes go their different ways for the season. Alfonso crosses the field and casts an expert eye over his realm; noting with satisfaction that the hay and straw have been delivered. Meat and vegetables for the animals will already be in the cooler. The canteen wagon is open for local merchants to deliver their goods – enough to feed thirty people as well as re-stock audience-refreshments. Alfonso always pays cash. His policy of straight down the nose and no messing has spread through urban grapevines. A prompt payer is well served, which puts him in mind of the outrageous incident concerning Mohammed and Labi earlier that season, when a local farmer had mistaken them for thieves and, armed with a shotgun, had chased them away.

Times are getting hard for local producers in their struggle against foreign imports on supermarket shelves. But one can't chase a world-famous pyramid-act down the road and threaten to blow off their arses. Such mortal insults! Not only for the Moroccans, but their forefathers and other family members in circuses scattered about the globe. They'd never heard the likes of it and would be taking steps if it was the last thing they did. Honour must be defended and dignity returned. Wrongs must be righted – a matter of pride!

"It's not the first time that circus people have been mistaken for gypsies," Alfonso remarked to his wife after the Moroccans had quietened down and retired to their caravans. "And what is the matter with gypsies, might I ask? Nothing!" he had answered his own question and continued – "There are some very fine musicians among them!" Clementina, behind her office desk, had nodded in agreement while counting the tickets for the evening performance.

Alfonso laughs as he crosses the field, remembering the incident as though it was yesterday, instead of last year. He had gone to the local police-station to straighten out the matter, and the ruddy-faced constable had nodded understandingly, explaining that a group of wandering gypsies had been suspected of stealing old William Bartholomew's young bull from the field. "But there was no trace of it – not even a hair when we caught up with them! Just imagine, a bull disappearing into thin air! You can't get rid of an animal like that, without leaving some kind of trace, can you?" the policeman had said.

"Never heard of a bull hiding in a caravan!" Alfonso had remarked, his imagination running at full speed, with a bull as a circus act. *A Corrida!* He had seen himself, proudly entering the ring, swishing his cape and presenting himself to the public. Two *Alguacilillos* on horse-back would open the *puerta de los toriles,* followed by the bull. What a spectacle! What a great thrill it would be – the crowd roaring with excitement at the bullfighter's skilful turn of *Capote* to the rhythm of their shouts. Olé! Olé! – They'd go with him, until the picadors entered the ring, armed with a lance to perform *la suerte de banderillas.* Imagine the *banderilla,* sticking out of the bull's back; it would chase around the ring; the signal for the *suerte suprema,* displaying his mastery of the bull being driven to death by the *muleta,* the small red rag drifting artistically around the animal before being killed by the sword.

Olé! Olé! Alfonso's Spanish blood had boiled with excitement but British sobriety had finally prevailed. There had been a moment's silence while Alfonso had gathered his wits and asked the two policemen if they would accompany him to William Bartholomew's farm to restore his artiste's good reputation.

Alfonso's laughter can be heard spreading across the field, as he remembers William Bartholomew in his shirt sleeves and his shy wife in a dark blue apron, standing in the shadows like dithering ghosts, and then scuttling off to find the firearm license for the police. "Circus artistes are law-abiding people," Alfonso had bellowed. As a gesture of goodwill, he'd presented the farmer with two tickets for the evening performance, which his wife had mistaken for the firearms license and handed them to the officer, who'd returned them to Mr. Bartholomew, just before the billy-goat had butted his arse.

Goat's milk had been the face-saving idea! The Moroccans were always on the look-out for goat's milk, and Alfonso had then placed an order with William Bartholomew for three pints a day

"I'll be auctioning 'em off! But you can have some milk 'till Jack Hawkins collects 'em," the farmer had explained. "I'm not thinkin' of keeping 'em much longer!"

Alfonso, always keen to make a good deal, purchased William Bartholomew's small herd of good old British Alpine goats consisting of one doe, a buck and four goatlings, for fresh goat meat, milk and cheese, rarely found in British food shops and highly appreciated among southern-born folks.

Now, on reaching the lions's cage, Alfonso thoughts turn to his son, who will be leaving for America to perform with his lions since human artistry is growing more popular in Europe, due to the high-performance quality of Russian and Chinese circuses. If there are to be no more wild-animal acts, at least he has recognized the potential of the clowness and athlete, and there is no doubt in his mind that Sally will soon be a brilliant performer. He will keep her under contract, as well as Gerti and Charlie's disciplined son Ron, who has re-arranged his parent's routine, into his own first class performance.

Maintaining high standards is the key! Alfonso doesn't want the locals on his back and has called a hasty conference of artistes and workers, concluding that first impressions are essential. In exchange for a favourable story, stressing the new circus motto of 'keeping the circus tidy', more free tickets have been distributed to newspaper offices. Meanwhile, lines of washing and piles of equipment have disappeared from view and rubbish bins appear in strategic places before visitors enter the ground.

...

"Where the hell is Zasto?" Alfonso never speaks quietly, but yells at the tent manager, who was once a professional boxer with a flattened nose to show for it. Being in charge of the 'uniformist' troop – dressed in bright red fantasy uniforms, they set up the props between acts – he firmly believes the circus won't function without him.

The tent manager smiles the secret smile of a sinner among men. "Zasto?" He stops what he is doing and has a whimsical expression on his face. "He's gone to visit a relative, living nearby!"

"Aaah! Visiting a relative is he?" replies Alfonso.

"Tell us another…!" shouts one of the tent-hands with a knowing wink.

Sally, previously unnoticed, emerges from the shadows. She has been helping Juan and Mejandro Santino to fix up the trampoline. "He's visiting an aunt," she explains, her voice soft and sweet.

Sensitive souls pity her, although she hasn't made any friends and there is no-one she'll confide in. Those of more realistic disposition regard her love-affair with Zasto as frustrating.

"Nadja says he's got her sleeping in his caravan," remarks Annie to Doreen who gives her a knowing look in return.

"To tell you the truth, we've already noticed! Just another affair for him, boyo – but not for her!" interrupts Marie from the Flying Santinos who is in the kitchen doing her washing and collecting the gossip.

"Now just watch what you're saying – uphold the non-interference rule, Doreen warns Nadja who are both part of the grapevine.

"I'll tell you something, now this is true is this! Alfonso wouldn't allow *his* daughter within ten feet of Zasto – not for all the clowns in the world!" says Andrea, Gerti's daughter-in-law, sitting at the kitchen-table with a cup of tea.

...

Chapter 9

When the circus moves northwards, Alfonso still hasn't got around to sacking his agent. Occasionally, they've detoured to the east, and then westward, slowly making their way towards Scotland, where winters are cold and early.

Alfonso has already predicted that the weather will be frosty and comfortless. Tents are frozen stiff and difficult to lace. Whatever they touch, coldness burns through men's hands and artistes prepare for their performances wearing thick coats.

The Moroccan women, never wont to socialize beyond passing the time of day, keep to their caravans. Nobody sees much of their husbands either, until it's time to perform. They stamp across the frozen field wrapped in thick woollen blankets, dark brown faces now dark-blue and pinched with cold. Circus life is tough and arduous; it has lost its magic, the summer warmth has deserted them and life is a treadmill.

Soon, it will be the last performance before winter. Animals will be taken to their winter quarters and artistes will leave for other engagements, or become reunited with their families abroad. The Poppis are planning to return to their home in southern Spain, where Clementina will transform herself into 'the British Mother of the Bride' in the bright blue wide-brimmed hat decorated with silk orchids, and a matching, loose fitting coat over a blue and white organza dress.

Alfonso has inherited the enterprising genes of three generations before him. He saves money where he can and spends it only when he has to. His credo of purchasing property and selling it at a profit has made him a wealthy owner of a hotel in his native Andalusia, with ocean views and a well-run kitchen, where he spends the winter months with his family.

As a young circus director, he'd seen the necessity of having permanent winter facilities for circus equipment and animals. He had purchased a lonely run-down farm at a bargain for the price, with what had once been a beautiful farm-house and stables for horse-breeding, situated on the North Yorkshire moors near the east coast town of Whitby. The irate estate-agent had been eager to get it off his books, since the previous owners, who had inherited the property, had packed up and left for New Zealand.

Alfonso had converted the farm into a hotel for summer-guests, and winter accommodation for his circus. It had almost ruined him by completion, although a solid investment, with six en-suite bedrooms, kitchen and dining room. Being the official circus winter-quarter, with ample facilities for animals and equipment, it now presents a first-rate opportunity for artistes to work on their acts in the off season.

All Alfonso's business ventures have been a success and Clementina is delighted with the small herd of William Bartholomew's goats; they remind her of her childhood and the small herd of goats that had fed them on their journeys. She still knows how to milk them and produce the traditional cheese, which is popular with the Moroccans. Accordingly, the herd must also be transported to Whitby, where the milking and cheese-making will be done by the caretaker's wife, and quartered in the neighbouring field with the llamas and miniature pigs. There are paddocks and stalls for the animals and a couple of barns for storing tents and equipment, vehicles and trailers. The indoor arena where they had once trained horses has since been converted into a well-equipped gym.

...

The last performance in the windy town of Ayr has taken the Toledano family to their limits. They yearn for their Moroccan home and are the first to leave, in a convoy of three gleaming Mercedes limousines pulling double-axel caravans, accompanied by a chorus of hoops and whistles.

Somewhere, a radio plays Frank Sinatra's *'The Party is over; it's time to call it a day.* Now that the trampoline has disappeared and Miss Flummi's somersaults are a thing of the past, a sad figure with a painted smile fights back the tears. Zasto, cheered on by the last crowd of the season and ignorant of her despair, finishes their performance by putting her away, into the box for the very last time.

She answers queries about her plans for the winter. "I'll be visiting my grandfather in Spain," she tells them, because no-one should feel sorry for her. No-one should call her the fool that she is, for relying on Zasto. She can't survive without him. A day without him is a day wasted. Even her concentration suffers when he visits some sick relative who happens to be living nearby, which is nothing to get excited about, he reassures her. "Haven't I promised we'll go through thick and thin together? What? Get married? Start a family of clowns, like other circus dynasties? Like who? Like Family Poppi? Hey! Don't get uptight now! OK, you can dream about starting a circus-clown dynasty; that's a joke for a start!"

"Hey Zasto, where will you be staying over winter?" somebody asks.

Zasto hates answering questions. "I'm off to the North Pole, to visit my Auntie.

"Which Auntie?"

"The one who's just moved there, from Newcastle!"

"You're kidding!"

"OK! I'm kidding!"

Pepe Santinos prefers moving forward on his hands rather than his feet, and cart-wheels over the grass. Other Santinos children are chasing a ball, circling around Miss Flummi and shouting excitedly. Marta and Marie have finished packing and stand in the door, watching their children discard surplus energy. Soon, they'll be leaving for Germany and an engagement with Circus Krone, which includes an appearance on television in the annual Christmas Eve variety show.

Good for them! So what? Sally couldn't care less if she's the only one left, in the middle of a field and as cold as ice. Her savings-book in the body pouch beneath her pullover gives her comfort. Her savings have grown, although not as rapidly since there's been no time to listen to Gerti's sorry tales. She won't be repaying the money she has borrowed – at least not yet – perhaps later – depending on the room at the local YWCA, and the waitress job from the employment agency which is making her feel sick. It must be the prospect of working as a waitress that is making her feel sick. On the other hand, she'd rather die than return home. Her mood changes from one minute to the next when she thinks about the mother she hates, and her weak, spineless father. At least *they* can't kid her any longer! She might be mouldering in a lime pit for all they care. Now she wishes she was leaving with the rest of the circus and will be bawling her eyes out before very long, if she doesn't start changing her thoughts!

In the half-dismantled Big Top, Zasto collects their props. "Hi girlie!" he says in greeting. "I've been doing some serious thinking."

Can he be serious for once? Sally remains silent. She doesn't want him to notice her trembling lower lip.

"We need to build more into the routine," he remarks casually as he fills the box with his props and closes the lid. "You must learn to move more like a wooden puppet. Alfonso can show you. He did it when he was a kid, but now he's too fat. Hey Alfonso! Come over here will you?"

The circus director raises an arm in acknowledgement; his attention is still fixed on the Big Top and the minor repairs that must be done before transferring it to Whitby for winter. There are matters to be discussed with the infallible tent-master, necessitating the usage of limbs as well as the rest of his body. He hurries towards them, arms wide open, beaming with obvious pleasure.

"Darling, how are you? I've been looking for you all over the place! Where have you been?" he enquires innocently, since nobody in their right mind had wanted to interrupt proceedings in Zasto's caravan. Not even Alfonso Poppi, Circus Director of the famous Circus Poppi, would interrupt a girl getting herself screwed (although if she'd been his daughter, he would have!) But never mind! He's had enough of arguing with Clementina about the girl. One must let sleeping dogs lie and mind one's own business! He takes a deep breath, "I've been meaning to speak to you, but haven't found the time, due to end-of-the-season finalities, not to mention the Inland Revenue who have taken the best part of my earnings. I just want to tell you that I love your performance and ask if you are willing to sign a contract for next season."

There is a sudden brightness in her eyes and she feels slightly dizzy as her pale face flushes with excitement, which he curbs with the shake of a finger. "But – and there is a big 'but' here – there's something we must discuss! Wassamatter Zasto?" he enquires impatiently.

Zasto hasn't told Sally about his plans for improving the routine for a first-class performance, having no intention of explaining half-baked ideas which might come to nothing. "I'll leave you to explain the details since you've let the cat out of the bag." Alfonso ignores his pettiness being accustomed to the whims and quirks of his clown.

"But... Why didn't you tell me I can stay with the circus?" she gasps.

"Just one moment please!" says Alfonso, rubbing his chin with a gold-ringed finger and regarding his feet, there being much plotting and counter-plotting behind dark bushy eyebrows, and all for the circus. He turns to Sally and lifts a warning finger, aware of theatrical effects when making one's point.

"Because you'll have to put in some really hard practise before you can call yourself a top-number-performer! How would both of you like to spend three months at Whitby? If you're not going home, there's no better place for you to practice than at Whitby. I'll be down to arrange about the animals; then I'll demonstrate 'the wooden doll act' which Zasto and I have been speaking about. It's an 'odd-joint performance' I did with my granddaddy, an' I'm certain you'll master it with practice. Another thing!" Here the warning finger, "you must put more humour into your trampoline performance – make it more entertaining! Forget the competitions! There are no competitions in a circus. People need to get excited and be entertained." Alfonso turns to the invincible tent-master, cups his hands, and bawls into the far corner of the rapidly decreasing Big Top. "Hey Pete! Get this trampoline packed right away, will you? It's goin' to Whitby!"

Alfonso's face creases into an appeasing smile, ignoring men's shouts and the deafening noise of machinery. "Just imagine! My baby is getting married. You remember my little Karina?" His head drops to one side as he cooes about her marrying into Circus Petronella. "You know Jules Petronella don't you?"

"Sure I know him," Zasto answers. "We were together in Copenhagen for a season – nice guy and good experience it was, working with him. It was my first engagement as a carpet-clown; a real stroke of luck, since the accident stopped me from working on the ropes."

"Yes! The accident! Is your back strong enough now?"

"I've had no problems this year. The trampoline is a good alternative. I've never considered working on a trampoline, but thanks to Sally…," he puts an arm around her and draws her close, "…within the next three months, we'll have a top act."

Within the next three months we'll have a top act. Is he speaking seriously? One never knows, with Zasto! Sally has her suspicions, but there's no sign of teasing as he discusses the routine with Alfonso, who is nodding his head in agreement. Silently, she leaves the dungeons of despair, swearing to herself that she won't disappoint them. *Dear God! I won't disappoint them! I'll make it to the top of the bill, if it's the last thing I do!*

…

Nadja and Doreen are sitting on packed suitcases and observe her indifferently when she asks if they're leaving.

"Looks like it!" they chorus sarcastically. Although they've been sharing accommodation, they'll never make friends with someone as secretive as Sally, who is as mad as anyone could be. They turn their eyes in silent entreaty. To avoid their spitefulness, she leaves the trailer and walks across the field.

"Jeysus, doesn't she tell bloody great lies!" remarks Nadja for the thousandth time.

Doreen announces there's nothing worse than a habitual liar. "You can't believe a single word of what *she* says. It's like believing a confidence trickster innit? Yea! A bloody confidence trickster! That's what she is – telling people she's broke when her purse is full. She's as rich as Rockefeller is that one!

"Broke? Huh! If she's broke, I'm a bloody Chinaman," agrees Nadja. Looking through the window, she watches Sally walk away. "And what's this in her drawer?" She walks over to the bedside table at the far end of the cabin next to Sally's bed. "Go on, open it further, she won't know! Cor blimey! Take a look at that! A pile of notes! From Gerda's piggybank, no doubt! She'll be paying them into her bank, the next time she's in town. How much is it? Go on! Count the money! Twenty bloody quid? Listening to shit about unhappy childhood makes people generous. That's how she does it! A right bugger, that one!"

"At least we'll finally get some well-deserved rest," says Doreen, the light sleeper, busily zipping up her luggage. There'll be no more mimicking the soft voice and starry-eyed-look that makes Nadja roll on the floor and wet her knickers. "Hmmm! Hah! Sorry for waking you, but I haven't had time to clean. Zasto had been making me rehearse my act. Which act? You know, my little bouncing act!"

Nadja chuckles and looks out of the window. "Ssssh! Be quiet! She's on her way back, and Nicko is here too!"

Sally, having already returned to the trailer, waits outside, watching them drag overfilled suitcases down wooden steps and into the car which belongs to Doreen's boyfriend.

"See ya!" They chorus, raising limp hands in farewell.

"See ya!" replies Sally to the disappearing car and immediately forgets her previous roommates because her thoughts are with Zasto, on his way to Newcastle to visit his Aunt. Of course she understands that he must visit his Aunt. Of course, it is *she* who must start practising right away. They're as good as engaged to be married and she'll be part of the family she can't wait to meet. It will be wonderful belonging to a family again.

Memories are painful and Zasto had laughed at her tears. "What's the point of getting upset?" he'd muttered as she stood there miserably, watching him stack luggage into the back of the jeep. "I'll see you in Whitby. When?" his face had darkened at unwelcome questions, "Don't ask me when!" He'd climbed into the driver's seat and closed the door, regarding her intently, yes, even provokingly, proving that contradiction is useless because there's no quarrelling with Zasto; he won't argue back; he'll shrug his shoulders and do what he pleases.

Her mind jolts into the present. There are still things to do! The remaining equipment is ready for transport. Adam, who belongs to the Polish family of horse-trainers, has already collected her luggage and stacked it in the lorry behind the passenger seat, which is still hers when they take to the road. Now she must say goodbye to Annie and Luke, who will be leaving within the hour for an engagement in Blackpool. Sally makes her way across the field towards the caravan in the far corner and waves to Antonio. He salutes absent-mindedly, preoccupied with preparing his lions for the engagement in Las Vegas and giving them the correct dosage of tranquillizers they'll need for the flight.

Annie takes the costumes from the temporary washing-line and examines the fringes on Luke's suede jacket as he sharpens his knives. They've even repainted the spinning-board and checked the fixing straps, which secure Annie, trapped and ready to meet her fate. When Luke aims his knives around her body, the audience holds its breath, wondering with morbid excitement if they'll soon be seeing blood.

"Come inside now, and have a cup of tea!" says Annie, who is no fool and braces herself for another 'poor tale', which will come as sure as the knife in Luke's sheath. A cold breeze accompanies the girl inside the cabin; she is always in a hurry and invariably out of breath. Annie is familiar with the same old explanations – that she'd have come earlier if it hadn't been for the dirt in the trailer she has since cleaned. "Now that doesn't say much for my room-mates, does it?" she remarks, examining her watch. "Zasto makes me practice all day, so I can only clean the trailer at night." She lets out a long sigh, throws herself onto the settee and lowers her voice into a more confidential tone. "You wouldn't believe how dirty they were!"

"Drink your tea and you'll feel better, I don't doubt." Annie places two cups of tea on the table and sits down to regard the girl over the brim, wondering if she might be hearing more stories.

"Can't go through all that again," the girl announces dramatically and punches the brocade cushion to underline her point, "…which is why I'm saving up for my own caravan."

"Your own caravan! And how will you be transporting your own caravan, might I ask?"

"That's the problem! I need a car and don't have a driver's license because I'm never in one place long enough."

"One of the disadvantages of belonging to a circus!" remarks Annie.

"…and having no money." Sally sighs. It's worth a try! Unfortunately, the ensuing frosty silence suggests the strategy of gaining money which has been highly successful with Gerti, doesn't seem to be working with Annie. Gerti and Charlie have since left the circus to realize their dream of a cottage in the country and her conscience is pricking for missing their retirement party in the Big Top. But it had been her last night with Zasto and not even an extra bonus from Gerti could have kept her out of his bed. She hadn't got around to speaking to Gerti about paying back the money, which is probably why Andrea had given her the look. On the other hand, they'll be back from their Blackpool engagement in spring and she'll give Ron the money – that's if he asks!

"Have a scone so you won't starve to death." Is Annie being sarcastic? , she wonders as Annie opens the tin and puts it on the table.

"Thanks! Perhaps I should eat more! Zasto says I'm too thin, but don't Orientals prefer plump women?"

"Zasto isn't Oriental!"

"Isn't he?" Sally straightens her neck and looks surprised. "Where does he come from?"

"Hungary! Didn't you know?"

"I thought his father was a Sheik."

"A Sheeek!" Annie roars with laughter. "He's a big teaser, that one! Zasto's father was a clown and his mother a foot-juggler before they fled from Hungary during the uprising when Zasto was a child. As far as I know, his mother returned home after the death of his father." Annie is eager to change the subject. "Now tell me where you will be over winter!"

…

Chapter 10

It must be the last curtain-call, since they've already returned for four encores and the last bus will be leaving the town square at eight minutes past the hour. Majestically, Nickbone wraps his robe around his sturdy bulk, and takes another deep bow. The audience applauds for the fifth curtain call, but not quite as frenetically. A few are already checking their watches and there's a scraping of chairs as they leave their seats to make a run for their coats, despite it being 'The Bowling Green Amateur Dramatics' Society's closing performance of a well-produced Richard III. They have played to a succession of six full houses and been favoured with excellent critics in the 'Evening Herald', as well as the church magazine, which is always reliable for an over-the-roof critic.

Nickbone feels like he's reaping the reward for time invested in his role as Edward the IV – though he has often fancied himself as the staunch Duke of Buckingham, instead of a sick old king who is no use to anybody.

The heavy dark red curtain remains closed – at last! Company members troop up creaky wooden stairs to join the rest of the audience for a cup of tea and home baked buns, served on an ancient oak table with an enamel plate notice screwed onto the centre that reads – 'do not put hot plates on this surface'.

His eyes scan the crowd for Patricia, who is a staunch supporter of local cultural gatherings along with most of the ladies in her 'Musical Movement' Thursday evening classes. He finds her in deep conversation with the vicar's wife, outside the cloakroom.

"A splendid performance – The RSC couldn't have done better," somebody mutters at his elbow as he peels off his beard to make way for the scone. Carefully balancing his cup of tea, he guides his plate above the rapidly expanding and jostling crowd towards the stranger, who stares in surprise at the unexpected hospitality of Edward the IV offering scones. The stranger is unable to decide whether he'll have one or not.

"Go on, be a devil! They'll be all gone in a jiffy!"

The stranger takes a floury scone and thanks him profusely.

A pleasant fellow, thinks Nickbone, and notes the stranger's habit of lowering his head, regarding his counterpart from a subordinate position when speaking. Nickbone considers the distinct inclination to agree with everything being said, could get annoying. He recognises the type as being the typical fraud-victim; one who believes in the goodness of mankind and will turn a cheek to be slapped on the other.

The heavy cloak and pompous crown fixed to his wig to prevent it from slipping is making him sweat. His eyes search the crowd for his wife, who has since moved along, from the vicar's wife to the producer.

"I greatly admire those able to perform in front of a large audience." The stranger bites into the scone and chews with gusto, waiting for Nickbone's attention to revert to him. "My daughter joined the circus about a year ago."

"Ah yes," Nickbone replies thoughtfully. There's something about this fellow's daughter..! His intuition has always served him well, both during the war in military intelligence and later, on the Force. It tells him there's something familiar about somebody's daughter joining the circus and is ringing a bell at the back of his mind. He'll bet his retirement gold watch that right at this moment, he is talking to Sally Foss' father; the impassive parent of a daughter gone adrift; the long-suffering husband of an unfaithful wife. Jesus, what a coincidence!

"How fascinating!" Nickbone subdues an urge to question the man; reminding himself, with the obligatory pang of regret, that he is no longer a policeman but an old age pensioner with a penchant for amateur dramatics and a fine collection of wooden spoons, among other things.

"My wife loves the circus," he continues, "we went to see it not long ago, when it was here." He finds his statement banal. A detailed description of their visit to the circus; their fruitless attempts at contacting Sally, would seem ridiculously out of place in this jostling crowd.

The stranger's face lights up. "Circus Poppi! That's the one she's with! They were at Battingley the second week in April."

"Your daughter is Sally Foss, right?"

The stranger nods vigorously. "Right!" he yells proudly over the noise.

Nickbone deposits his empty cup on a window-sill, places a friendly hand on Matthew's shoulder and guides him towards the temporary quietness of the cloakroom. "My name is Nicholas Lightbone and Patricia, my wife, was Sally's trainer. Does that ring a bell?" he enquires casually, with the hint of a smile.

The stranger stares at Nickbone and shakes his head unbelievingly. "M-M-Matthew Foss!" he stutters. "How do you do!" He offers his hand.

Nickbone shakes it vigorously and waits politely until Matthew has found the right words.

"Mrs. Lightbone! Sally used to talk a lot about Mrs. Lightbone. Isn't it a small world?" Then, as an afterthought, "Did you speak to Sally? How is she?"

"We didn't get a chance to speak to her, unfortunately. I think she's well. At least, she looked alright to me," Nickbone added and laughed. "She's a very good clown!"

"A clown?" repeats Matthew slowly, as though greatly surprised.

"Yes! A circus clown!"

Matthew Foss examines his feet and looks up awkwardly. "Unfortunately, due to my wife's severe illness, we didn't get around to seeing her. Been very ill, has my Missus; very ill indeed! Sally never 'phones, you see." He speaks rapidly now, with an apologetic hint in his voice. "Circuses don't have telephones. She sends postcards instead, that is – when she has time."

Nickbone reassures himself that his wife is still talking to Jack Finch, an intense man with strong principles who needs plenty of time to express his opinions. He doesn't want Patricia meeting Matthew Foss yet. Why? He has his reasons; there's a time and a place for everything! "I'm terribly sorry, but I simply must get changed and leave," he announces, checking his watch. "I have an appointment in less than half-an-hour at the other side of town and am already running late. Perhaps we could meet soon and talk about your daughter. My wife will be delighted to tell you about our visit to the circus." There's a pregnant pause while Nickbone regards Matthew Foss closely. An invitation will follow or his name isn't Nicholas Lightbone.

"Oh sorry, sorry!"

The man is a great apologizer. Seems OK though!

Foss continues, "Ah! Yes! Well! Would you care to visit us?"

"We'll be delighted, absolutely delighted! That is very kind indeed!" Nickbone puts great emphasis upon being delighted. "I hope your wife's health has improved."

Matthew Foss regards his shoes once more and there's another uncomfortable silence. "She's been much better lately. News about Sally will perk her up!"

"Well then..!" Nickbone looks significantly at his watch.

"Goodbye! Ah yes! And please do visit us!" repeats Matthew Foss hesitantly.

"Love to! Any special time?"

"Perhaps next weekend?"

"Next weekend? Splendid! Thanks, old chap!"

"Erm – Saturday evening, at about seven? Would that be alright?"

"Certainly! Looking forward to it, tremendously! Goodbye for now and see you on Saturday at seven!"

...

'All things come to him who waits.' Matthew Foss considers there is plenty of sense in his mother's words of wisdom, although he has to admit, there's also a bad side to her wonderful truths, if one has no idea what one is waiting for, and he hasn't had much idea either, until now. At least his patience has been rewarded and Charmaine belongs to him again. On the other hand, he has paid a heavy price to win her back and had to forfeit just about everything dear to him, including his family – his brothers and sisters – since she'd refused to allow them over the threshold the last time they'd visited.

Keeping an eye on Charmaine is one hell of a task and has finally cost him his job. *It's a mystery how she manages to get her hands on all that alcohol: probably 'phones the off-license and has it delivered when I'm out shopping.* He has even resorted to begging the bastards not to sell her the stuff.

"Sorry!" they tell him. "It's no use refusing! She'll only get it elsewhere – walk for miles in the pouring rain, if she needs it that badly!"

He has already saved her life twice – although she'll never thank him for it – on arriving home and finding her in a state; choking on her vomit and gasping for breath.

"Blood alcohol content of point forty per cent – enough to kill an ox," the doctor had said. "She'll be dead within a year if she goes on like this – or end up going psycho. Try to get her into dry dock! If she refuses, take my advice and let her land in the gutter. Sometimes, when they get that low, they start picking themselves up," he had added.

He remembers her fury, the second time she'd been admitted to hospital, after he had tentatively broached the subject of finding her a place in a clinic; and winces when he remembers how embarrassed he'd been, trying in vain to quieten her down.

"Me? On a level with drop-outs, drug-addicts and trash? Are you joking?" she'd yelled through the ward, causing people to stop what they were doing and stare. "I can stop drinking whenever I feel like it. Only thing is, I don't feel like it at present! So take those bloody forms and stick them up your arse, 'cos I'm not signing anything! Is that clear? *Is that bloody well clear?*" Her voice had now reached the hysterical pitch. "And another thing! That young nurse down there, the one pushing the trolley, has been giving me the 'you're-a-real-bitch-look' since I had her picking up those forms I threw on the floor. One more disrespectful word! One more disrespectful word and she'll be out of a job!"

I can't allow her to land in the gutter! It's all very well for a young doctor, freshly scrubbed, glowingly healthy from a well-to-do background giving me advice I can't take. He says she might pick herself up, but I wouldn't like to bet on it! Besides, what will people say about a bloke who neglects his wife and leaves her in the gutter?

But now he has found a new pastime – a strange kind of pastime! It gives him more pleasure than he cares to admit.

He has almost become addicted to the morbid enjoyment he experiences when secretly filming his wife, with the brand-new 'Super 8' he has treated himself to, as a reward for the suffering and sorrow.

He sets up the screen and arranges the cushions on the brown velvet settee – in the imaginary first row – reserved for special guests, he assures her, guiding her like an usherette to the place where she'll sit. Soon he's running the film of which she's the star. Can he be so cruel as to present her with the bloated features and the saliva trickling from her mouth-corners? Why has he filmed her pissing into the wardrobe instead of the toilet; taken shots of the urine stain, spreading from the crotch to the back of her pants? Now she is crying bitterly. Her eyes are red and swollen and he feels like crying too, because he doesn't have the guts to ride his bike into a bus and put an end to it all.

Would Sally care if he died? Why, for God's sake, had she suddenly left home to join a bloody circus of all things? Must have been some reason but he can't make it out. That's women for you… never know what they'll do next!

He finds no comfort in the fact, his wife needs him now more than ever. One must be grateful for small mercies, his mother had said. But he is losing the battle against doom and disaster and to make matters worse, there's a financial problem showing its ugly head on the horizon since Charmaine lost her job. They'd called it 'internal structuring'. He'd called it 'boozed-up at work and getting kicked out on one's arse.'

He'll have to take the initiative and make the far-reaching decisions he's been avoiding for too long. Doesn't he have the right to occasional enjoyment? , he asks himself. Social contact is what he needs. Having taken the plunge, he has stepped over his shadow by inviting the Lightbone's to his house – and surprisingly enough, they've accepted!

Have I been a tick too spontaneous? Too late! I'll have to go through with it! A cup of tea and some buns should be enough to keep them happy. I'll have to keep an eye on Charmaine; make sure she stays sober; have her hair done and get rid of those lanky strands that make her look old. I'd do anything to turn back the clock.

...

The deepening crease between his eyebrows implies that Nickbone is in no mood for conversation. His wife knows better than to interrupt his deliberations, despite the question poised on her tongue as to how he has got them invited to the home of the most unsociable family in town; after she'd ferried their daughter across half of the country without getting as much as a foot through their door. She'd rather wash her hands of the whole situation after overhearing in the school-library that 'holier than thou' history-teacher, Sandra Blunket, with the gob-stopper figure describing her as a 'do-gooder' – a do-gooder, indeed! "And what about the whopping great lies Sally Foss tells?" she'd overheard Miss Blunket saying. "I've never met a girl who tells so many lies! There's a name for it!"

"Nut-case," Julianne Weaver had replied, the art-teacher with lilac-coloured streaks in her hair.

"A psycho-job if you ask me..!" Their voices had grown fainter as they'd walked down the corridor.

The car has reached the top of the moors and they stop to admire the view; the weirdly-formed outcrops of rock between thick tufts of vegetation. Far below, where fields are separated by ancient dry stone walls, a solitary wanderer slithers his way down the slope towards an impenetrable carpet of bracken and bogs. A small flock of sheep grazing on rough pastures lift their heads, idly contemplating escape. A skylark protests against sudden interference and triggers a swarm of sparrows. Far off to the right, a group of distant die-hards swing golf-clubs, braving the blustery wind.

The reservoir at the top of the hill has filled since the end of the drought. They drive over the hill crest and down the bumpy road towards the small town, appearing to the oncoming visitor as a chequer board of red and grey roofs around a desolate mill-chimney.

"You might at least tell me the reason for this strange visit!" Patricia remarks stiffly, annoyed at his perpetual silence. "Don't you realize what a strange position this puts me in? Not once, considering the numerous times I've picked the girl up and driven her to an event, have I been invited over the threshold of that house. It's unbelievable!

And all you do is give Matthew Foss a doe-eyed look and get us invited – just like that!" She snaps her finger.

He clears his throat and takes a deep breath. "I'm looking for the answers to questions which have been burning on my mind for some time." He pauses for a moment allowing the announcement to sink in. "I'm convinced there's some kind of link between Sally Foss and Jeff Nelson – you remember the upheaval after he was killed in that cycling-accident?"

"I remember!"

"You'll say I'm mad, but I can't get rid of this weird feeling, the girl is in some way connected with his death." After another short pause, during which his wife has remained silent, he continues. "Like I said, I've got this weird feeling…!"

She fixes her eyes on his face, wondering if he is out of his mind. Never in her life has she heard anything so utterly unbelievable. Sally Foss wouldn't kill a fly! She considers whether it might have been manslaughter… in effect…or accidental death? What is she thinking about? There have been cases of mishandled children murdering their parents. Sally, mishandled? Is Nickbone in full possession of his senses? Has retirement gone to his head? Might he be simply *inventing* a crime? On the other hand, her husband is shrewd – and seldom mistaken.

Nickbone concentrates on the traffic ahead. Then, in a casual voice, he informs his wife that Jeff Nelson had been having an affair with Sally's mother. "...been going on for years, so I'm told! Which way do we turn at this junction?"

Unbelievable! This is too much and she'll think about it later. In the meantime she'll consider the times she has driven down this road; past this row of semi-detached houses to collect her protégé for yet another competition supposedly vital to an athlete's career.

Mum and Dad are hard-working people! They don't have time to drive me around, because Dad works overtime and Mum attends important meetings involving large amounts of money, which is why she's never home! Patricia recalls the abundance of complicated explanations for dramatic situations which had seemed to dominate the girl's life while Nickbone parks the car on the paved driveway.

Later, his wife will wonder why she has never met this mild-mannered man who opens the door and welcomes them inside.

"Pleasure to meet you at last; never had the opportunity; my wife will be delighted!" He shouts up the stairs, "Charmaine, come down, my dear! Our visitors have arrived."

Nickbone notes the dark red hall carpet and the empty white square on the wall. "Might I congratulate you on your good taste? We have exactly the same wallpaper in our hallway," he lies. Patricia raises an eyebrow but remains silent.

"Oh yes!" Matthew Foss laughs uncomfortably. "It needs doing again." His eyes wander over the wall and he adds, almost apologetically, "Since Sally's picture disappeared, leaving this awful white patch, I'm afraid it's become obvious."

"What needs decorating?" A woman's voice, hoarse and encrusted by excessive habits, rebounds from the top of the stairs. Charmaine appears, no longer the cultivated, well-groomed career woman, but now abnormally thin, almost skeletal and undernourished; a ghostly apparition at the top of the stairs. Loose, bedraggled strands of hair rest on her shoulders; a thick layer of make-up camouflages blemished skin; lipstick, applied too thickly at mouth-corners by an unsteady hand, lends a petulant look to her features. Watery eyes find it difficult to focus on the visitors she has no wish to meet – prying visitors – eager to interfere in other people's lives.

"What needs re-papering?" she repeats.

Matthew fixes the visitors with a pained smile. "The hallway, my love!"

"What's wrong with it?" Her head wobbles in a vain attempt at focusing on her husband. He takes hold of her arm.

"Nothing, my love!" He gestures towards the empty square. "It's just the white spot on the wall where Sally's picture used to hang."

"Does Sally paint?" Nickbone cocks his head.

"She once did paint a beautiful sailing-ship, didn't she love?" He turns to his wife who ignores the question. It disappeared some time ago; quite mysterious, really, isn't it love?" Matthew's voice trails off in another vain effort at bringing his wife into the conversation. He attempts another pained smile and for the hundredth time, regrets having invited these people to his house.

"What a shame!" remarks Patricia, thinking it's time she joined in the conversation. After all, she was once the girl's teacher.

Charmaine stifles a yawn. Matthew is eager to change the subject and guides them into the lounge. There are onion-flavoured crisps in a large glass bowl on the coffee-table in front of the brown velvet couch. He announces his intention of making a nice cup of tea.

Patricia's gaze moves towards the beige tiled fireplace and the fake flames of an electric fire. "These Beatrix Potter figures once belonged to my mother," says Matthew, nodding casually towards the row of figures on the mantelpiece. "Oh, sorry!" He hastily removes a pile of magazines from the couch and puts them on a shelf, at the same time keeping an eye on the television and the last race at Aintree. The commentator's eyebrows twitch nervously, his mouth moves excitedly over the silent screen.

Nickbone, a keen observer of human behaviour and blessed with a penetrating mind's eye, imagines the late-night-sittings in a worn-out armchair, of a tired man in a rut, keen to replace life's monotony with an artificial world. His thoughts are interrupted by Matthew, who tears himself away from the horses to help his wife with the tea.

"She's probably forgotten to put on the kettle," he says, and leaves them with another pained smile. Nickbone and Patricia exchange meaningful glances, triggered by the subdued whispers and clattering of crockery, before Matthew appears to repossess his chair. "Did you read about the shopping mall they're planning to build down Lumb Road?" he asks, grateful that his guests are easy talkers.

Patricia says she prefers the friendly atmosphere of small, privately owned shops. "My husband has been doing the shopping since he retired. He likes to flirt with the salesgirls and taste anything going for free, which saves me from cooking his lunch."

"At least we all agree that the outskirts of town is an unsuitable place for a shopping centre," remarks Nickbone, eager to steer the conversation away from his own shortcomings.

Matthew looks at his watch, sighs impatiently and excuses himself once more to continue the whispered conversation in the kitchen. Apologizing profusely for the delay, he re-emerges carrying a tray filled with cups and a tea-pot, followed by Charmaine, who insists upon laying the table. Crockery rattles in trembling hands and there's the sweet sour odour of something stronger than tea.

It occurs to Patricia that they've hardly mentioned their daughter. She puts down her cup. "Training youngsters can be highly rewarding, especially when they're as talented as Sally," she announces pointedly, which is followed by an uncomfortable silence, broken by Matthew.

"We seem to have lost track of Sally. It's difficult keeping up with a circus; you never know where they'll be next." He twists a teaspoon through his fingers like a marching trooper with a baton. "Until now, she's only sent us one postcard, telling us she's well. Where was it from?" He asks his wife who shrugs her shoulders, intent upon reading tea-leaves in her cup.

"I hate circuses," she suddenly announces, looking up, but still ferociously stirring what is left, as though beating an egg. "Can't understand why Sally wants to be with one."

"Perhaps she's proud that her forefathers were circus artistes." Patricia remembers Sally being proud that her mother had once walked the tight-rope. Charmaine shrugs her shoulders and leaves the room, announcing she'll be back in a minute.

"It was a nervous breakdown," Matthew whispers, looking unusually concerned after the door has closed behind her. "I've had to give up my job to look after her. The doctor says she's suffering from depression and shouldn't be alone in the house." He leans towards them, almost mouthing his words. "Her nerves haven't been right since the accident." His lower lip trembles as he sits back in his chair.

"Which accident?" Nickbone enquires in the gentle tone described by Patricia as 'luring'. Somewhere in the depths of the house there is the sound of a flushing toilet.

"My wife's boss was killed in an accident...fell off his bike and smashed his head on the day that Sally left home." Matthew regards them almost beseechingly. "Can do funny things to your system can shock, oh aye!" he explains, reverting into local dialect. "Fancy more tea?" There's an oppressive silence as he refills their cups, and Charmaine re-enters the room inside a spirituous cloud.

"This is a delicious cup of tea!" Nickbone picks up his cup with a flourish and, intent upon easing the atmosphere, takes another demonstrative sip. He is growing weary of their sufferings and would rather tell a funny story. "Ever been to see the The Pan Jam Orchestra?" he suddenly asks.

Matthew racks his brains because he has never heard of The Pan Jam Orchestra and even worse, Charmaine's face is growing dark with confusion. He hopes she won't make a scene.

"Saw them at The Alhambra last Christmas!" continues Nickbone, "–started the show with some serious performance of classical music, until the cellist fell off his stool. He hit the drummer who lost his balance and knocked over the cymbals, sending a clarinettist into the row of violins. They all fell over like dominoes and carried on playing, flat on their backs.

Chapter 11

Who cares about animal odours and other displeasures, when the proverbial track of trials and tribulations has merged into a lush and green alley, leading Sally Foss to the pinnacle of stardom?

Adam is driving the lorry, with Marek next to him; he keeps a silent eye on the road, leaving their passenger on the back seat, to the pleasant thoughts of a clown. She dreams that all will be well. Of course, all will be well when Zasto returns. Clementina has told her about the hotel on the North Yorkshire moors near the fishing town of Whitby; once a horse-breeding centre owned by a wealthy wool-merchant and in a dilapidated condition when Alfonso had purchased it eight years ago.

When approaching the two-storey stone-built house with twin gables above latticed windows and imposing stone columns framing a carved oak door, one might contemplate that owning a circus must be a lucrative business. Since converting the place into a reputable hotel, Alfonso has added a car park, separated from the house by a low stone wall.

Adam parks the lorry and trailer in front of the house, lights a cigarette and climbs down. Sally follows him from the passenger seat and examines her surroundings; the stately house has already impressed her, situated upon the gentle slopes of the moorland countryside, slowly unveiling through the ocean mist against an emerging sun. The landscape stretches to the horizon over a dark pink carpet of late autumn heather mottled with brown, beneath grey blankets of dampness and white crystals of an early morning frost. Intimidated by the size of the property and the beauty of the countryside, she can hardly believe she'll belong here.

Barks and yelps herald the arrival of Madam Pinkie and her dogs, inside the red and blue trailer parked at the back of the house. Men are shouting and Adam relaxes, relieved that his brothers have arrived with the horses and there are no injuries to attend to. The animals can be left with the groom during their absence, when the Polish brothers return home for Christmas to their wives and children, and attend Holy Mass to thank Julian the Hospitaller, the patron saint of the circus, that all has been well.

A small wiry man in a green apron appears from the back of the house. "About time you showed your faces in this part of the country again," he yells to Marek and Adam and Miko who are already attending to the trailer with the horses. There's much back-patting and shoulder thumping, bantering and ragging about Marek and his two brothers being a family of rogues and other light-hearted insults, before he turns his attention to Sally. "Me and the wife are the caretakers and if there's anything you need, just ask old Harry," he says, thumping himself on the chest. "Now excuse me a minute while I show Adam where to park the trailer, 'cos he's a messy bugger an' never puts anything in the right place!"

Adam laughs. "It's worse here, than in the army! – still thinks he's a sergeant-major!" Adam and Marek, the horse-grooms and their brother Miko, the trainer, speak with strong polish accents. They joke in their native language, doubling over with laughter, and Sally suspects they're poking fun at Harry, who walks with a bow-legged gait.

Adam climbs back into the lorry and drives the vehicle down the gravel path, carefully keeping an eye open for the dogs. He parks the vehicle near three large stone barns built parallel to the neighbouring field.

Sally follows on foot. The sound of crunching gravel under her feet reminds her of walking across the circus field, where paths are temporarily gravelled because of the mud. From the adjoining field, a red grouse flees into the distance, protesting loudly over the intrusion, disturbed by the unfamiliar sound of a trumpeting elephant somewhere inside a building. Sally is oblivious to calamities in the lives of wild birds and mammals as she watches the two men guide the wooden trailer into a huge barn where stalls have been erected.

Alfonso had said she must stay over winter, so where will they put her? Where will she sleep? She feels the strong urge to clean. Perhaps she should ask Harry, this chirpy little fellow coming towards her with the friendly, encouraging smile.

"Staying here over winter too, are ya?" he enquires offhandedly, pushing a thin strand of hair from his forehead.

She nods, without speaking.

"What's your job – training the 'orses as well, are ya?"

The girl relaxes. It amuses her that they should think she's an animal trainer; she, who'll avoid being near animals because they stink. Cleaning their stalls had given her nightmares!

"I'm a clown!"

"You're a clown!" repeats Harry, whistling softly. "Well I never! I always thought Zasto was the only clown in this circus!"

"We work together... he'll be coming here too, very soon."

"...known him for years..." continues Harry as though thinking aloud, as they make their way to the back entrance of the house, "...he's a real rogue is Zasto! Emileee! Here's another clown looking for her room!"

A thin "Yeeees!" reaches them from the depths of the house.

"Can't go inside wearing my wellies," Harry explains. "Get yourself settled in an' I'll see you later – when that rascal of a clown arrives." He goes off chuckling and Emily, who seems in a hurry, appears in a bright red pinafore and green headscarf which is her usual mopping attire. She smiles at Sally and removes her rubber gloves. "So you are a 'Clowness'!" she greets the girl breathlessly. "Come with me!" She guides Sally through a spotless kitchen, past stainless steel cooking equipment and through a swing door. "This is where you take your meals," she announces with a wave of the hand as they enter the dining-room. The ceiling, in medieval-style, is of roughly cut beams. The polished pine wood floor supports solid furnishings; deeply cushioned dining chairs. The long bench-table covered with an assortment of animal magazines and newspapers, is where circus people take their meals.

Impressive! The comfortable yet genuine opulence of the place reminds her of a party she once attended, a long time ago at a rich girl's house. The strangeness of wealth is a cause for discomfort and dark memories are threatening to spoil the pleasure she finds with open fireplaces at each end of the room; the hide of an ox on the wall and the row of latticed windows overlooking the drive. It must be wonderful to dine in this exclusive atmosphere – a pleasure for others, but never for her.

"One room has been taken by Miss Clark (Madam Pinkie). The large suite is for Mr. and Mrs. Olsen, Danish acrobats who'll be arriving tomorrow. Yours is the first room on the left."

Wow! Did she say my room is the first room on the left...? It hasn't entered her head that she'll be entitled to a room of her own. She follows Emily across the hall and up a winding staircase leading to a conference room and two bedroom suites. "The remaining suites are on the second floor, Emily explains, irritated at the girl's lack of response, thinking she could at least open her mouth and make *some kind* of remark. The caretaker's wife, being a good-natured woman, continues showing her around. "Attic rooms are accessible through a side door and separate staircase, to accommodate animal grooms during winter and hotel staff during summer. We've put Jack Iski in with the grooms this year because he can't behave outside the circus," Emily explains with a withering look as she lifts an imaginary drink. "We thought Alfonso wanted rid of him. Has he signed up for another year?"

Emily considers the best way of finding out is to ask a straight-forward question. But Sally merely replies with a shrug and disappoints Emily once more, who is a virtual vacuum cleaner for sucking up information and hates one-sided conversations. "I don't really know," the girl answers shyly after a while, and her face suddenly brightens. "Where's Zasto's room?"

"Second floor; same as last year!" Emily takes a key from the bunch fixed to the chain around her ample waist, reminding the onlooker of some quaint prison warder. "Open Sesame!" she announces on opening Sally's door, triumphantly noting the girl's enraptured features with the thick brocade curtains in pale yellow and matching bedspread; the deep rugs covering gleaming marble tiles; polished wood furnishings and a sideboard with a lid unfolding into a dressing-table mirror. "Here's your own private bathroom!"

Sally gasps with delight as Emily opens the adjoining door to reveal the gleaming fixtures against marble tiles and pale yellow towels. Here it is! , the beautiful bathroom she has never had before. She'll start right away – getting rid of the filth, which might be invisible, but always remains until she has cleaned it away.

...

Zasto drives slowly down the gravel path to the back of the house and the tiny workshop in a corner of the barn which is his during winter. He bangs his foot on the brake and parks the jeep outside the garage, still feeling angry and frustrated at what should have been an erotic weekend with a sexually frustrated woman. *Did her goddamned husband have to return unexpectedly just as his seducing act was reaching its zenith, for Christ's sake? Bloody cold it had been, hiding beneath that laburnum bush, stark naked and in the pouring rain. And to make things worse, the stupid cow had taken her time about getting his bag through the window. Look at the state of it now! No big fat horny weekend this time, old boy! It'll have to be a 'quickie' instead! If she's not in her room, I'll be desperate...*

Still in a savage mood, he removes the soiled and dripping wet bag from the back-seat of his jeep and his thoughts return to Sally. Working alongside a talented partner does have its drawbacks, and she has shown exceptional talent on the trampoline, as well as working with the Santinos kids. *I've got a cuckoo in the nest! She'll be getting too big for the boots that are already gigantic, and stealing the show. I need a frame for my performance and not somebody stealing my show.* He carries his bag through the entrance and in tune with the sardonic thinker, contemplates Alfonso's intentions of promoting Miss Flummi as a solo performer and rubbing his hands at the price! *Watch out Alfonso! Nobody pushes old Zasto off his pedestal without paying the price. I'll secure my position as 'top of the bill Carpet-Clown' and there's no way she'll take the front-line.* Life on the road has its advantages. One can move from one love affair to the other; another town, another woman, like jumping stepping-stones across a stream and keeping one's feet dry. He knows exactly how to give them the hots, focusing with the strong hungry eye and the swift exchange of a telephone number coupled with more of the eye and the promise of excitement for what they'll find under the clown's baggy pants. It's time to put on the charm – and his cheek against the green headscarf.

Emily comes towards him with open arms and smiling broadly. "Welcome back! Ah Zasto, it's so lovely to see you again!"

As his arms enfold her, he wonders if she ever takes off these dreary rags. *Does she ever take off anything?* Zasto holds her at arm's length, examining her face in a theatrical manner.

"You're looking as beautiful as ever," he assures her, which makes her laugh and they are still laughing when Harry enters the kitchen.

"Which room have you given me this year?" He yawns noisily and rubs his eyes as alibi for a quick departure.

"The same as last year!" Emily hands him the key and subdues the motherly feelings surging within. After more effusive greetings, Harry offers to give him a hand with the luggage.

"Naw! I'll leave the rest of the luggage in the car ''til tomorrow. By the way," he adds, almost as an afterthought, "has Sally arrived?"

"Aye! She's up in her room, right now. Making a real job of cleaning, she is. You'd think someone had ransacked a dustbin in her room, the way she's going on! Emily had already given it a good going-through and there wasn't as much as the hair of a gnat before she moved in!"

Jesus! This cleaning tick! That's all I need! A screwed-up cleaning woman after a messed up rendezvous and I'll be impotent within a month! Cursing silently, he shoulders his bag and marches up the stairs, following the rumbling noise of a vacuum cleaner.

He flings open the door. As he watches her pushing the cleaner, as well as wiping and dusting the furniture, his anger turns into rage when she turns off the cleaner and wonders how to greet this statue, standing in the doorway with the menacing look. For a moment, they stare at each other in silence. The storm comes unexpectedly.

"Here I am, after a long and tiring journey, and what do I find? A crazy psycho with a cleaning tick! I'll tell you something, Miss bloody Flummi! You're loony! You need a psychiatrist, and a damned good one at that! Why the hell are you cleaning again, eh?"

Is this Zasto? Why is he yelling like someone gone crazy? Is she in the wrong film? She watches dumbfounded as he strides through the room and demonstratively empties the bucket of suds onto the tiles. Grinning spitefully, he turns to watch her reaction.

"Stop, stop! You can't do that! You're re-infesting my room," she almost screams and bursts into tears. She can't allow him to re-infest her room. Isn't it her job to get rid of the alien's filth and prevent it from re-entering the house?

Sally moves about frantically, mopping the water as it spreads. Suddenly, she senses him behind her, but it's too late to avoid his clasping grip; too late to prevent him from pinning her against the wall. His mouth clamps down upon hers; she feels his teeth against her lips and there's no stopping the biting. With the fury of the abused and downtrodden, she thrusts a muscular knee against his erection and regards him dispassionately, knowing he would have mistreated her, had she not put her knee between his legs. He rolls on the wet floor, hands on his crotch, crawls towards the bed and pulls himself up, cursing and swearing, spitting abuse.

How silly he looks, moaning and groaning like some kind of pimp; one who has overestimated his manhood, disqualified himself as a lover and even worse, has betrayed the ethics of a clown by forfeiting his innocent magic. There'll be no mercy for polluting her paradise. He'll have to be punished!

"Alfonso is coming tomorrow," he pants, in a vain attempt at redeeming his pride. "He expects us to have started practising the new number."

The new number? There'll be no new number with Zasto! Until this moment, she has ignored the threads of overheard gossip, the knowing winks and whispered insinuations; the truth being a cruel commodity. But situations can change. Of course, they can change! It's unbelievable how her situation has suddenly changed!

"Don't expect me to work on a new number with a woman who is low enough to kick a man in the balls." He sends the mop catapulting through the room, leaving a trail of grey suds.

"Suit yourself!" she replies, ignoring the mop which has landed against the far wall with a grey watery thud.

"And another thing," he says, thinking there can be no better punishment, because nothing can hurt more than cutting her out of the act, "There'll be no more training for Miss Flummi the Clown. There are plenty more where you came from!"

She straightens the pillow, retrieves the brocade bedspread and folds it neatly onto the foot of the bed. Images of loneliness cross her mind. She'd do anything to put back the clock. In the meantime she'll clean away the threatening words rebounding in her mind like a ball bouncing from one wall to another. He'll sabotage her act? She won't allow him to sabotage her act! Miss Flummi is no longer dependent on Zasto the clown. Zasto will be leaving sooner than he thinks! Nothing will stop her from becoming a star.

...

When Alfonso arrives the following morning, there's an air of breeziness as he swirls through the building as well as checking room reservations for the coming season; a couple of wedding receptions and menus to be composed by the chef. The kitchen-chef runs a restaurant with his father during winter, and returns to the hotel for summer. That is when Emily sits behind the reception-desk, looking unusually smart, and Harry wears a dark green uniform with polished black shoes because being a hall-porter is a profitable job compared to the menial work which will then be done by seasonal workers.

Alfonso goes to see Wanda and Loftus in the elephant house, the partitioned half of the animal quarters. He speaks to Jack Iski and the elephant trainer argues loudly, which doesn't intimidate Alfonso with the louder voice and explosive temper. These days, elephants and other wild animals are becoming a problem and Alfonso doesn't want any more trouble in *his* circus. Times are a-changing. Animal protection has a strong lobby and wild animals don't belong in a circus, they claim. "It won't be long before there are circuses *without* any animals at all," he tells Clementina that evening. "The circus family Poppi, has a reputation to keep; a hundred-and-fifty-year-tradition to be handed down to future generations, or my name isn't Alfonso Poppi. I've made my decision and there's no going back! The elephants are being donated to the zoo and there's an animal transport on its way! Jack Iski can work as a stable hand, but not as a groom. He has no respect for animals – no respect at all! "

The following morning, Alfonso makes for the gym expecting the clowns to be there, already practicing a top-of-the-bill routine to replace dwindling animal numbers. He badly needs a new attraction since Antonio, his son, and the lions left for Minneapolis. He greets Sally with the usual gushing effusiveness which she still finds embarrassing. "Where's Zasto?" he demands, favouring the direct approach because there's no time to lose.

Sally doesn't answer. She stands next to the trampoline looking helpless. In his present mood, Alfonso doesn't need helpless women. "What the hell is bothering you now?" he asks, unceremoniously.

As though waiting for his cue, Zasto appears in the arena, smiling and relaxed, and Sally wonders if yesterday's incident had happened at all. Had she been dreaming?

Alfonso points, with great satisfaction, to the newly erected equipment which the Flying Olsens will also be using. He signals Sally to climb the ladder and she obeys, and then fixes herself to the climbing bar with the safety belt, her limbs hanging loosely.

Now far below, Alfonso is ready to give his commands. "Imagine you're being pulled by an invisible string fixed to the top of your head. Your body must move only very slightly to one side, just to emphasize the movement. Now, bend your knees loosely in the same direction," he bellows through cupped hands, "…then imagine your arms are also fixed to the string and pulled upwards. Imagine the strings fastened to your wrists and another to your elbow. Good, good, my darling," he says, watching critically, adjusting her movements. "And now! Legs move on strings attached to your knees, so your steps will be controlled from the knee. Get it? Yes, my darling! You've got it right! Hey folks, look at that! She's got it right!"

The Danish couple who enter the barn wearing black leotards are blonde and beautiful; the top-class aerial-performers Alfonso has bargained for with an uncompromising agent. Ole and Irena have supervised the setting-up of equipment, and Sally has admired their strength and precision. In turn, they watch Sally with a professional eye, wondering how long it will take before the wooden doll's movements seem involuntary, and her show will be polished for the critical audience. They stand next to Alfonso who scrutinises her performance and corrects imperfections with short sharp commands. "Imagine your legs move only on strings tied to your knees, so your steps can only be controlled from the knee."

Sally imagines the heavy weights fixed to her limbs, and her arm shakes slightly as it drops.

"Good girl! That was really good!" Alfonso calls. "Now make all your limbs move separately so that they have their own swing at the pull of a string."

Sally concentrates on moving her limbs like a puppet, trying not to think about Zasto, who is part of the show and can't imagine herself for one minute accomplishing the performance alone. The situation muddles her thoughts and impedes concentration; a great deal of self-discipline is needed when doing it alone.

Unaware of her predicament and now deep in thought, Alfonso rubs the end of his moustache between finger and thumb, scratches his head and then springs to life. "I've got a sudden idea! If you perform this on the trampoline – a bouncing puppet on a string – it could be even better. What do you reckon?" He turns to Ole Olsen, who is silent for a moment and also deep in thought.

"With more acrobatics it could be a top number," he answers, to which the circus director responds by throwing a fist in the air.

"You try it, my darling, you try it!" He looks around. "Where the hell is Zasto? Zasto, you come over here! Now this girl will have a damned good act if she spends the next three months working on the routine and getting it polished. You'll have to develop the choreography yourselves, but, by Jesus, we've got the basics of a successful show here. Watch her move! Sally, my darling, show him the movements!"

An invisible hand pulls the strings and Sally moves her wooden steel-jointed limbs in bizarre poses. A left arm shoots out and slowly descends down the back of her neck, followed by the right arm which also disappears behind her body. Legs, bent at the knee, slowly move towards her head and a string pulls her feet. With slow, jerking movements they are put in position, joining her arms. Legs and arms seem to be tied into a knot and the audience applauds as she unwraps. On one single string, guided by the invisible hand, her limbs move to an imaginary rhythm.

"What do you think?"

"Good!" Zasto takes a ping-pong ball from his pocket. It appears in his mouth. Oh, surprise! Another ball rolls from his trousers! The Olsens laugh loud and heartily – big people with big laughs! Alfonso complains that a serious conversation is impossible with this guy.

Sally loosens the harness and Alfonso examines his watch, thinking there's no time to lose if he'll make the midday train to London. He needs to negotiate the fee for the illusionist he'll engage for a season. *Meanwhile, I'll take Clementina's advice and keep an eye on the clowns.*

"Don't trust Zasto," Clementina, his wife and advisor, had told him in the privacy of their bedroom. "He won't be sharing the limelight with the girl when he's finished with her – and the girl has potential. She'll be going places if we don't put her where she belongs."

"At the top of the bill?" replied Alfonso as he climbed into bed.

"You've said it, kiddo!" said Clementina before turning out the light

"Hey, listen now!" Alfonso turns to Sally, recalling the conversation with Clementina. "I'll be back after Christmas to prepare for the season, which means we'll need to polish your act before mid-April for the opening in Blackpool." Is he asking too much? Can he rely on the girl to master the number in time for the opening? He needs the illusionist! "I've been considering another attraction. But if you and Zasto can work out the routine, you'll have a permanent job. Besides, we need a good solo to replace the elephants."

"...replace the elephants?"

"No more wild animals in the ménage from Circus Poppi!" he states, ignoring their astonishment. "Even Antonio is leaving with his lions and won't be coming back," he adds sadly. "So don't you guys let me down – eh? You've got six months to get your act together, ready and polished, so keep practising until you can do it blindfolded!" He underlines his words with a plump gold-ringed finger.

...

Shit! There's no key under the doormat! Sally rubs her hands against the coldness and breathes clouds of frustration into the early-morning air, wondering if Zasto is still in the workshop, fixing the tyres on his jeep. She walks around the building and looks through frosty patterns on the window into an empty workshop.

Back in the house, she knocks on the door of his room and turns the handle, surprised to find it unlocked. The bed is still made and luggage only partly unpacked. Judging by the half-emptied bags and clothes on hangers lying on the bed, he must have left in a hurry. Her anger rises. To her, practising the routine is a holy ritual; her first step to stardom. But she cannot begin! An invisible cord laces her throat; unpleasant memories surface once more. There are questions which cannot be answered. Where is the clown with the key to her dreams? For the moment she needs him – but for how long?

From the chimney of the neighbouring cottage, a thin spiral of smoke signals early morning activities when the girl knocks on the door, attempting to appear calm. If they realise something is wrong it might cost her job.

Harry rubs the sleep from his eyes. "And who has thrown you out of bed at this time of the morning, young lady?" he asks.

"Sorry, Harry!" She smiles trying to sound casual. "I got up early to practise, but can't get into the barn."

"Your friend Zasto has a key!" Harry says, raising an eyebrow.

"I don't know where he's put it and he's not in his room."

Low blood-pressure hinders a man's thoughts in the early hours of the morning and Harry is too sleepy for far-reaching conclusions. Ignoring undertones of panic in the girl's voice, he gives her the wink. "Probably shacking up with that widow again, Jean Whatshername – worse than a sailor is that bloke; got a girl in every town…!" Then he disappears into the dark depths of the cottage to search for the key.

A dark shroud transforms light into dark, joy into sadness and love into hate. It causes the inward cry of pain, but allows no display of emotion when Harry returns. *Everything is fine! Put on the happy face because you don't want his pity. Don't listen to his warbling either, about not losing the key because it's the last one he has. Take no notice of the unspoken questions through raised eyebrows and a suggestive nod.*

The darkness, once locked away and forgotten, has infiltrated her circus world, stifling the gaiety and contaminating her surroundings. It is the evil cloud which once took her mother and transformed her father. Now it has returned and is moving towards her while she jumps, up and down and roundabout: higher and higher, floating on currents of air, twisting and turning. Her body is lithe and flexible; her mind is filled with passionate intensity. Miss Flummi's limbs are going in different directions. Anger and hate swells inside like an ugly giant balloon, driving her forward. She almost reaches her goal – the trapeze. The double somersault must be performed at great height – much higher – more and more, until she finally touches that tantalizing swing, dangling over her head.

A ray of sunlight enters the barn through the great sliding door, outlining the silhouette of a woman in black tights. Her blonde hair is a halo of gold transformed by beams of sunlight. The sudden apparition watches intently as Sally achieves her goal – the high spring and somersault between the side ropes of the trapeze. The apparition applauds vigorously, truly impressed. "That was very good!" Irena Olsen speaks with a pronounced Danish accent, pleasantly soft to the ear. The door opens further and more sunlight enters the barn.

"You've brought me luck," announces Sally gratefully as she draws to a halt, her face suddenly brightening when dark thoughts are gone. "I've been practising for a whole hour," she starts jumping again, "and reached the trapeze for the very first time, just as you came through that door."

Irena's head moves to the rhythm of the jumps. "I can check your movements, if you like. I used to do a double somersault in aerial flight, so why shouldn't I coach you – help you get there from the trampoline."

Sally doesn't answer. She continues jumping, her movements are almost hypnotic.

Irena, distinctly annoyed and with dwindling patience, observes the clockwork-figure on the trampoline, unaware she has been transformed into the image of Patricia Lightbone, standing where she is now standing, sending images of training-sequences through the girl's head. In her imagination, officials wearing track-suits dash about the gym. Trainers cradle their check boards, noting final results before the competition begins. The rhythm of her movements induces pleasant feelings of success, becoming almost a trance. Keep going! Keep going! Such a beautiful rhythm!

How long has she been like this? Had she fallen asleep while moving? She jumps from the trampoline and recovers her balance, intent upon concealing the lapse of awareness. What had she said? "Would you do that for me?" she asks breathlessly, looking around the barn as though some kind of explanation might appear from the far corner.

Irena has a forgiving nature and smiles to cover her confusion, enjoying the sacred moment of offer and acceptance. Life is taking a turn for the better after being on the road with her brother, whose homosexual friend will be joining them shortly, leaving her out on a limb.

The door opens wider. A white Jack Russell follows a yapping Yorkshire Terrier into the barn; an orange poodle and three larger dogs race behind, followed by Georgina

Clark as Madam Pinkie wearing blue working drills. A red scarf tied into a huge bow covers most of her orange hair and her face is so heavily rouged that she looks feverish. She chases her dogs as they sniff around the barn in noisy abandon, apologizing profusely for the noise. Finally, she blows the whistle taken from a bulging breast pocket which induces sudden and unexpected silence, apart from the sound of panting animals with pricked ears, attentively awaiting the command.

"Would you mind if I take over a quiet corner of the barn, to rehearse my new act?" she turns to face the two women, who laugh delightedly at the surprise performance, which is daily routine for Georgina Clark. "The dogs get *sooo* excited at this time of the day – as happy as pigs in shit, you might say! Where are the kennels? Don't tell me they're still in the barn next to the stables! Oh God! There'll be all hell let loose when my dogs see the horses being led into the field. They'll want to get out and start barking. The grooms will hate my guts because of the noise! It's the same every year! Ah well! That's life!" Georgina's one-sided dialogue continues as she sets up the row of hurdles. Her dogs watch intently, wagging their tails with excitement.

"It's better than Blackpool, mind you. Last year's variety season was hard enough." Georgina makes an appreciative gesture after a quick look around. "Couldn't wish for a better place, could you? There's nothing better than a bit of peace and quiet mixed with clean country air for getting one's act together. By the way, I'm driving into Whitby this afternoon! Wanna come too?"

Irena says "Oooh! I'd love to come!" and turns to Sally. "How about you?"

...

Alone in her room and free from bad thoughts she fingers through the local telephone directory in search of a driving-school, blissfully unaware her door is still open.

When Irena appears, she is startled, then horrified at the sudden and unexpected intrusion. With Irena, the filth has returned and she'll be spending the night cleaning once more. "You've given me a shock!" The directory falls to the floor as she jumps to her feet, eager to prevent Irene entering the room. "Be careful, the floor is wet! You might slip!" Sally warns, panic in her voice, arms wide open, blocking the entrance or she'll be inside like a shot.

"You reckon I might slip? Do you know how well-balanced I am?" Irena giggles, then doubles over with laughter, the idea being so ridiculous that going into a fit is the least one can do. "If I can balance on a rope, surely I'll keep my balance on your wet floor!" She stops laughing and coughs, looks at her watch and regards Sally impatiently. "Hurry up! Georgina is waiting downstairs. By the way, guess what's in the back pocket of my jeans. The Master of the Keys has given me the job of getting a barn-door-duplicate and you know how caretakers are fussy about keys."

Sally makes an effort to appear light-hearted as she locks the door of her room and walks arm in arm with Irena down the corridor, giggling at some trivial remark about Georgina and her dogs.

They squeeze into the back seat of a Morris Minor with 'Doggies on Board' splashed across the rear window. Georgina, whose red hair matches the poodle on the passenger seat, concentrates on starting the car. The dog hangs its head through the half-open window, snapping at the wind as they drive into town.

After Georgina has parked the car, Sally makes a point of consulting her watch. "I have to be at the driving-school in about fifteen minutes," she informs them, "Does anyone know where it is?"

"Good for you!" says Georgina. "A driver's license is essential in a circus." Georgina knows her way about town. "It's down the road and to your right!"

Irena says she fancies a pair of ballerina shoes that are coming into fashion.

"There's a good shoe shop in the centre of town," says Georgina, "and a café around the corner that does freshly ground coffee. Shall we meet there in an hour? Would that be alright?"

She'll keep it a secret! Sally can't wait to get to the bank and check her account which is not in keeping with the 'poor little girl' image she has painstakingly built. At the bank, a middle-aged woman in a figure-hugging beige

141

costume returns the savings-book with a business-like smile, having added the interest to the total amount which balances at five thousand two hundred pounds. Sally sends a silent message to the grandfather she hasn't yet met. *Thanks Granddad! One of these days, I'll visit you in Spain.* The clock in the bank tells her it is half-past three. The driving-school is around the corner.

The man behind the desk says, "Fifty pounds booking fee and ten-pounds an hour."

He might be asking for the earth! There's no way she'll part with that kind of money! She faces the elderly man, who never tires of talking about the retirement insurance he deserves, having taught two generations of Whitby residents how to drive cars, trucks and motor-bikes which is enough to drive a fellow around the bend; although the creases on his face suggest he is a man of great patience.

"The problem is," she takes a deep breath before explaining the problem now forming in her mind, "…being an orphan and belonging to a circus which doesn't pay regular wages, I don't have much money at present – and desperately need a driver's license to pull my own caravan." Her eyes fill with convenient tears, due to the necessity of sharing a primitive wooden trailer with a couple of dishonest kitchen workers who regularly steal the little money she has.

"I'm very sorry about that!" The sympathetic driving instructor, whose name is Bartholomew Bell, has a soothing manner and cringes at the unlikely vision of his two daughters and three grandchildren in a similar position. A little indulgence might be appropriate here, he considers, always a willing helper, especially when a damsel is in distress. He smiles at Sally. "With a bit of luck and regular lessons – say five days a week – you'll have your license within a month," he suggests. "How about two o'clock in the afternoon?"

"But how am I to get here from a lonely hotel on the moors, when there is no bus-service in winter?" she wails.

"Ah! There's the problem of getting into town on time, is there? Well! That shouldn't be a problem if I can manage to pick you up. By George lass! I must be having one of my good days, 'cos I don't usually go out that far to pick up my clients."

"Oh! Thank-you so much! I would love to take up your offer, but there's another problem, which has been causing me sleepless nights. I don't like to mention it! It is so embarrassing!"

"Go on then! I'm all ear, and cross my heart, I won't say a word!" he adds jovially, wondering how such a pretty girl could have so many problems.

"I don't get paid regular wages out of season, during winter, when the circus earns no money and the director is in Spain." She takes out a handkerchief to wipe away the tears and finishes the performance by blowing her nose.

He can bear it no longer. In his opinion, the whole set-up is a scandal! She can't even pay the booking-fee, poor lass! Whoever heard of such iniquity? "Now dry your tears, my dear! It will all work out in the end!" he says as she signs her name at the bottom of the form and he adds her name to his dwindling list of customers. A new driving school has opened in the town centre, with a modern driving simulator and art deco lounge.

...

A rusty freighter and small fishing boats list on the freezing mud in the harbour, waiting for the tide to come in. On a long bank outside a small shed, a group of fishermen wearing waterproof capes and earflap caps brave the cold as they wait for the tide, and watch idly as she walks by. A flock of gulls swirl overhead, sharp eyes continually moving in search of a morsel. Their high-pitched screams remind her of their ability to float without obvious effort on currents of wind and she yearns to join them, gliding through the air, with the turn of a wing higher and higher; leaving the trials and tribulations of life far below. On reaching St. Mary's Church, it comes to mind she has never gone sightseeing in the towns they have visited. One town is like the next, circus people say. There's no time to waste on trivialities! No time for sightseeing when there's a schedule to keep!

There's this overpowering odour of fish. An old sailor in rubber togs hoses down the fish market floor, reminding her of a previous visit in a different life; a Sunday-School trip as a reward for the group who'd reeled-off the Ten Commandments without a mistake. It reminds her of eating shrimps from a paper-cone bag with a tooth-pick. Where are the shrimps? The stalls are empty and the market deserted, which is just as well because thinking about The Ten Commandments reminds her of the sins she has committed. There have been too many sins for forgiveness; too many demons at the back of her mind, who'll be out if she'll let them. Who cares? Let her be punished by the gulls! But there again, better not! Their dropping will be covering her head if she doesn't quicken her pace.

There's a long row of villas along the sea-front; some converted into elegant hotels and boarding-houses, which she admires – the last time she'll admire, or gain pleasure in anything now that she has spotted the familiar figure a short distance ahead. Zasto is not alone! She watches him from a safe distance, flounce with his head to one side in a typical pose, through the hotel's swing doors. and happily descend the steps. Her heart turns cold as she watches him put a protective arm around the woman's waist. "The Newcastle Aunt," she whispers through the dark cloud that enfolds her. The tall, slim and blonde beauty presses her hip against Zasto's loin, tossing her shoulder-length hair and smiling the smile of the satisfied lover. They are the lovers with eyes only for each other; who'll advertise the fact to the rest of the world. "Thank-you, darling, thank-you for the wonderful night!" they seem to be saying.

There are scratches on the dull black surface of the monster in the convenient telephone-booth with the flattened cigarette butts covering the floor and the telephone-book in shreds. Could there be anywhere worse to look for cover? Is there anything more vindictive than the truth? The remaining curtain has been pulled from her eyes, and the anger follows, cold, remorseless and vindictive.

Having shivered for a while in the telephone booth, she retraces her steps, draws up her collar and pulls the beret over her ears, dreading the sound of their footsteps behind her. The wind freezes the blood in her veins as Zasto's jeep cruises down Royal Crescent Street, past the figure sitting huddled on a bank.

...

"Where on earth have you been?" demands Georgina from a corner table in the empty café. Her face is blushed with subdued anger. Significantly, she examines her watch while Irena stirs in her coffee without looking up.

It can't be helped! Sally throws herself onto the remaining chair and extracts the long and meaningful sigh of having done the heroic dead, cost what it will. "You wouldn't believe what I've just been through. An old lady tripped over and fell onto the pavement, so I tried to help her but she couldn't move her legs, so I couldn't leave her there, could I?"

Georgina and Irena agree that she'd done the right thing; regard each another meaningfully and Sally, having a strong antenna for atmospheric impressions, feels encouraged to continue. "Some bloke came and said he'd ring for an ambulance," (now she is well into her story and knows exactly how it will end), "...so we waited for a while, but it didn't come. Then I went to a nearby telephone booth but there was a woman inside who wouldn't let me in to dial an emergency, so I grabbed hold of her arm and pulled her out. You can imagine what a fuss *that* caused..." she rolls her eyes towards the ceiling and shakes her head in disgust, "... when she started to scream, attracting a crowd. Then I explained about the poor old lady, lying injured on the pavement further down the road and waiting for an ambulance. A man in a bowler hat told the woman to stop screaming and said she should be ashamed of herself for being hysterical and preventing help for an injured old lady who might die of shock if she's left on her own. Then everything happened so quickly. The ambulance arrived within five minutes, which just goes to show how fast they can be in an emergency, when you dial 999 and give them the correct information about exactly where you are, who you are and what has happened. You can imagine how grateful the old lady was – said I'd saved her life and wouldn't let go of my hand. The ambulance driver said I could accompany her to hospital, but I told them about meeting my friends. They won't wait forever, I said."

She rummages in her handbag, muttering under her breath, on the verge of panic while wondrous silence prevails at such an impressive account of selflessness and presence of mind. 'Penance' enters their thoughts, for the frightful passion they've worked themselves in to, not to mention the bitchy things they've said – and the longer they've waited, the more hateful they've grown.

"Oh no! Someone has stolen my purse. I'd saved three hundred pounds for my driving-lessons, and it's gone!" she wails tearfully, tipping the contents of the bag onto the table. "And what's more, I'm starving!" Sorrowful tears roll down her cheeks. "It must have been that man with the beard, who claimed to have called the ambulance – standing behind me as I attended her leg." It had happened! Of course it had happened. That's how it had been! She admires her own courage and experiences genuine anguish; the atrocity of the Good Samaritan, the victim of robbery while doing a good deed. Tears flow more freely when one believes one's own lies. She wipes them away with the back of her hand, takes a tissue from her pocket and dabs her eyes, looking at them appealingly. "A whole month without a penny to my name – how can I possibly exist?"

Irena hands over a fresh tissue. "Don't worry; I'll lend you some money! When you have finished drying your eyes, we'll have another cup of coffee, some of these delicious teacakes, and the world will seem a much better place, wait and see. In Denmark they say, food is cooked hotter than it is eaten which means a situation is never as bad as it seems. Yes?"

Later, she sits on the back seat of the car, next to the red poodle. Sensing her aversion to the odour of his fur, her lack of interest in his rear parts and unwillingness to scratch behind his ears, the animal capitulates at making a new buddy and curls up on his cushion. Irena and Georgina, in the front of the car, talk about collecting the duplicate key from the ironmongers, admire the six new leather dog-collars to be decorated with sequins, all of which is of no interest to Sally, who stares out of the window because Zasto's punishment is going through her mind.

Who can resist a new pair of shoes? Irena removes the light-blue ballerinas from the exclusive shoe bag decorated with pink and white stripes and shows them to Sally, who won't show her sorrow and with great deliberation she admires them effusively. "Can I try them on? Oh how wonderful! They fit perfectly, lucky you!"

"Well! They don't fit *me* perfectly, so you can keep them, honey," says Irena, eager for repentance and ashamed to admit she can't recall having been so biased. Egotistical and definitely weird – that's what she'd said about Sally, who'd kept them waiting for more than an hour. Let that be a lesson! Never jump to conclusions. Let her keep the shoes! God knows, she's deserved them!

"Oh! I can't possibly…!"

"Sure you can, honey! I've got loads of shoes. These are really too small. They'll kill me! I'm giving them to you as a present!"

Such unexpected generosity! How should she cope with it? Extreme tiresome, accepting presents and feeling obliged to give in return. She has nothing to give, which is why she'll do without them, thanks very much!

For some inexplicable reason, since trying on the shoes, the dog has become restless, sniffing around and contaminating her clothes. She'll wash them right away, as soon as she's home. Tears prick her eyes as she stares through the window. Her body is aching because Zasto will die. The ghost of a girl looks through the keyhole and watches the rhythmic movements of her mother's body beneath the alien, while Gloria with the permanent smile dances on her bed, allowing the pollution to spread through the house. The dog's eyes illuminate in the darkness, focusing on her as though waiting for something, as she listens to her companions, talking about shoes.

Circus people love to gossip and she can well imagine what they've been saying. *Hey listen! I'll let you into a secret! She's at the end of the line! She's the fool for a clown!* That's what they've been thinking; she knows what they've been saying and thinking. *He has been telling his lies to silly little Miss Flummi. But Miss Flummi no longer needs him. Others will help Miss Flummi achieve the performance of her life, when Zasto has joined the alien who once stole her mother.* Vigilant eyes gleam through the door. He examines his watch and disappears from her vision.

...

Mr. Bell is even more sympathetic on hearing she has been the victim of theft. "How low can you get?" he asks in the compassionate tone reserved for the doted-upon grand-daughters and young female customers. "I'll make you a generous offer, since you were kind enough to help an elderly woman in distress, which shows great strength of character in my opinion, and deserves to be acknowledged by paying a rate of one pound per month for your driving lessons, and the rest within the next two years. How about that?"

What the hell, just keep going! The big aim is the driver's license and a contract with Alfonso.

Her luck has returned. Even Irena and Ole are kind and generous to the poor, downtrodden helper; the victim of infamy. They have given her a loan on her salary, with no conditions attached. When shall she repay them? Will she repay them? Ole is a reliable and dedicated coach. He waits for her every morning in the gym, determined she'll be gripping the flying bar before very long. Soon, she is finding it is easier than she'd imagined and even better, Ole continually praises her talent as though she were some kind of genius. The wooden doll has sprung to life, and Ole never tires of reminding her that the figure must have soul. "Give it soul, honey!" he repeats until at last, the doll has achieved her goal; has reached the swing. Her gloved hands grab hold of the ropes. Triumphantly, Sally pulls herself up. "You need to practice the timing," Ole, the perfectionist, explains. "The somersault must be done on the split of a second and at an exact height, otherwise you won't land on your feet."

Why they are eager to help her attain such achievement? Are they fools, or simply 'do-gooders'? She smiles, thinking, *if they knew how much money is in my account, surely they wouldn't be so generous!*

Today is the day and a cause for celebration! She has passed her driving-test and is one step nearer her goal. The taste of success is sweet, around the long wooden table after the evening meal, in the company of well-meaning people. Harry brings a crate of bottles from the cellar, there being no draught-beer storage in winter and Ole drinks his beer with the usual intense demeanour before leaving the group to drive into town and visit his lover.

Ron, the one-wheel juggler and his wife Andrea are passing through on their way home from an engagement in Scarborough and sitting at the far end of the table. Ron says he's looking forward to seeing Zasto. "Has the old scoundrel gone bird-catching again?"

Bird catching? There's an awkward silence. Andrea nudges her husband who looks startled and begins an intense examination of his feet.

In the adjoining office, the telephone rings. Sally jumps up and wishes she could flee; run outside – go anywhere, rather than listen to echoes of the past resounding through the building.

"Sorry! I mean clown-catching," adds Ron sheepishly, forcing her back to reality. "I mean Zasto chasing you … or rather you as Miss Flummi… around the ménage, of course…"

There's suppressed laughter and another uncomfortable silence while she savours the pleasure of secret knowledge – the advantage of knowing what will happen. They don't know he'll be leaving – sooner than he thinks, and won't be returning! She shrugs her shoulders, eager to appear unconcerned about the clown who is a traitor, and thinks about what had happened to Gloria. Everyone should know what happens to a traitor...

"Saturdays and Sundays when he's here – that's when we practice." She stands up and pushes her chair under the table ready to leave, but the telephone has stopped ringing and she sits down again as Harry enters the dining-room, red in the face and looking jolly.

"You won't believe this, folks!" he slaps his knee and doubles over with laughter – a frequent occurrence because it doesn't take much to start him laughing and circus people consider him an easy audience when it comes to appreciating their art. "Did you hear the telephone ringing? Guess who it was! Lord Soandso himself! Booking in for three weeks in summer."

"Lord Soandso. Who the hell is Lord Soandso?"

"He's the one who pisses in t' paper basket ...blind as a bat! Thinks it's the loo!"

Harry finally takes a seat and, having calmed down, says he's real proud of our little Miss Flummi for passing her drivin' test an' all.

"Thanks Harry! Have a beer on me!" says Miss Flummi, realizing that generosity is a satisfying attribute. Georgina Clark had reminded her that passing her driving-test would cost her a round.

"What? Do I have to pay for the drinks?" she'd asked Georgina in amazement.

"Pay for the drinks – what a weird question!!! Of course you have to pay for the drinks – where have you been all your life? – on the moon?"

Harry is in for gossip; telling the tale behind a pint of bitter, even if it comes from the bottle. He bangs the palm of his hand on the table and makes the announcement. "Jack Iski's elephants were collected by the zoo early this morning."

"Thank God for that!" someone says and there are nods of agreement – and what about Jack?

"He's a stall cleaner!" mutters a tall, silent man, one of the local animal grooms.

"Fancies himself as a balancing performer," says the silent groom's girl-friend, who exercises the horses when they're out in the field.

"He once asked me for a few tips – about balancing on one leg of a stool and doing a handstand," says Ron. "I said it's dead easy! Start practising when you're four years old and keep going!"

Harry said, "I've heard from the locals, he spends most of his time hanging around the tables in 'Snooker's Den', making out he's the famous animal trainer who's retired to Whitby."

"Where's Zasto?" asks one of the grooms.

"Should be here soon, to watch Miss Flummi's new 'wooden doll' act," says Irena glancing appreciatively across the table. "Wait 'till he sees her on the swing, like she's been doing it all her life: I can't wait to see his reaction!"

"Ah ha! What d'you think he'll say?" asks the groom.

"He'll tell her to take off the weight she's been putting on just lately, or she won't fit inside his box," answers Irena lightly.

"I'm tired, off to bed, good night!" Sally doesn't want to hear remarks about her figure; doesn't want to know why her periods have stopped and her figure is changing. She feels an overwhelming longing for the vacuum-cleaner; it's the old friend, waiting in her room. Let them say what they like about her hands being rough and calloused; her fingernail-beds swollen and flaky through too much hard work. Without those flesh-coloured gloves she wears during training, they'd already be bleeding.

...

Here they are! The soldiers from Emily's cleaning cupboard; bottles of liquid lined up on her window, with the brushes, rags, mop and a bucket, preparing for the battle which she can't wait to begin. The murmur of voices and occasional bursts of laughter are far away and irrelevant to her mission. She must free herself of the filth; work at great speed before it contaminates her bedroom and destroys her new circus-life.

Take the duster! Oh, these specks of dust, swirling about the room and spreading evil and damnation while searching for somewhere to land. The mutters and whispers are swelling; becoming louder, rising into ranting and raving and swearing. These are the noisy profanities that erupt if she'll allow them. Under normal circumstances they would never enter her head, let alone pass her lips.

A welcome breeze, cool and refreshing, spreads through the room as she opens the window. It's time to hang out the bedding; an opportunity to rest. The scrubbing, washing and wiping at a great pace, is making her dizzy. She leans over the sill to watch the headlights of a car approaching the building and feels her heart beating. Standing behind the curtain, she watches it enter the drive.

Four car-tires piled into the back of the vehicle are visible in the light of six Victorian-style lamps bordering the drive. Straining her ears, she catches remnants of conversation between Zasto and the groom. Zasto kicks idly against a front tyre, his head to one side as though seriously considering whether to change it or not.

Who cares about changing car-tyres when the dressing table needs polishing and the bath must be cleaned before mopping the tiles?

Forget the cleaning for a moment and take another look!

Latticed patterns project from the barn window onto the gravel. Reflections of fine drizzle beam through the light. Raindrops sparkle like floating diamonds against the blackness of night. The light shining through the tiny workshop window reveals he is inside. She remembers his aversion of being disturbed when 'screwing his jeep'. It's a labour of love, so he claims.

There's something to be achieved and no time to be wasted.

The figure in a dark jacket, the hood pulled over her face, emerges from the room and silently closes the door. Wearing the new ballerinas she steps silently along the corridor, down the steps leading to the deserted kitchen, past shelves stocked with dishes, stainless-steel cooking utensils and the softly humming freezer. The back door is unlocked and she opens it quickly. A cool draught enters the kitchen as she slips into the night.

Standing framed within the open barn-door, she waits until her eyes have grown accustomed to the dark. Silent silhouettes of circus equipment come into view. A soft light seeps through the half-open garage and into the far corner. She hears the rhythmic strains of reggae music. The clown's feet project from beneath the vehicle through the half-open door. She'll have to step over them to get inside.

'No, woman, no cry'; sings Bob Marley from the transistor radio placed on a stool in the corner. A step over the protruding legs and she's almost there. *Hadn't it had been his idea? – only a joke, but he'd said it!* "Don't turn the handle when I'm changing the wheels or you'll squash me to death! And if you squash me to death, there'll be no more sex! You wouldn't like to put an end to all that lovely excitement, would you?" His mouth had laughed; his eyes had been dark and impassive. The fool for a clown

remembers, as she stares at protruding feet beneath the vehicle without wheels.

Bob Marley sings the words of little sister shedding no tears and the refrain of 'no, woman, no cry'. She turns up the volume. Shadows freeze against the whitewashed wall. The electric bulb flickers against a spider's web on the ceiling. With the stoic determination of a hangman and eyes filled with hate, she opens the trapdoor to death and turns the jack handle.

Such wonderful music! Someone has turned up the volume. Who can it be at this time of night? The weight of the car suddenly slumps on his body. He can't breathe – shut down the music – he can't bloody breathe! He'll die if he can't free himself of this overpowering weight squashing the life out of his body. He moves his arms, making one last inhuman effort to push up the car. If he could reach the hammer, he might prop it up. But the hammer is out of his grasp and his strength is weakening. His life as a clown is dwindling away; the ménage is out of his grasp. *My beautiful jeep is killing me! Oh, my beautiful jeep!* He remembers the words; *don't turn the handle when I'm changing the wheels or you'll squash me to death!* The music drowns the gurgling scream; his very last breath.

Chapter 12

Nickbone is offended; unaccustomed to people nodding off while he's speaking. The old boy's head, second to the left in the front row, has been drooping over his stiff white collar for some time. Nickbone takes a deep breath, an effective pause, lending the atmosphere he needs to emphasize the drama of the battle of Dunkirk. He allows his eyes to run over the six rows of grey and white heads, counting fifty three listeners, mostly in their seventies and some well into their eighties, within the communal lounge of the 'Nethersted Nursing Home.'

Sister Louisa stands in the doorway, head to one side, giving the impression of intense concentration as he leaves the battle of Dunkirk, and with a few well-chosen words, changes the subject to J.B. Priestley''s *'Postscripts'*.

The amateur actor succeeds in returning his listeners to their stronger days, by reciting in the familiar Yorkshire dialect, the written words of the famous novelist and wartime broadcaster. Is it sadness or pleasure which causes the slight quiver in his voice when worn faces lighten with happy memories, or darken with the tragedy of war and life-long struggles? Now, having reached the final destination, they wallow in déjà vu.

"My Walter didn't come back," a woman murmurs as a handkerchief meets the eye.

"I was on t' 'Brighton Queen'," announces Arthur Dickinson, a sprightly old soldier with a phenomenal memory and a mine of information on local history, "a flimsy thing like a box of matches, but it got us back over t' Channel alright … lot of us left behind, though." Whispered reminiscences of lost comrades bring sadness to the room. A hoarse voice breaks the spell.

"Now I'll tell you summat about Mr. Priestley. My uncle used to know him." The fresh perm nods energetically and a thin frame springs to life. "Now I'm not into discussing politics, but did you know he was a Labour man?" A bony finger stabs at the air; a striped woollen shawl is drawn tight. "They say that's why they stopped his broadcasts."

"I never knew that!" remarks someone from the back row.

"Oh aye!" A bright-eyed lady shrugs indignant shoulders and nudges the white-collared sleeper leaning dangerously starboard.

The neighbour awakes with a start and grasps the wrong end of the discussion, referring to the rationing of food. "Two ounces o' butter, – wasn't even worth wrapping!"

Wartime experiences are shaken and dusted. Uncertain details, dates and places are confirmed; heroic acts acknowledged before routine returns with the ring of a bell announcing supper. An overall fluster fills the room as they eagerly rise. Meals are a highlight in homes for the aged and infirm.

"Thank-you, a nice cup of tea is just what I need to lubricate my vocal cords." Nickbone pushes Jonathan, the forty-year-old car-accident victim, in a wheelchair into the dining-room with the firm intention of remaining at his side of the symbolical fence. There's no room in his mind for his own vulnerability. He takes a hungry bite into the soft white triangular sandwich, chews heartily and helps himself to another before registering the transportation of food into other, unconcerned mouths. Jesus! He'd swallow the whole plate in one piece…well, almost! – manners permitting. He looks through a mirror into the future, seeing himself in twenty years' time as the old boy at the other end of the table, placing crumbs into an empty mouth with a trembling claw-like hand.

Don't dwell on unpleasant facts! Nickbone tells himself, just like he had advised junior officers. *A cup of hot tea is what I need!* He refills his cup from an oversized pot on the table and makes a mental note to speak to matron about a newspaper-reading-session.

Passing half-open doors, a world of embroidered cushions and walls hung with family portraits, he takes a seat outside Matron's office and a newspaper from the pile on the table. *'Attack on British vessels heightens Cod War'*, he reads. Well! Who's interested in phony wars? His eyes fly over an article on Northern Ireland, reminding him of a rainy holiday spent in County Antrim when he'd won a fancy-dress competition wearing the apparel of a local fisherman's bright yellow raincoat and galoshes and displaying a poster advertising holidays in Ireland. Still smiling at the memory, he turns to the back page.

'Tragic death of a clown'.

Removing his glasses and muttering that he can read better without the damned things, he examines the reportage subtitled, *'Circus clown dies in an accident.'*

Circus Poppi's popular clown has been found crushed to death under his car, in a garage adjoining a hotel on the North Yorkshire moors owned by circus director Alfonso Poppi. The hotel is home to the circus' artistes during the winter, when it is closed to the public. Mr. Poppi has since returned from Spain and says he is "absolutely devastated". The coroner is expected to issue a verdict of accidental death.

Nickbone skims the editor's note, warning against crawling under a jacked-up car without extra support after removing the wheels. As he folds the paper and puts it into his pocket he has already decided on a day trip to Whitby. He hasn't been there since he was a lad – a long time ago, he ruminates peevishly. His grandparents once ran a boarding house nearby, in Cullercoats. He distinctly remembers the sea-view.

His correctness being almost pedantic, he informs Matron that he has pocketed the newspaper and hopes she won't mind if he keeps it for a while.

"Of course not!" the woman with the kind face and tired smile assures him.

"I've got a lot on! – can't take any more engagements at present. But I'll keep in touch!" he announces vaguely, his eyes glittering with suppressed excitement making it obvious there's something else on his mind. Matron raises a questioning eyebrow and wonders about a retired policeman who has done his duty and still gets excited about reading the newspaper.

The unbuttoned raincoat billows behind him like an open parachute as he leaves the building, checks his watch, unlocks the car door and decides to catch up with old colleagues.

'The Malt Shovel' is the unofficial meeting place for police officers, taking a pint to wind down. Hugo, the flamboyant barman with the hair dyed blond and wearing leather jeans, says 'it's the will of God' when a snatch of information comes his way. From whom? Nobody asks!

Nickbone feels the urge to share his thoughts and with a bit of luck, he'll catch a snippet of information which hasn't reached the press: often the lurid details of a crime; seldom, the frivolous problems of life.

"Hello old man!" Detective Inspector Jack Douglas has taken his usual place at the bar and watches his former superior hang up his coat. "We were wondering when you'd be showing up again – even laid bets on it, didn't we?" He turns to the young police officer sitting next to him. "So I've just won a couple of rounds, old man! – reckoned you'd be here within the week."

Nickbone, enjoying the experience of friendly acceptance, climbs onto the vacant stool, greets Hugo the barman behind the highly polished bar, and orders a pint of bitter before acknowledging the colleague whose company – he has to admit – he still badly misses.

"Jacket's getting a bit tight!" Jack Douglas observes, watching him undo the buttons for a more comfortable pose.

"Seems to have shrunk!" Nickbone replies. "Dry-cleaners aren't what they used to be."

"I've heard that pot-bellied policemen are a common sight in India," the young police officer with the quick wit and well-trained muscles remarks. Jack Douglas gives him a look and a nudge for 'putting his foot in the shit'.

"Sorry! I'll bite my tongue! Heard a lot about you, Nickbone! It's a pleasure to meet you!"

"My pleasure!" Nickbone answers casually and turns his attention to the task of lubricating his throat. "Tea's no bloody good after long-winded recitations," he announces after the lengthy swig follows a sigh of deep satisfaction. He replaces his glass on the bar, wipes his mouth with the back of his hand (which he'll only do in male company) and slowly removes the folded item of news from his inside pocket which he places, without comment, in front of Jack.

Jack studies it carefully and without a word, passes it to his junior partner, who also reads it in silence.

Thumbs up! Nickbone's silent request for background information on the death of the clown requires no further explanation, and they nick their heads furtively while Hugo renews their damp beer mats and wipes the bar, grumbling about Saturday's match: Leeds United against Manchester, which he'd seen live. "Don't know where all this hooliganism is leading to! Sup up lads!" he says.

…

"What have you been up to lately?" asks Patricia.

His frequent visits to the 'Malt Shovel' haven't escaped his wife's attention. Without a word, he leaves the breakfast table and reappears with the newspaper clipping.

"Oh dear, how sad!" says Patricia as she scans the article, regards her husband and sees the suspicious gleam in his eyes. "This refers to Circus Poppi," she points out. There is an oppressive silence as she gathers her thoughts. "I know what you're thinking – I can see it written all over your face! You suspect that Sally Foss could be involved in the death of the clown, which is ridiculous! – it just can't be possible!" Her voice mirrors her distress. She regards him fearfully as he sips his coffee, carefully replacing cup upon saucer to avoid the rattle and she strangely remembers he'd rather do without saucers.

His voice interrupts her thoughts. "At least ten per cent of suspected accidental deaths have been proved to be murder, another ten per cent are murders which can't be proved, and another twenty per cent are cases of manslaughter."

This is all a bit much! Now she has lost her appetite and even feels sick! *Thank goodness there are no lessons today. Is he still trying to prove Sally Foss is a criminal? An innocent girl, a promising athlete – could have reached Olympic standards if she hadn't run away. To hell with it all, this is intolerable! Where is my handkerchief?* "Girls like Sally don't murder, unless…"

"Unless what?"

"Unless there's something wrong upstairs." Patricia taps her forehead.

"Do you think she is," he clears his throat, "wrong upstairs?"

"I don't know…" her voice trails off. "Don't let us talk like this."

He waits, thinking how naïve she is. He has seldom shared the pressure of his work; protected his sanity by listening to her instead, talking about her pupils, the school, evening gymnastic classes for women and the hours of weekend training for talented students while he has silently relieved himself of distressful cases, brutal murders, family tragedies, delving into the depths of the human soul. Perhaps he should have shared them with her after all!

"You know how rumours spread."

"What kind of rumours?" A spiral of smoke makes its way from the toaster to the newly painted (egg-shell white) ceiling.

"Can't you switch the damned thing off? Are you planning to set fire to the house, as well as inventing a murder?" She enjoys blowing her top now and again. It clears the air and she prefers to be open about things. Secretive behaviour isn't her thing. On the other hand, she wonders if he is interrogating her. Of course he's interrogating her, with or without intention; asking pointed questions; and against her better judgment, she must give him the answers.

"I did enquire after Sally, without making too much of an issue about her leaving school. After all, one doesn't forfeit a promising career for no obvious reason." Patricia pours herself coffee and Nickbone declines her offer. "I spoke to a couple of girls in her class – separately – you know how people relate the same story differently. They told me a few things. Teenage girls can be unbelievably cruel. They started calling her 'Bloody Mary' when her period soaked through to her dress and she thought she was dying. Just imagine! She thought she was ill! Where was her mother, for Christ's sake?

"To get out of being called 'Bloody Mary' she invited half the class to her birthday party. They got excited about it – said they couldn't talk about anything else because she'd never invited anyone to her house and they were inquisitive. There's an unspoken rule among girls of that age. If you don't invite, you don't *get* invited – they'll leave you out – don't talk – except behind your back, which is what happened to Sally. When they arrived at the house, she didn't open the door. But they knew she was home; they could see her reflection in the mirror next to the window, hiding behind the curtains – weird, eh? Makes you feel kind of sorry for her!"

Patricia shakes her head and falls into silence while Nickbone examines what seems like a document taken from his pocket. He looks up. "Know what, Pattie? I haven't been to Whitby since I was a lad. Lovely place! Come to think of it, I wouldn't mind seeing it again; staying over for a few of days. What do you think? Fancy coming too?"

"You know very well that I can't take time off during mid-term," she answers without emphasizing the fact that she's more interested in encouraging new talent, than chasing ghosts.

Nickbone embraces his wife. "I enjoy acting as much as you enjoy teaching," he mutters in her ear, having spent half his life delving into human structures and inscrutabilities. He kisses her cheek and she returns his affection with a smile. Later, he replaces the newspaper in the drawer of his desk, with the official and detailed report on Zasto Furninski's death.

...

Chief Inspector Jack Douglas had no serious qualms about handing over the report on Zasto Furninski's death, although he'd wondered about old Nickbone's intentions and decided his previous senior officer would be hardly breaking the law after spending so many years with the force. Although it hadn't been a top-secret document, he didn't suspect for one moment that Nickbone would disclose the source of his information should anyone ask, which was highly unlikely. "Unofficially, mind you," he had said, handing it over and trying to make himself understood despite the live performance. 'The Country Fiddlers Quartet', accompanied by the rhythmic tapping of studded soles on the Malt Shovel's ancient floorboards, and country and western yodelling had made conversation impossible, so he'd smiled gratefully and pocketed the paper while listening to the music and tapping his feet.

Now he's having his doubts again. Could these accidental deaths, strangely related to the clown, have been a chain of tragic coincidences after all? But his instinct tells him otherwise. Tomorrow, he'll set off for Whitby.

...

"Once a copper, always a copper," he mutters to himself, having crossed the Hambleton Hills onto the rugged plateau of the North Yorkshire Moors, at least according to the roughly sketched directions taped to the dashboard of his car. The rolling landscape of outstanding natural beauty opens like the pages of a book; heather smothered moors with interspersed dales and patchwork fields, bordered by dry stone walls upon which a group of hikers are resting. Defiant of the fine drizzle, they laugh and wave as he passes and he is reminded of pre-war hiking holidays, which again, cause a sudden twinge of conscience, bringing his chain of thought to Patricia's notion about his back pains being the result of lack of exercise. *"Too much sitting on your fat bum,"* she had said.

He speculates on the trials and tribulations of old age while turning a sharp corner, bringing a cluster of stone buildings behind an elegant country house into view. This is the place he is looking for, according to a roadside board advertising first class accommodation, and the flyer saying they'll be closed until Easter. It is a solid two-storey stone-built house with twin gables above latticed windows and imposing stone columns framing a carved oak door, built at the turn of the century well back from the road and further up the heights and in pretty good shape.

He is the travelling salesman passing through; an easy role to play for a member of the Bowling Green Amateur Dramatics' Society. He locks the car before making his way up the gravel path towards the main entrance; rings the shiny brass bell on the reception desk (which reminds him of The Malt Shovel's bar) and admires the rustic charm of a converted country house, beamed ceilings, whitewashed walls and wooden floors, radiating an atmosphere of homely comfort and easy-going luxury.

"Emily! There's summat out front! Oh! Sorry sir!" The western-style bar-door swings open and a small wiry figure in a bright green apron makes his entrance. "We're expecting a delivery an' thought you was the veggie man!"

Nickbone confirms that he isn't the veggie man. "Actually, I'm looking for someone," he explains politely, "in connection with the tragic accident that happened here recently. We read about in the newspaper."

Harry thinks, *that's the last thing we need at the moment – people snuffling around the place!* He regards the stranger suspiciously. "I can't help you, sir!"

Nickbone is well aware that hotel deaths are usually hush-hush affairs, corpses being quietly removed down the back stairs and taken outside through side entrances. He lowers his voice and continues, "When my wife read that Zasto Furninski had appeared in the circus ring with a clowness as partner, she said she'd bet her bottom dollar they were referring to Sally Foss!"

Harry regards the stranger with credible suspicion, having sworn (to Emily) that he'll say 'nowt', not to anyone! He has no intention of going back on his word.

Nickbone recognizes the stubbornness and continues, "My wife was Sally's trainer in Trampoline Jumping – took her up to international level until she suddenly threw it all in and joined the circus instead." There's a short silence before Nickbone continues. "I'm passing through and thought I'd look in to confer our best wishes. She was Junior Champion in Trampoline Jumping? Did you know that? No? Well, she was, you know! And..." Nickbone raises a knowing finger "...she has my wife, Patricia Lightbone, to thank for that!"

Now greatly impressed due to the 'knowing finger', Harry feels out of his depth about how much he should or shouldn't disclose to a stranger. "Hang on! I'll just get the Missus! Emileeee!" He sticks his head through the kitchen door. "My wife will be able to help you much better than I can, sir! She'll be here in a sec.!" The perky head goes from one side to the other, reminding Nickbone of the synonymous movements of spectators at a tennis-match.

Emily appears, her hair tied up with a bright green headscarf which matches her husband's apron. She puts down the bucket and although giving the impression she is still in a hurry, listens patiently as her husband explains.

"I'm just passing through on business," Nickbone resumes cheerfully.

Harry looks at his feet and then at Emily, while Nickbone wishes someone would turn off the Viennese waltz on its third time around.

"Sorry, Mr. Err…"

"Lightbone, Nicholas Lightbone."

One of Harry's principles about not confiding in strangers is beginning to wane. This fellow seems to be one of the seldom species one might trust. Besides, he enjoys a pleasant chat with a gentleman and this fellow's a gentleman alright! One can tell by his clothes.

"She's gone to Spain, sir!"

"Gone to Spain?" Nickbone has no intention of mentioning the follow-up article in his inside pocket, describing Zasto's rise to fame with Circus Poppi; the double act with a talented female clown who has left the hotel for an unknown destination. "Gone to Spain, eh?" he repeats thoughtfully, rocking backwards and forwards on the soles of his feet, which he swears will stimulate his brain and focus his thoughts, enabling him to confront a problem with logical consideration.

"It was the accident! Turned that girl about it did, when we found Mr. Zasto under his car. He didn't jack it up properly – radio still going t'next morning at full power – didn't hear it in here, being out at the back." Harry signals towards the rear buildings. "Don't ask me how he looked when we jacked it up again an' pulled him out; flat as a bloody pancake is a mild description for how he was! Follows you, does something like that! I've seen some nasty things – 1956 in Kenya with the 'Yorkshire Lights' – kind of expect it then, don't you?"

Nickbone considers it obvious. Ex-servicemen who have been in combat hold themselves differently.

"Don't expect something like that in a nice place like this though, do you?" Harry shakes his head at tragic assertions.

His wife stops the silent sobbing and wipes her eyes with the handkerchief kept tucked up her sleeve. "Such a nice fellow was Mister Zasto – always playin' tricks; made little white balls come out of everywhere." She laughs at the memory. "We had some lovely evenings in the dining-room after they'd finished practicing, an' had their supper. It was like having a circus all to one's self." She sheds a few more tears and blows her nose on the handkerchief she hasn't yet replaced. "It'll never be the same again! We'll always be thinking about Mister Zasto, won't we, Harry?" The handkerchief finally disappears up her sleeve and she regards her husband through swollen red eyes.

Nickbone smiles his schoolmasterly smile. "My wife never forgets a student," he hurries to explain, "especially one as talented as Sally."

"She and Mister Zasto did a two-man clown act. They were very close, if you know what I mean," he gives Nickbone a knowing wink. "After the accident, Mister Alfonso came over from Spain and took Sally back with him. And as far as I know, she's convalescing at her Grandfather's place. What's it called Emily?"

"Andalusia."

Nickbone stops rocking on his feet and can hardly contain his excitement. "My wife will be relieved to hear she's in good hands – likes to keeps track on former students, you know, especially the talented ones."

"Oh aye! She's talented alright! I've never seen anyone do a triple somersault from the trampoline onto the trapeze. Aye! She got it right in the end – you can tell your wife about that, despite Mister Zasto not having the time..."

"Not having the time?"

Harry gave him a knowing look. "I've known Mister Zasto for five years. Now I don't hold with speaking ill about the dead, but I'll tell you this much; he was a ladies' man, with a roving eye!" Harry laughs. "There was some talk about him havin' it off with a wealthy widow down the coast, an' I overheard Irena saying something I won't repeat", he places a demonstrative finger upon tightly closed lips and signals a change of subject with the close examination of his keys.

After forty years of questioning 'just about every type of human-being under the sun,' Nickbone has no intention of being deferred by a bunch of keys. "Irena is Sally's friend?" he enquires politely. Obtaining information 'from a friend,' can be revealing.

"Oh aye! Sally's had a lot of help from Irena. She and her brother are trapeze artists and I don't think she'd have managed to jump to that swing and stay there without their coaching. I don't go around eavesdropping, but artistes like to talk about their performances at mealtimes, and you can't help overhearing what they say. Irena and Ole helped Sally rehearse on the trapeze, because Alfonso wants her as a solo performer, despite the planned duo with Zasto."

"But according to the newspaper, Zasto was the star of the circus."

"That was the problem! They say Zasto was jealous," said Harry softly, his voice taking on a more intimate note of disclosure, finding it necessary to get something off his chest which he hadn't disclosed to the police. "It seems he was trying to sabotage Sally's performance."

"In what way?"

"He refused to give her keys to the gym, so we had to get a duplicate made," he sighs impatiently. "Zasto didn't care about anybody! He trained irregularly, and sometimes didn't turn up at all."

"That seems a bit selfish!"

"Selfish, you say? It was a catastrophe for her. Alfonso, having thrown out Jack Iski and his elephants, was billing her as a solo number; he made her promise to get her act perfect before the coming spring season. That's what upset us, but you can't interfere, can you? Mind you, she was like putty in Zasto's hands! Wouldn't say a wrong word about him, would she Emily?"

Emily agrees unwillingly. Harry is off again! His tongue is getting too loose for her liking.

Nickbone wears a friendly smile. "They seem extremely nice people. I'm sure my wife will be delighted if I could meet them. What are their names again?"

"Irena and Ole Olsen; known as 'The Olsen Twins' – Danish, I think."

"At least I can tell my wife that I've met Sally's friends." Nickbone decides he can't use more pressure without being overbearing.

"They'll be in the gym if I'm not mistaken. Emily'll know – been tidying up the equipment room."

"Aye! But they won't be disturbed while practising. I'm on my way to the kitchen, to put on the kettle. Fancy a cuppa, sir?"

"That's very kind of you. As a matter of fact, there's nothing I would appreciate more, at the moment."

"If you don't mind taking it on the kitchen bench."

"Not in the least. Show me the way," he adds gallantly, following Harry and Emily though the Western bar-room door and into the hotel kitchen.

"And what brings you down here, sir?" inquires Harry politely for something to say while crossing the yard. He stoops to pick up the yard-brush and leans it against the wall.

"I'm a passionate collector of fossils, among other things; on my way down the coast to inspect some new finds."

"And what else do you collect, apart from fossils?"

"Wooden spoons," he replies, looking around the spotless kitchen, thinking it wouldn't hurt his stomach to dine here with Patricia. He'll book in for a long weekend after all this has finished. They might even do a hiking-trip over the moors.

"Wooden spoons? Well I never...! What's so interesting about wooden spoons?"

"For instance, think of the tales they could tell."

Emily fills their cups from an earthenware teapot and then turns to Nickbone. "See that old spoon on the window sill over the sink? It was involved in the accident and we should have got rid of it after they'd finished investigations." Emily's teaspoon rattles on the saucer and she produces her handkerchief. "It upsets me to look at it. You can take it and add it to your collection if you like. It'll only land in the bin!"

"Thank-you indeed! It'll be a pleasant reminder of my visit, which I'm thoroughly enjoying, thanks to your hospitality." Nickbone springs from his stool, takes the spoon and examines it, turning it around in his fingers, noting the handle stained with a rust coloured substance, and the hollow covered with oil.

"It's no use in the kitchen any longer; no good for food either, since Mr. Zasto stirred his paint with it."

"Rust protection!" confirms Nickbone, still turning the spoon.

"A good guess! A very good guess indeed! Aye, you're right, sir! There was an open tin of rust-repellent on the floor next to the car."

Nickbone remains silent, trying to recall the accident report he'd been given. There'd been no photographs provided, but the mention of an open tin of paint on the ground, two and a half feet from the car, and at an angle of thirty five degrees from the front right wheel. Parallel to the tin had been the lid, at an angle of forty eight degrees. Balanced upon the lid, and without floor contact at both ends, had been a wooden spoon used for stirring paint, hence the untypical brown/red colour of the handle and traces of oil. According to the witnesses (Harry) Pearson, James Crockett and Peter Dempner, who had re-jacked the car and pulled out the deceased prior to aid arriving, the body had been lying at an angle of almost 120 degrees to the front right wheel and almost parallel to the exhaust pipe, suggesting that the deceased had been working on the vehicle before it had crushed him. Forensic investigations have since proved these accounts (see sheet 3). The spoon has since been returned to the owner, after coroner's verdict of accidental death (see sheet 4).

His tea, which he drinks in one gulp, is almost cold. Emily sets about rinsing the cups. It is time she continues her duties. Harry is eager to return to the stables and demonstrates the fact by shaking his keys.

"What a beautiful place this is," remarks Nickbone looking around, in the hope someone will show him the place, because he is not yet ready to leave. "I'd like to return here with my wife for a short holiday." *That should encourage them to show me around. How can they refuse?* "Such a friendly, relaxing atmosphere," he adds, considering the wooden spoon will look good next to the Kung Fu freak's spoon, which had smashed Nick Lawson's lower jaw with an upward thrust and put an end to his burgling.

"Future guests are always welcome," assures Harry courteously, one foot already out of the door. "I'll be glad to show you around, Mister Lightbone. Come with me to the stables, although the horses are being exercised in the far field." Still jingling the keys, Harry leads the way through the back door and crosses the narrow courtyard to the stables next to the typical Yorkshire closed-in field, with an iron gate in a dry stone wall. "All right Jack?" shouts Harry as they enter the stables.

Jack Iski stops shovelling hay into the stables, leans on his fork and regards them sullenly. "Jess has taken them out for a run in the field," he points an unwilling arm towards a group of horses at the far end of the field.

"A beautiful sight it is, six white horses running around the field as happy as Larry," says Harry, pointing into the distance at the animals, manes flying in the wind as they begin to race around the field.

Nickbone is reminded of a painting they'd almost purchased at an auction, of a herd of white horses galloping across a snow covered mountainside.

"Jess needs the key to the equipment room," says Jack Iski to Harry. "Miko asked Jess to bridle them occasionally to keep them in practise."

Harry removes a key from the bunch and hands it over. "That's where they keep the equipment," he explains to Nickbone, nodding towards the stone building. Nickbone takes note of the coloured trailers and a couple of bright painted trucks, subduing an urge to take a closer look through the window. A retired policeman can't shake off habits that easily! Perhaps he should have been a bank clerk instead!

The third building, once an indoor arena for horse-training, has been transformed into a gym, providing refugee artistes from behind the iron-curtain, or those who can't return home for the winter, with ideal training and rehearsing facilities. "Mister Alfonso converted it into a gym six years ago," Harry explains as Nickbone looks around him. "The Olsens, who worked with Sally before she left, are starting their first season and will be finishing for lunch. Fancy meeting them?"

Nickbone attempts the casual approach to disguise his mounting excitement. "If you don't mind," he says, nodding vigorously.

A wave of warm air, from the central heating connected to the main building, meets them as they enter the gym and Nickbone unties his scarf. There is a system of ropes and swings fixed to the ceiling and the huge trampoline functioning as a safety net below. A wooden bench runs down one side of the building and ends at a door. It is the side-entrance to the workshop; large enough for a vehicle and also accessible through a red, white and blue-striped garage door at the rear of the building.

The eye of the observant ex-policeman recognizes the remnants of red sealing band and traces of chalk under the door, revealing the position of the body. This sudden confrontation with unexpected death, may it be through crime or accident, makes him suddenly aware of his own fallibility and doubt returns once more. Might he be on the verge of making a fool of himself after all? He recalls Patricia's accusing words, calling him 'a retired policeman who can't let go'. It had hurt more than he cares to admit.

Doubtful thoughts are diverted by the couple on the bank: typical Scandinavians, tall, slim and blonde, wearing bright red tights, black T-shirts and black clogs, which Nickbone finds look decidedly clumsy when they walk around noisily, wood clattering against wood. The woman throws a wrap over her shoulders and smiles at Harry. Nickbone (the amateur actor) concludes that brother and sister radiate the confidence of the accomplished performer. But does he have to imagine a crime behind every closed door?

"Irena and Sally have been very good friends," Harry explains with a hasty introduction. After the usual greetings, Nickbone explains that his wife had been Sally's trainer."

"Oh really, how interesting!" The Olsens speak in chorus and seem genuinely interested.

"Where do you come from?"

"Denmark!" answers Irena, her mind preoccupied with other things. "It's a shame about Sally! We were about to invite her home for Jule – that's Christmas! – our cosy traditional Christmas which we try not to miss. Last year, in Monte Carlo, it was all champagne and glitter and not in the least bit Scandinavian. This year we've no Christmas engagements, which doesn't make much difference because we won't be happy whatever we do. It's this awful tragedy! – can't get it out of our heads!" Irena looks sadly at the closed door.

Her brother continues, "Circus people are superstitious; avoid tragic places and we hate practicing here, in front of this door where it all happened. Perhaps we should get hold of a clergyman to bless Zasto's soul," he looks genuinely scared, "before one of us falls from the trapeze."

Harry tells him to take it easy because it's the first and last time for tragic accidents; he knows what he's talking about, having been through the war and come out alive. "Emily will have lunch ready in about half an hour. Fancy a plate of sausages and baked beans with fried potatoes, Mr. Lightbone?" he asks, all in one breath.

Nickbone feels the urge to move on. "That's very kind of you, but I have an appointment to keep. I'll be back here in summer with my wife; she loves the open countryside of the North Yorkshire moors."

Irena, who has put aside her dark reminiscing for the moment, says, "If you happen to know Sally's address in Spain, I'd like to send her the new pair of shoes I gave her. She left them under her bed."

Nickbone has a sudden inclination he might need the shoes, but for what? He doesn't know yet! Could this be the last link in the chain? "We know Sally's parents very well. I'll pass them on, if you like," he replies hopefully.

Irena returns with the light blue ballerinas and hands them over. "They were too small for me and because Sally admired them, I gave them to her as a present. I bet she's kicking herself!"

Nickbone, with an eye for fashion, examines them closely and experiences the familiar jolt of excitement caused by the thin black oily streak which surely must be machine oil, running along the right outer side and overlapping the edge of the thin leather sole. He stifles a gasp, his mind now working at full speed.

"Anything the matter?" Harry enquires.

"No-oo! Nothing's the matter!" He sighs and shakes his head vigorously. "No, not in the least!" he ascertains, eager to be alone or go to the lab; eager to analyze the substance on the shoe, on the wooden spoon, which is burning a hole in his pocket.

…

Chapter 13

She remembers exactly how it happened. It reminds her of the nightmares she'd had as a child; it reminds her of closing the window and drawing the curtains to shut out the sound of the telephone ringing; the flashing lights penetrating the curtains and the blanket over the window. She remembers a woman's high pitched wailing; the slamming of doors and the rumbling of a vehicle driving off in the night. If she'd known about the master-key enabling them to enter, she would have barraged the door to prevent their filth from contaminating her room. She'd been dizzy and hungry. There's never time to eat when she's cleaning!

They had come. She'd expected them to come at some time or other; the sound of their footsteps on the corridor tiles, drawing to a halt outside her room, banging their fists on the door. She remembers their mouths more than anything else. It's the mouths that stick in her mind; the doctor's mouth when he'd finished the examination, the uncertain expression on his face as to whether he was imparting good or bad news. Did she want the baby? Which baby?

She'd tried not to listen until they'd posed the question – the question she'd been dreading. Home? It doesn't bear thinking about! Home is the dark shadow following her through life; sometimes present and other times absent, depending upon the situation she is in. It comes and goes, leaving her mind in a state of disorder which disappears when she cleans. Return home? Home only exists in unpleasant dreams.

"It's amazing what a change of wallpaper can do," she had overheard someone say.

Inform my family? "No, no! There's my Granddad; he's waiting for me in Spain. I'd rather die than go home to my parents! What do you mean, I can't stay here? Why can't I stay here? Family? Of course I have family! My grandfather is my family – the High and Mighty Don Libella who lives in a village in Spain and that's where I'll go if I can't remain here. Ask Alfonso! He knows the village where grandfather lives. Go away! I'm tired! Leave me alone!"

They had arranged it all while she'd slept and now she is above it all; flying through the sky, over the clouds and out of reach.

Alfonso is sitting next to her. He has covered his face with a newspaper, signalling sleep; unwilling to be disturbed while recent events pass through his mind. Of course, he is aware that tragic accidents happen in circuses, despite the necessary precautions one takes. But a clown squashed to death beneath his own car is not only an unpredictable disaster, but a horrific turn of events – a tragedy! Harry had 'phoned to tell him the bad news and for the first few moments, he'd been unable to comprehend what had happened. Then he had taken the next flight to London, and a taxi to Whitby, where officers investigating the accident had almost completed their enquiries. The local doctor, an elderly Scotsman who'd been attending Sally, had told him the news, asking questions and speaking in short sharp sentences. Alfonso had hardly understood the broad Scottish accent and the doctor had then spoken slowly, patiently repeating himself. "The girl refuses to contact her parents! Ach! Strange circumstances, eh? Doesn't sound good to me! Only her grandfather, lives in Spain...know all about him, and where he lives, do you? Good! Perhaps you could inform him! Something must be done!"

"Dicho y hecho!" It shall be done, announced Alfonso, made the necessary enquiries and then put a long-distance call through to Donald Libella which he had immediately regretted. The old man was hard in concept, so it seemed, not understanding a word, continually demanding in a thin, high-pitched voice that he repeat what he'd said until Alfonso had been almost shouting, slowly and clearly explaining the situation his granddaughter was in.

To Alfonso's great relief, he'd suddenly found himself speaking to Conchita, the Spanish housekeeper, and in his native tongue. She told him she'd been with Senor Libella since his accident. "Of course, the girl is welcome to stay as long as she likes," Conchita had assured him over the 'phone. "People know me here! I look after the old and sick in this village. I will look after the girl. We have an experienced midwife in the village. I'm sure that Senor Libella will be delighted."

Alfonso has been having nagging doubts about having made the right decision. Has he misjudged the situation? A grandfather, a stranger, is beyond his comprehension. He imagines how it might be, passing one's grandfather on the street without knowing who he is. On the other hand, the girl demands to be taken to her grandfather and refuses to contact her parents. And then there's Conchita, who looks after the grandfather and has promised to look after the girl – a trustworthy woman; he has made enquiries and gathered information through the grapevine.

Sally is unconcerned about the trouble Alfonso has taken; ignorant of the fact that he and Clementina have had long telephone conversations, to solve the problem of where she should go. Clementina can be adamant at times. "Sally has mysterious moods," she'd complained over the telephone. "I don't believe all these stories about her family. Where is her family? Why doesn't she go home? Why is she always cleaning and asking for money? The stupid girl has allowed Zasto, may God rest his soul, to take over her life instead of joining circus life and making friends with the others! You'd think she comes from another planet!" Later, Clementina regretted her harsh words. "We must ignore her strange habits and let her come to our villa, should the situation with the grandfather prove unsatisfactory."

Sally regards the newspaper covering Alfonso's face, fluttering in the rhythm of his breathing. Outside the aircraft is the illusionary landscape of sun-drenched peaks above the pure whiteness of cotton-wool plains. They are clean and pure, the surroundings she loves. There's no bitterness and loneliness, no pollution here. She closes her eyes and steps out of the aircraft, balancing on air and revelling in the purity of it all. Now she is dancing upon them; flying over virgin snow; floating from one heavenly canopy to the other; sheltering beneath the curling wisps of a suddenly formed cave. And there is Grandfather, strong and proud, gazing into the hollows of the ocean. Dark thoughts fly over the clouds like a swarm of black crows, and burn in the sun.

Alfonso nudges her elbow, indicating the sign instructing her to fasten her seatbelt. The aircraft shudders in the turbulence of air-currents as clouds open like a stage curtain, revealing an azure-blue ocean, deep and mysterious, covered with thin, cotton-wool-like wisps. She experiences the panic of the first-time passenger; is reassured by Alfonso the frequent flyer and the smiling stewardess walking up and down the aisle. Alfonso will bring her to the grandfather she loves and the hero she admires. All will be well!

A sudden jolt and the revving of engines closes memory's door. Alfonso stretches and folds his newspaper. "We'll be landing soon."

...

All circus artistes must have a passport, Clementina had stated a long time ago. So she'd written a short letter home requesting her birth certificate, which had arrived at the post-office before they'd moved on.

The handsome customs official rummages through her bag, giving her a look on the side. "What's it like living in a circus?"

"The best life in the world," she answers and tells him she is proud to be a circus artiste, proud of being a clown; proud to make people laugh, jumping up and down on the trampoline which is the best thing for getting rid of your troubles. He smiles and gives her a wink, making her think there are plenty of good-looking men in the world, and she wouldn't mind having one of them all to herself.

An azure-blue ocean, a white hotel on a golden beach and the sun reflecting from a cloudless sky remind her of a film she'd seen with Zasto.

Don't think about Zasto! Put him out of your mind!

As they drive past spotless white villas with arched portals, surrounded by a lush green golf course stretching into the dunes, Alfonso goes into raptures about his beautiful country with the beaches, the warm climate and easy-going atmosphere which attracts plenty of tourists. She senses his love for his native country and the family he misses. When he talks about his daughter's wedding, it is as though he is speaking to no-one in particular. In such a mood, he'll provide the answers to his own questions and ramble on to whoever might be listening. In the passenger seat of the hired car, Sally listens, envious of his daughter's forthcoming wedding, being reminded of Zasto which clutters her brain as Alfonso describes in detail how the wedding is planned. She sees the beautiful bride wearing a slim long white lace gown, entering the church on his arm. They walk up the aisle to the strains of the 'Bridal March', swelling and echoing throughout the ancient church. When they arrive at the altar, Alfonso hands over the bride. He takes her hand and gives it to Zasto. Zasto is a lucky guy! Everybody agrees! They'll enjoy a happy and successful life in the circus.

Put him out of your mind! Lock him away and don't allow him to return!

She must forget the sleepless nights, the tossing and turnings, the hopes and dreams of the disappointed lover and listen to Alfonso talking about his family, where they live and how often they visit. Sometimes, they'll stay at a cousin's place if they've drunk too much wine. People sleep all over the place, on the floor, in the bath-tub, on the veranda! She has never heard of relatives sleeping in the bath-tub before.

Alfonso flashes a gold-ringed finger at the distant snow-capped Sierra Nevada, pointing out the route they'll be taking up the valley and into the hills. "I know about this village where your grandfather lives. It was once very famous. People used to go up there for the annual 'aguinaldo' – the ancient tradition of children singing Christmas songs." Sally feels uncomfortable with unfamiliar traditions and remains silent as Alfonso continues, "These days, only few children live in mountain villages since tourism began to rule people's lives."

Where is the excitement? Why the silence, the secret meditation, the sudden fear of the unknown when she should be happy and cheerful? Why this tightening of the stomach, this feeling of sickness and her refusal to acknowledge a doctor's diagnosis? Why this sudden fear of her grandfather? Could this be a premonition of what is to come and how it will end?

Nonsense! Grandfather, her distant benefactor, has been her idol as long as she remembers; on the faded 'photo, proud and strong, an artiste in the circus ménage dressed in a red velvet cape, with a dark moustache, twinkling brown eyes and a sack full of presents. *Go away, you dark shadows of the past! Go back to your dungeons!*

"Take a last look at the ocean before we leave the main road." Alfonso puts a stop to her muddled imaginings. "They say it's the arm of a greedy giant who stretched his arm into the ocean and it became a rock as punishment for taking all the fish."

Waves pound angrily against the rocky isthmus. The tumultuous roaring and swishing in a never-ending cycle grows fainter as they continue their journey along the serpentine road blasted into the hillside. The air is cooler. A refreshing breeze conveys the unfamiliar aroma of hillside vegetation. Here are none of the familiar dry stone walls, the abundance of green; the comfort of an English landscape, soothing and friendly. Gone are the Mediterranean palaces with pillars and balconies! Now she yearns for the familiar soot-grimed cenotaphs of an industrial revolution instead of the village, nestling into the hillside and barely visible from the highway. Having turned another corner of the road winding itself into the hillside, Alfonso steers onto a flat grassy patch and they leave the car to gaze at surrounding dark green hills dipping into the water, azure blue and sparkling in the sun like a thousand diamonds, framing the distant coastline. Far below, the clusters of buildings and townships become strangely insignificant; reduced to shapes on a distant skyline.

The stone wall surrounding the village, built against marauding pirates and later, brutal aggressors in a civil war, completes the splendour. Now, the distant ocean is blue and white and fluffy, wedged between hillsides, losing itself against the horizon, leaving the spectator to admire the valley below. Wild vegetation survives between outcrops of rock; bushes with pale yellow blooms decorate the hillside, stretching further upwards towards ancient terraces of olive trees and vines. Grey and white box-shaped houses have flat clay roofs where, in late summer, red peppers and tomatoes will be set out to dry between chimney pots.

An open entrance between crumbling walls allows direct access to the square. Alfonso parks the car in the shade of three vast palms and Sally follows him to the old fountain which has stopped spouting water and is centred in a basin, decorated with traditional Andalusian mosaic tiles.

"The village sleeps during the Siesta, as well as the water-supply," Alfonso remarks as he examines the double-tiered fountain with stonework carved in oriental patterns – a legacy of Moorish culture – clear and blue, reflected by the tiles. Opposite a deserted café, where rickety chairs and tables await the evening philosophies of old men, is a massive church built on a plaza of rough paving stones. Beneath the square tower, a carved figure of the Virgin Mary and her child in a protecting alcove, overlook the heavy wooden door. A loudspeaker, an unfitting intrusion among the abundance of historical relics, is fixed to the wall above a row of solid wooden banks. They return to the car and Alfonso reverses it out of the square to bump along the cobbled surface of the main street, past overhanging passageways and the sagging walls of aged stone houses. Rows of flowering geraniums in rusty paint-tins decorate stone walls of tiny gardens and an odd splash of pink and white oleander enriches ancient walls.

There's an old man with the weathered face beneath the battered straw hat, leading a donkey down the road. The car stops and words are spoken in rapid Spanish. "Aaah! Senor Don Libella," replies the old man with the wide toothless smile, gesticulating wildly towards a solitary house, hardly visible from the road which ends on a flat ledge where a couple of tethered goats are on their hind legs, tearing at a chestnut tree.

"The old man says that is your grandfather's house." Alfonso gestures towards the far end of the village and the roof of the solitary building. The old man still speaks in rapid Spanish as he bows and crosses himself and Alfonso continues, "He wishes us a long and happy life and says may we be blessed by the Holy Mother herself."

Sally smiles. The old man continues his journey, then turns and waves his hat.

The lulling nature of a sleeping landscape in the mild temperatures of early afternoon renders them silent. Winter is no more than a refreshing breeze rustling among dry vegetation, or a sudden heavy shower of rain, turning the countryside into a lush colour of green. They observe their surroundings; listen to the crunching of gravel beneath their feet as they make their way towards the house, through an open gate and into a levelled-off courtyard.

The sudden chimes of a telephone within the depths of the house disturb the silence and cause her to shudder at the shock of unexpected intrusion. *Surely this can't be happening; the ludicrous opening of the door, the sudden appearance of the alien where he doesn't belong. She has seen him before, through the keyhole, white and naked on top of her mother. She'll close the door, but not on her mother. Where is Dad? He's far away and pathetically indifferent. She can't tolerate the alien for refusing to leave her alone. Now there is Zasto with the bright red nose, wearing the silly yellow jacket. She'll destroy them both if it's the last thing she does!*

The roses alongside the path are red and yellow. These are the flowers of love. These are the colour of Zasto's red nose and his silly yellow jacket. She attacks the heavy blooms with her bag, intent upon destroying them, pulls out the petals until they are spread like confetti. Alfonso watches her in dismay; takes her by the arm and shakes her, his face close and eyes filled with anger. "What are you doing?" he whispers hoarsely. She looks at him in surprise and her bewildered gaze transforms into light-heartedness. "I'm only getting rid of these flies! They're buzzing around my head all the time and nearly driving me mad!" She hesitates for a moment. "Come on, Alfonso! Let's go inside. I've been looking forward to meeting my grandfather, the one and only, high and mighty Don Libella, for years," she adds dramatically, hooking onto his arm as though nothing has happened and ignoring his obvious bewilderment as they enter the courtyard.

To the stranger, a spacious stone-built house surrounded by beautiful gardens suggests a wealthy owner. Sally's mood has suddenly changed; the demons have left her, along with the misgivings and dark thoughts which have muddled her brain. It's a wonderful thing being the granddaughter of a famous circus artiste, moreover a *wealthy* retired circus artist who will take her back to her roots. Here they are, in this beautiful house, these wonderful surroundings; the authentic background she has yearned for. All this is hers! She belongs to the family of circus artistes whose forefathers once travelled the world. Her grandfather will give her the advice she badly needs. He will tell her what to do and how to do it. She is happy and excited; she can hardly wait!

Unaware of the turmoil in the girl's mind, Alfonso, having decided to ignore Sally's strange behaviour, casts an appreciative eye over the house. He admires the solid rough stone painted white, the red tiled roof sloping almost to the ground and the high stone wall surrounding the building. There are pots of flowering shrubs in the courtyard and bushes bordering the entrance, welcoming visitors with their red and white blooms.

A small woman, with a friendly smile and the dark, well-carved features of indefinable age, appears from the side of the house. She is wearing a colourful flower-patterned dress tied at the waist. "Hola! Cómo estás?" she cries gaily without introduction, and embraces Sally who stands awkwardly, still unaccustomed to spontaneous displays of emotion. The woman removes her gardening gloves and, with gay abandon, tosses them over her shoulder. A lavender bush sways under their weight.

"I'm Conchita and you are Sally!" She examines the girl appreciatively, holding her at arm's length. There's another quick demonstrative hug before she greets Alfonso, speaking in rapid Spanish. Walking down a narrow path alongside the building, they continue their conversation, stopping for a moment to discuss some point until they reach the patio at the front of the house, intricately tiled in mosaic patterns. From the patio, shallow steps lead down a sloping lawn to the swimming pool. Water shines like a mirror within a framework of white pebbles and pots of pink and white geraniums.

"Oh how lovely! Can I go in for a swim?" When was the last time she'd had a swim!

The memory returns and pleasure is gone with their coldness; their look of disgust; the smell of whisky in the car driving her home. *No more friendships! No more invitations for you, my girl! Your mother's a pavement whore. She'll drag you away, shouting abuses.* Can they touch her now in this colourful world of sunshine and warmth? Can they take away her roots, or the flair of the circus? No they cannot! She is safe at last! She will swim!

"Of course you can. But first you must meet your grandfather." Conchita consults her watch. "His siesta is over, I will bring him outside!"

The palms of the girl's hands are wet; she wipes them down the side of her jeans, examines her reflection through a window and wishes she'd combed her hair. There's a fleck on her jeans – a remnant of the airline-meal she'd hardly touched. Her big moment has come. Should she kiss him, or merely offer her hand?

"Now don't you fidget! You look fine, my dear!" Alfonso knows how to calm people's nerves before they enter the ring and he senses she is about to enter the illusory ring.

Whose voice is that? Muffled words rise into a crescendo of anger; the door swings open; the fanfare announces – the One and Only, High and Mighty Don Libella – like a ventriloquist's doll, huddled limbs squeezed into a wheel chair and wearing a Panama hat. Conchita wheels him onto the sunlit patio; laughs and chatters to no-one in particular. At the command of a silent finger, she pushes down the brake and the girl stands before him, shuffling awkwardly, unable to conceal the crushing disappointment she feels and unable to speak.

Where is the dashing hero? Where is the champion, the idol of her fantasies?

Conchita bows the low-sweeping pretence of subservience, having done her duty by delivering the goods, and then returns inside, ignoring hoarsely whispered profanities from the depths of the wheel-chair. The old man is now quiet; he straightens his hat and fidgets with the collar of his shirt before bracing himself for his granddaughter.

"Hello Granddad...! Pleased to meet you," she finishes lamely

"So, you're Sally are you?" The voice crackles as though seeking escape through a rusty exhaust. "It's about time you visited your old Granddad." Light green eyes stare at her blatantly as though considering her value, ignoring her obvious discomfort. "Tell me about your parents – my prodigal daughter and her pathetic husband, who I suppose, is your father. Have you lost your tongue, girl?" He taps impatiently with his stick. "Get on with answering my question girl – and speak up! How are they?"

Dear God, what should she say when disappointment has taken her voice and she'll break down and cry if she opens her mouth. Who is this petulant old man; this stranger? Where is the handsome man with the thick shiny brown hair; the athletic body, the bulging muscles and eyes, singularly alive in a youthful face, defying the onlooker's gaze? He has aged, of course, but not into the mellowed old man of her dreams who might have reached only Grandma Foss in goodness and benevolence, but doesn't hit the mark.

He has failed, and suddenly, it makes sense. She had done the right thing, destroying Gloria with the permanent smile who'd arrived at Christmas, who'd been his gift to her as a child, evil through and through and deservingly punished for allowing the alien to enter the house and steal her mother. The puzzle has fallen into place. She stares at the sensuous mouth, drawn into petulance beneath lanky grey strands. The light green eyes, solitarily lively in a sunken face, rest upon Alfonso.

"Alfonso Poppi at your service, senor!" Alfonso subdues his confusion, concluding Senor Labella has a weird sense of humour, or who would speak in such a tone to his granddaughter, if it wasn't meant to be funny? A joke gone wrong – perhaps he should laugh! He introduces himself in best ringmaster manner.

There are issues to be cleared about Sally. Now is the opportunity for posing the questions which have occupied Clementina – always concerned with the welfare of the troop – and the talented girl who had appeared from nowhere. "As you know, your granddaughter here" – with a ringmaster gesture towards Sally – "belongs to my circus. We have already spoken on the telephone about the reason for her coming." Alfonso registers the old man's interest; his sudden and undivided attention. He bows respectfully and continues, "She tells me you were a circus artiste before, erm, before you were incapacitated."

The old man cups an ear with a grizzled hand.

"You can be very proud of your granddaughter," Alfonso gestures towards the girl. "She'll be the star of the circus if she can fulfil our expectations – it all depends on the baby."The old man nods slowly, his mood suddenly improved. The baby! Ah yes, the baby! Sally pulls herself out of her pondering. Her pregnancy is becoming more visible. She hasn't wanted to think about the baby, until now.

"Have you found your tongue yet?" There's still a sharp side to his voice. He throws back his head and cackles. "Go on! Go on!"

Too high – her expectations have been too high, considers Alfonso. She has made a hero out of Don Libella, and got a crippled old man instead.

The old man has discarded his petulance and seems suddenly relaxed. He is thirsty! Conchita has made some ice-cooled Granizado which they can drink in the kitchen, if they'd care to go inside.

In the kitchen, Sally gulps down the liquid and quietly mourns her lost hero. *Manners, manners, don't forget your manners! I'll say thank-you for the Christmas money you've transferred into my account. I'll invest it sensibly, Grandfather. I'll invest in a driver's licence to pull my own caravan. There'll be no more polluted sleeping quarters for your granddaughter.*

She'd like to say it, but will leave it for later since Alfonso is speaking to Conchita in rapid Spanish and judging by his actions he's talking about the baby. She doesn't want to think about the baby. It reminds her of Zasto. She can bear it no longer and interrupts their conversation. "Can I unpack my things?"

"Of course you can, Sal-lee". Conchita's exotic pronunciation of her name rings pleasantly in her ears. Should she change her name to Sallee or better, Salliah? Salliah, the Jumping Clown doesn't sound right. Zasto had called her Miss Flummi and Miss Flummi she'll stay!

Don't think about Zasto!

"Thank you for bringing me, Alfonso." She looks at him through her eyelashes and ignores the old man, fussing over his glass.

"I'll return your Grandfather to his room," Conchita says, and winks good-naturedly, indicating things will go better without him.

Alfonso watches her silently as she wheels him off. Now alone for the moment, he turns to the girl. "Sally, do you have enough money?"

"Now that you ask, not really!" she answers, appearing suitably embarrassed.

"You must not be without money, my child!" Alfonso's eyes widen and his dark skin takes on a purple tinge. Being without money upsets him. "The accountant sends you a monthly cheque during winter, doesn't he?" Being a man accustomed to paying his debts, Alfonso is alarmed.

Her mind works fast. Here is the opportunity to blame expensive driving-lessons for situations gone wrong.

"Then why are you without money? No self-respecting artiste should be without money!" Alfonso sighs impatiently and attempts to ignore the batting of her eyelids, feigning innocence. "It's because of my driving lessons. The instructor charged me extra for picking me up. There is no bus-service into Whitby during winter."

Alfonso splutters indignantly; his broad chest growing broader. "Took all your money! What d'you mean, took all your money? How much did he take?"

The unsuspecting Mr. Bell, now visiting his daughter in Australia suddenly becomes 'a trickster of the nastier sort' – despite having written her off as a bad debt.

"One thousand pounds," she flusters.

"You gotta be mad, payin' all that money for a few lousy driving lessons. You could have practised driving around the field in a circus vehicle. What a damned waste of money! I can't bear listening to this!"

"I'm so ashamed! I fell into the trap. And to make things worse, it was the extra money I earned helping Emily with the cleaning," she lies.

Between wiping her eyes and blowing her nose, she watches his face soften into a benevolent mood. *I'll emphasize how hard I've been training, as well as cleaning for Emily, who still hasn't paid me for all the hours I have worked. Life is so unfair to the good-hearted!* Now she wonders about her own truth, convincing herself it is the real truth and nothing but the truth. 'Being used', is a subject she can talk about for hours. On the other hand, she would rather tell him about the progress she has made rehearsing her act.

"I know, I know," he replies impatiently, ignoring the delicate subject of 'cleaning', being one of the strange girl's half-truths he'll never understand. He carries on speaking, "Irena and Ole have told me about your performance, so dry your eyes because Miss Flummi looks on the bright side of life and I'm relying on you to be 'top of the bill' after the baby is born. By the way, have you thought about who will look after the child while you're working?" This is an issue which Clementina, his wife, has insisted must be addressed and Alfonso is not one for beating about the bush. There is a long silence and Alfonso wonders if she is as excited about the baby as she is about topping the bill as a circus performer. He has his reservations about the girl's capabilities as the mother of a child and is grateful to Conchita for the arrangements she has made with the midwife.

Did he say I'll be topping the bill? Sally's spirits soar into unknown heights as Alfonso opens the black leather wallet and hands over a wad of Spanish pesetos. "Clementina and I – we're concerned about the baby," he continues and the raised finger tells her she must listen to what he is saying. "We will be Godparents to your child and it must grow up in the circus, God permitting," He is insistent about this, and relieved at Sally's eager acceptance, because there's nothing better than a family of circus-artistes – and this child will belong to the family Poppi!

Conchita returns to wipe the table and remove Grandfather's glass, relieved at the girl's friendly smile, despite the hostile reception of an unbalanced man who'll change his moods from one minute to the next. Will she reap the benefit of her loyalty when he dies, despite the sudden appearance of his granddaughter and her unborn child? It is time to review her situation. This evening, she will visit the church to beg The Holy Mother for guidance. "I'll show you your room now, if you don't mind," she offers and puts a friendly arm around the girl's shoulder.

The sound of their feet on polished floorboards keeps pace with the ticking of a pendulum clock. Her room is at the far end of the corridor. Dark wooden furnishings contrast with white-washed walls and pinewood floors. Curtains are in alternating shades of blue, with a matching bedspread and brightly-coloured cushions. Her luggage is piled onto a stout wooden rack at the foot of the bed and she wonders how it got there.

"I brought it inside from the car. I'm a strong lady!" remarks Conchita with a grin. She heaves the bulging suitcase from the rack with the ease of Goliath, balances it on her head and crosses the room in the stately manner of native women heading heavy loads. "A remnant of my circus days. The only thing I can't do is swim!" she adds good-heartedly.

"You were a performer, too?"

"I was!"

"Aaah!"

"Didn't you know about me?"

"No!"

Conchita remains silent. One can't be diplomatic while balancing a suitcase on one's head. It lands with a gentle thump on the rack. "Make yourself at home. If you need anything, just let me know." She is eager to return to the kitchen because they seldom have visitors; opens the door and smiles at the girl. "Don't forget to say goodbye to Alfonso." Her smile changes into laughter, as though not saying goodbye to Alfonso would be a huge joke.

Relieved to be alone, Sally's gaze rests on the poster of a bullfight pinned to the wall behind her bed. The proud Matador is dressed in a bright blue jacket decorated with gold braiding and a knotted black sash, and he's wearing bright pink knee-high stockings. He brandishes a flowing red cape at the bull. Short spears decorated with colourful streamers protrude from the animal's neck as it goes in for the final attack, head down and front legs almost bent double. One can almost feel the hot breath blaring through flared nostrils; hear the last agonizing bellow of fury above the roar of a cheering crowd. It is a depiction of cruelty and even worse, it is polluting her room.

From the kitchen, low mutterings are interrupted by short outbursts of laughter as she unpins the poster, rolls it up and deposits it behind a curtain out of sight. She doesn't want to be reminded of the unpleasantness which puts her in mind of the elephants, Wanda and Lofty, triggering the desire to clean the floor around her bed. There's the familiar sound of chairs scraping on tiles. Alfonso is leaving. She must return to the kitchen. Conchita will laugh if she doesn't say goodbye.

Alfonso's voice rings down the corridor and she hastens into the kitchen, afraid of someone knocking on her door. "Have a nice rest, take it easy and 'phone me whenever you please." He gives her a knowing look, but avoids mentioning her pregnancy again, because pregnancies are a woman's business and he wishes he'd brought Clementina, who is up to the neck in wedding-arrangements. He reckons he has done the right thing by paying Conchita a large sum of money to look after Sally – this once-in-a-lifetime performer, who'd got hooked by the wrong guy – Zasto – the brilliant clown; the hard-headed scoundrel and incorrigible womanizer. He hugs her affectionately and hands over his card. "Don't hesitate to contact me immediately if anything goes wrong, or as soon as anything happens," he whispers, looking slightly embarrassed for a change. "Don't forget! I'll be back for you both," (and he emphasises 'you both') "so we can open for Easter."

From the patio she can see the road, like a giant snake winding down the hillside, meandering between high rocks and low vegetation until it reaches the coast. She focuses the binoculars on the car crawling down the hill. The binoculars are kept on a hook alongside the patio door, allowing her grandfather to check on the comings and goings of villagers. The shadowy figure of Alfonso melts into a fading dark fleck, disappears beyond the curve and then reappears like an ant on some downhill errand. The sound of the engine fades away, cutting her off from the world.

...

Chapter 14

Nickbone screws yet another hook into the wall, directly above the serving spoon with the metal scoop and wooden handle, from which Angelo, from 'Scutti's Pizza Parlour', had hurled boiling bolognaise sauce into the face of his attacker, who'd almost made it behind the counter with a knife in his hand. "This spoon saved my life", Angelo had claimed after handing it over and Nickbone had wound up the 'Pizza Mob' case. Angelo had been unable to identify his assailant, which hadn't made things easy. "Mama Mia! Dinna getta look at his face – covered with Bolognaise right down to his chin. Completto!" Angelo had waved his arms in the air, finding it impossible to give a detailed description.

The spoon, brought back from Whitby and sent to the forensic laboratory together with the oil-stained shoes, now hangs on the wall directly above Angelo's ladle. "Motor oil and red oxide, rust-repellent," Doc. Whittaker had confirmed as he'd handed over the wooden-spoon along with the ballerina-style shoes"

Which proves? What does it prove? Nickbone wonders. Does it prove that the girl had entered the workshop while the clown was fixing his car? Does it prove she was on the scene when the accident *actually* happened? Like hell it does! Does it prove she caused the accident on purpose? *You're at a dead-end old chap, which is putting it mildly*! He has heard it before, from a smart-ass lawyer hired to defend the thug charged with collecting protection-money. "Aw stop reading story books! I'll make mincemeat out of your story."

So what? She'd come into contact with motor-oil while wearing the shoes, which is all he can prove. He'll have to do better than that! She'd been on the scene and left before the accident had happened – he can almost hear the defence-lawyer's biting sarcasm, stating that fact, (they're only doing their job, his wife always says).

There had been no witnesses!

He'd studied the accident report, as well as the statement from the hotel-caretaker's wife about 'the girl going strange' after the death of the clown. (Emily had remembered the doctor's strong words, and kept her mouth shut about Sally being pregnant).

Strange? Had a nervous breakdown... locked herself in her room and started cleaning again ...cleaned day and night...wasn't normal!

Cleaned day and night? Were you there, in the room? Sorry, old chap, that's just not good enough! He can hear the defence-attorney again.

...

"I'll keep my promise; return the shoes and forget the whole thing!" states Nickbone the following evening and quite unexpectedly, having sensed the forthcoming storm. Patricia's eyebrows go up in surprise. "Besides, I've promised them another J.B.Priestley reading at 'Redfold' on Monday, and I don't want to disappoint them." Out comes his diary. "There are all sorts of Christmas events - Richard III for the very last time, at Hemley Town Hall next Saturday; ADA''s. Christmas Party next Tuesday." (Nickbone hasn't dropped the habit of initialising names, so the Amateur Dramatic Association becomes 'ADA'). "So I won't have much time before Christmas."

"For what?"

"Returning the shoes! I need the address fitting this number." He opens the first page of his diary, where he keeps his receipts, and removes a scrap of paper the size of a bus-ticket. "This is the telephone number Alfonso Poppi dialled when he spoke to the girl's grandfather after the accident happened. The call was put through from the hotel switchboard and, being the only international number on the list, I wrote it down, which doesn't say much for my memory," he admits.

Patricia watches him thumbing the pages of his diary. His hair is turning from grey to white; the silhouette of his stomach is protruding over his belt, the result of drinking too much beer in the garden-hut, no doubt, and listening to George's deliberations on rights and wrongs; amateur dramatics; World War 2; the Royal Family (he's a profound royalist) the local vicar (with whom he seldom agrees);

Sunday Church services with an electric guitar instead of an organ (what's the world coming to?) She has lost count of the times he has come inside after smart arse George has tired him out with lengthy monologues on cutworms, wireworms and millipedes. He could, of course, join the 'Senior Men's Gymnastic-Group' – they put on an excellent show in the church-hall last summer, parallel to her 'Ladies Gymnastics' so they could drive home together – at least he wouldn't be wasting his time investigating people for no reason. She knows he'll scorn the idea – but perhaps, with a bit of friendly persuasion...?

"By the way, they're casting for 'The Importance of Being Earnest' next Tuesday," he remarks casually. "I've read it through – not up to doing 'Algernon', though – too time-consuming, learning all that text." He has no intention of biting off more than he can chew, which might result in forgetting his lines and being continually prompted by Sheryl, in the souffleuse box at his feet. Besides, he can't start private investigations on a suspected murder and study Algernon at the same time. It will have to be one or the other. Rehearsals start in three weeks. He closes his diary, aware of having broken his pledge.

Patricia says, "Ever heard of 'brain-jogging? You've always had a good memory! It needs oiling, or you'll end up like Walter Chapman searching for his slippers in people's front gardens."

He can't bear to think about old age dementia. Perhaps he should try for Merriman, the butler. He is too old for Algernon, the dandy, who finds it awfully hard-work doing nothing.

...

Chapter 15

If there's one thing she enjoys, it's digging into people's lives and discovering what they've been hiding from the rest of the world. Despite the smell of urine that hangs like the mark of a dog among the few clothes he possesses, the chest of drawers in her grandfather's bedroom emits an air of great promise. In his wardrobe there are four striped shirts hanging above a pair of brown shoes, and a beige poplin coat, fraying at the sleeves. On the shelf, carefully folded, is the tweed cardigan which Conchita has knitted. She says that's all a stubborn old man will wear to protect him against the cold; these sneaky cold breezes which crawl over the hillside after the sun has gone down.

The wardrobe doors creak as Sally closes them. The glass door opening onto the patio reminds her to keep an eye on the road. For a moment, she looks across the valley to the wedge of ocean sparkling in the sunlight and further out to the horizon, where the sail of a distant boat protrudes into the sky. A fishing boat plods down the coastline like a sluggish beetle on an arduous journey. Later that evening, there'll be a whole fleet of fishing boats, spreading their lights like a sequined cover over black water.

The dark-stained wooden chest of drawers is an exact copy of the one in her room. She struggles to open the bottom drawer, which doesn't run smoothly and is reminded of her father, going about the house with a candle, waxing roughened drawer-runners.

Don't think about Dad! Lock him away! Lock him away!

There are piles of underwear, handkerchiefs and brand-new woollen socks still paired together. A selection of photo albums in varied stages of decay draws her attention. The prospect of examining old photographs thrills her, and she remembers examining old photo's in an album, together with Gloria.

The past is an unwelcome guest. What tale will they tell? – these uniformed men with dark moustaches, staring grimly through the years, hypnotizing her with the whites of their eyes – gone forever; dead, buried and forgotten!

Something is moving inside her womb, but she has no intention of thinking about the baby and has made no plans to accommodate this unwelcome addition to her life. So she ignores the movements, having grown accustomed to disregarding what can't be accepted and turns her attention to the child on the photograph; a miniature John Wayne between two older girls, their hair in pigtails, wearing tiny western boots and frilly checked dresses in contrast to the boy's matching shirt and bootlace tie. A soldier in the background, his parade-uniform decorated with girdles and medals, stands to attention outside the tent. She closes the album.

There is a pile of envelopes, yellow and brown with age, addressed in spidery writing and difficult to decipher. The black leather document-case is locked. She removes the envelopes and places them at the foot of the bed where she can examine them and keep an eye on the road. The neat circular handwriting is vaguely familiar but hardly comprehensible.

'Greetings from Brighton' is printed on the black and white postcard. Two vintage cars are parked in front of the pier. There are spirals and towers, galleries and portals beneath the bowl-shaped room of an amusement arcade, illuminated by an armada of light-bulbs. A smaller ornate building resembles a circus tent. On the back of the card in written in spidery letters, *'This is where we're appearing – a great season! Wishing Alma a speedy recovery. Love Zelta.'*

The postmark, the year 1945, is faint but unmistakable. Her mother must have been about fifteen years old at the time.

'Wishing Alma a speedy recovery'. Had her grandmother been ill?

Nimble fingers remove the tiny key from the trinket-box and the fragile lock springs open. Neatly folded circus flyers, yellow with age and old-fashioned in print, depict 'Lovely Lulu' virtually flying through the air holding an umbrella; and 'Funny Freddy' hanging upside down from a swing, wearing blousy bloomers over his tights. She spreads them onto the floor, to examine more fascinating images of clowns, trapeze artists, bareback riders and balancing acts which, the reader is informed in swirly eye-catching print, will be presented by 'Luton's Variety Show' in Leeds. There are a couple of sideshow freaks, 'Freda, The Fattest Woman in the World' in a bright red frilly dress, who'll perform an escape routine. Sitting in her pocket is Tessa, The Tiniest Woman in the World, both due to perform in the Gaumont Theatre on Christmas Eve.

"CIRCUS ARTISTE ACCUSED OF CAUSING WIFE'S DEATH.

Her hands tremble as she opens the clipping, yellow with age, of The Saturday Evening Post and reads the blurred caption - '*A photo of better days'.*

The famous circus performer Don Libella beckons towards his wife, Alma, as she crosses the ménage on a tight-rope, with their daughter balancing on her shoulders.
It has been rumoured that Don Libella was planning to divorce his wife due to his affair with another circus artiste, as well as other problems caused by Alma Libella's bad health. It has also been rumoured she was suffering from a brain tumour.

The local doctor has declined to give further information on the case, apart from confirming that Alma Libella shouldn't have been performing in her present state of health. It has since been claimed by members of the circus that Don Libella had dragged her into the ménage, despite the serious illness she'd been suffering. Another witness has even gone as far as to accuse the performer of 'regularly maltreating his wife'. The coroner will be investigating the case.

She remembers…

"*Oh Gloria! Just imagine! An elephant rolls Grandma Libella into his trunk and carries her out of the ring. The applause was deafening. They thought it was a trick. Nobody knew she was dead. Come on Gloria! Let's join the circus and travel the country with funny clowns and artistes from foreign countries. Do you feel the magic, Gloria? Look! I can do the splits! I'll clear away your doll's things to make room for the pirouette, and the elegant hand taking the call. Then I'll open up the pillow-case and turn into Miss Flummi..."*

Sally stares at the performing child, fairy-like and sparkling, dressed in a tutu. There is no emotional link with this child who is her mother, her facial expression displaying nonchalant distrust. The scene changes and she sees the child now looking happy on her way out, wearing the light blue suit she has bought for the office – always looking happy on her way out. Suddenly, the familiar sadness returns, the dark cloud falls around her and she pauses, allowing the demons to return where they belong, before closing the drawer on distant tragedies. It is time to pay attention to the road below. There is the distant pinprick of a car in the valley. Through the binoculars she sees the dark silhouette of her grandfather sitting behind Conchita who is driving the car. It disappears around the final bend and then reappears, along the straight stretch of road leading up to the village.

...

"All this shopping!" she remarks ten minutes later, appearing from her bedroom, yawning and stretching her limbs. The car is packed with bags, boxes and a couple of crates of fruit and vegetables bought from the market, parked in front of the door and ready to wheel the old man inside. "Why don't you buy at the village store?"

Conchita shrugs, ignoring the old man's accusing glance as she proceeds to push him into the kitchen. Sally is still unpacking the car when Conchita returns. "Nobody in the village will sell food to your grandfather," she mutters behind the open car-boot.

"Would they rather you left him here, alone in the house?"

She sighs. "They don't understand...all these years... I was with your grandfather as part of the performance. I'm committed to him and he is committed to me. It's as easy as that!"

"You were part of his act?" They stop unpacking the car and stare at each other in silence as the girl feigns surprise. Yet another piece of the puzzle has fallen into place! Who could believe it? Conchita had replaced his daughter – or had she replaced his wife too? Her grandmother's dramatic death had been described in the newspaper clipping? Amazing! The whole story is unbelievable! Now she feels angry, although the reason for her sudden anger is not yet apparent. How dare Conchita take the place of her grandmother! Thoughts about money swirl through her head. She'll put them away for a while.

"But that doesn't explain why they won't sell you anything."

"I'll tell you, my child. The trouble began when your grandfather bought the land and diverted the spring-water into the swimming pool. Since then, they have been unable to irrigate their olive trees and vines and lost their source of income. Shhh, my child!" She puts a finger to her mouth, "That's why they hate him," she whispers. "They wish he was dead and I'm frightened. But sometimes I tell him off! Wait and see, how I tell him off!" She claps her hands aggressively, and lifts her chin."

"He has diverted their water into the swimming pool!" the girl repeats slowly, her mind swirling once more. "But how could he do that?"

Conchita removes more shopping from the car, forbids Sally to touch the rest and carries the cardboard boxes inside, her shoulders sloping under the weight. Then she rejoins the girl who is still standing outside next to the car, open mouthed, as though in a trance. "We had visitors last summer," Conchita continues while unpacking the car, "two men in dark suits representing a company who are planning to build a hotel complex further down the valley. They need the land and the water and have paid your grandfather a large amount of money to divert the water. I don't know exactly how much, but it must have been a lot, since the bank-manager almost fell over while checking the account."

"He has signed a contract to re-divert the water?"

"Go inside, my child. Think about your health! It is getting cold!"

Grandfather is in the kitchen, unaware of their conversation and reading 'The Times' which he always collects from the newsagent next door to the bank. He folds the paper and regards Sally with a troublesome expression; an old man in search of something to complain about.

"Got the latest newspaper, have you granddad?" Sally enquires in the hope of extracting a few friendly words.

"Conchita never buys the right newspaper if she's left on her own to do the shopping," he grumbles. "That's what happens when you're dealing with idiots! And now, where's my coffee? What's the world coming to with two women in the house and having to beg for a cup of coffee?" The newspaper lands on the floor as he bangs a fist on the table with astonishing strength.

"Two beautiful signoritas in the house, looking after *you*!" says Conchita jokingly, "and here you are, whining and nagging like Petro's old mule! Out there," she pokes a finger at the empty courtyard, "are a thousand hombres fighting for a place in the queue."

"Yes, yes!" says grandfather dispassionately as he bends over his wheelchair to pick up the newspaper, avoiding defeat.

"What do you say about that?" asks Conchita, pointing at the newspaper. "Wouldn't read about it would ya?" She stands in the middle of the kitchen, hands on her hips. "Spoilt, downright spoilt!"

"Doesn't know he's born!" agrees Sally

"…had plenty of time to notice, hasn't he? Go on! Give her the letter!" Conchita shouts at the old man and carries on muttering like she's mad about something.

There's the rustling of paper; the Christmassy envelope skids over the table and lands next to her cup. Just at that moment, the idea suddenly hits her that being his granddaughter, she might inherit his wealth. *Of course, I'll inherit his wealth! I'll inherit his wealth if it's the last thing I do! How come I haven't thought about this before?* She glances around warily as though they might be reading her thoughts; opens the envelope and removes the letter inside. The card displays the nativity scene, hand-painted and signed by Clementina.

"Thank-you Granddad, the letter's from Alfonso," she reads the letter without looking up and then replaces it in the envelope. There is silence as they wait. Surely she'll be telling them her plans! How long it will last? – these troubles with the girl they hardly know and don't understand "We'll be opening the middle of April in Blackpool," she adds.

Conchita looks like she's working something out. "That fits!" she announces triumphantly. "The baby is due in January so you'll be fit for the show!"

Sally would rather flee from the kitchen and take refuge in her room. Why do they have to keep reminding her about the baby? She doesn't want to know when it's due, for Christ's sake!

...

She walks through the village, past a group of old women wearing black clothes and head-scarves. They meet to gossip; sit on rickety chairs outside the village store and nod their heads in greeting at those passing by. They whisper knowingly, again nodding their heads, this time in agreement, as they watch her disappear through the crumbling arches of the ancient wall.

The delicate fragrances of wild rosemary and lavender remind her of someone she once knew – had it been Grandmother Foss who has long since faded away in a lost world, who had given presents of embroidered lavender linen-bags during an earlier life? Light grey and blue are the season's colours, blooming against the blazing yellow of early buttercups. The surrounding hillsides are tranquil, with fertile spaces; mysterious green shadows between clusters of firs, low bushes and outcrops of rock.

Somewhere among hillside bushes and a row of bee-hives, a man is singing in low, intense tones; the lyrics of a love song. She feels something inside her moving. It pains her to be reminded of love and romance and she won't be reminded of Zasto. Her attention wanders towards crumbling walls of ancient terraces and deserted vineyards and the love song is a background of mechanical noises reminding her of a telephone-bell destroying the tranquillity of an empty house. There is the swishing and crackling of branches, far away or confusingly close, echoing around the hillside. She listens to the rhythmic sound of her shoe-soles upon a bitumen surface; breaking the silence and echoing around the crevices of weirdly shaped rock. Clap, clap, clap – the sound of her feet is the sound of Grandfather banging his stick on the floor, enforcing his refusal of her offer. "Conchita drives the car!" he had roared in a tone defying any argument. "She knows which medicine I need better than anyone else! No! Conchita will push the wheelchair to the car park behind the church. She knows every hole in the road and besides, one has to keep an eye open for those stupid young bastards on scooters."

Does she hear the voice of her mother?

Thud, thud, thud! – There's still the rhythmic vibration of leather on bitumen. Now, the white-washed clusters of tiny buildings come into view, splattered across the hillside like a giant bird's droppings, protected by a dominant church-spire.

…

Sally climbs out of the swimming-pool and carefully treads over the wet and slippery tiles to rub down with the towel before the shivering begins, even though the high stone wall shelters the patio from the cold wind. It descends from the snow-capped heights, wiping its cold fingers over the hillside, defying the sun and cooling everything in its wake. If she forgets to replace the pool-cover, Grandfather will go choleric again; get red in the face and tell her nothing can come of a child whose father is a loser and a mother who has a brain like a sparrow.

Conchita is visiting old 'Tia Maria', and has taken a bag of plums to 'get her going', as well as the sick neighbour, 'La Abuelita', who refuses to get out of bed. She collects their bread and listens to news about old Juan's son, who has emigrated to Australia and works in a coal mine. Apart from that, she cleans the 'Iglesia' on Monday evenings, since the housekeeper from 'el cura' went sick, and helps the village midwife, who also keeps a check on Sally and listens to the baby's heartbeats through an ear-trumpet.

Conchita will be back within the hour, she'd promised before leaving; although she's never been back within the hour as yet, which doesn't matter, because as soon as Sally has slipped into dry clothes, she'll get rid of the demons. Grandfather is dead to the world. He'll sleep though the hustle and bustle and the mopping and dusting; the roar of the vacuum cleaner, the continual shish of running water filling buckets and the washing-machine; blissfully unaware of soapy suds in the open drain meandering down the valley; the washing-line dipping under the weight of a dripping rug, curtains and a bedspread, making her heart brim with happiness at the cleanliness and purity of it all.

She hears the door open and Conchita's voice rings through the house. She claps her hands as she enters the kitchen. "How was your swim today? Are you cleaning again? Muy bueno!"

Sally pulls out a chair and curses under her breath because Conchita has returned unexpectedly early. The old bastard will soon be awake and searching for something to bicker about; the missing teaspoon in the sugar pot, or using two tea-towels instead of one. To be honest – and it's important to be honest with oneself - she hates the old devil and wishes he were dead. Excitement overcomes her as she imagines his body in the middle of the road, squashed beyond recognition, or drowned in the pool, which is something worth considering. And what about Conchita? Conchita is after his money! She'll have to carry it through and put an end to it all! Money is so warm and comfortable.

With the promise of wealth and determined to carry out her plan, her step is light as she leaves her room to go about the house, singing under her breath, collecting things and putting them away, thinking how wonderful it will be, living in her own brand new caravan with a car to pull it. Never again, she tells Conchita over a cup of coffee, who shows great compassion, will she share living-quarters with obnoxious circus hands like Doreen and Nadja, who'd filled up the sink with used tampons and left overflowing urine-pans for her to remove when they'd left. She deserves more than a grimy second-hand caravan. Now is the time for posing the questions she has been meaning to ask. "Do you think Grandfather will lend me ten thousand pounds for a caravan and car to pull it?"

"Oh! That's a lot of money, even for the girl I love like my daughter."

For Christ's sake! That's the last thing she wants, to be loved like a daughter. She'll kill anyone who tries to put her through all that again. They'd given her Gloria and Gloria had been a traitor. Ten thousand pounds will make amends for Gloria; ten thousand pounds for a new caravan with fitted carpets, rose-patterned curtains and matching upholstery. It will have built-in kitchen units and a pink-tiled bathroom. A sparkling candelabrum will hang over the table. It is equally important that there'll be car to pull it.

"I'd be proud to have a daughter like you." Conchita's voice trembles. She reaches for her hand, but the girl drags it away, embarrassed at such an unexpected outbreak of emotion. She'd rather gulp down her coffee, return to her bedroom and wait for Conchita to leave the house and get on with cleaning the church, so she can finish turning out her room and disposing of the demons. But she'll stay in the kitchen. Now is the time to go through with her plan. She'll need Conchita's support in persuading her grandfather to give her the money.

Conchita, wishing to alleviate the tense atmosphere, checks the coffee-pot and refills their cups. "Let your grandfather sleep. He has been very tired recently." She stirs her coffee thoughtfully. "One mustn't get old these days." After another short silence she adds, "How are your parents?"

"They're fine, although I haven't seen them for a while. You know what it's like, travelling around. Every minute of my spare time is spent practicing." She doesn't want speak about her parents, but Conchita is eager to reminisce.

"I knew your mother when she was young. She left the circus because you were on the way and married your father instead. So I took her place and have been with your grandfather ever since."

Sally puts down her cup, her head spinning. "I didn't know my mother was pregnant before they were married."

Conchita's hand goes over her mouth; eyes wide open on realising her faux-pas. "Oh! I'm so sorry! It just slipped out!"

"Probably the reason why she was unhappy…didn't want me either, do doubt!"

"I'll put in a good word about the money," Conchita promises, eager to make amends.

…

Conchita will soon be leaving, to collect the aged and bring them to the square for the Christmas celebrations. "Tonight is the blessed night," she reminds Sally. "The luminarias is waiting to be lit and the traditional play of

'The Adoration' will take place in the church, so don't forget to place a burning candle above the door before you leave. Look! There is a special niche for it," she points to the whitewashed stone shelf above the outside door, "and an adequate supply of candles in the cupboard."

Sally would rather get rid of the filth, but cleaning her room offers little satisfaction for a change, now that children are running down the road outside, with sausage-dog balloons under their arms, laughing and shouting, going from door to door, singing and reciting verses and filling their sacks with the chocolates they've collected. They have wakened her desire to make people laugh; reminding the clown it is time to perform.

A suitcase, and three large bags filled with presents at the side of the door which will be opened the following evening after they have eaten their meal, reminding her of a picture; a sailing ship pasted onto cardboard at the bottom of a murky canal. She doesn't want to think about Christmas presents either, but Conchita has opened the door and Gloria with the permanent smile has come out to dance.

"She was such a beautiful doll," says Conchita.

There's the tin of Whitby toffee in Sally's bedroom, which she wraps in a serviette and gives to Conchita.

"Buenos Gracias! Buenos Gracias!" says Conchita, holding it like some precious stone. "When I open it tomorrow, I shall say a prayer for you." She embraces the girl, who never fails to feel embarrassed at such unaccustomed displays of emotion. "I have also spoken to your grandfather about the money you need."

When the stars come out, they light the bonfire. The village is alight with hundreds of candles reflecting through windows and onto the street. A group of boys pull a heavy log tied with a thick rope up the hill and collect chocolates and nuts for their efforts. Later, they sit in groups around the fire, on the low wall surrounding the village square. The church door is wide open, leading into the square with the ancient figures of the nativity scene, fresh straw in the manger, radiant in the candlelight. Old people flock into the square accompanied by Conchita, others with visiting relatives who have left their commercial lives for a short while, in an attempt to save ancient traditions from the destructive mouth of a growing economy.

Everybody knows Pablo. He is ninety three years old and never alone because his place is a wooden bench outside the village shop. Conchita has often mentioned his phenomenal memory; his widespread knowledge of Spanish history; the local hero who'd saved the village from fascist rampaging during the Civil War, the village prefect and avowed pacifist who'd known them all. Now he is sitting in an armchair outside the church, surrounded by a delegation of village personalities.

Are they looking at her? Does she imagine that even the children are glancing shyly in her direction as they dance around the fire? She stands on the periphery of the crowd which Miss Flummi would like to entertain if she could, with her painted face and red nose. But the guitarists have never heard of Miss Flummi, and neither have the parents, who are laughing and singing as they dance with their children.

Old Pedro, the peasant farmer she sometimes meets up the hill transporting bundles of hay on his donkey, beckons her over to the group of old men who sit on the bank in the square, leaning on their walking sticks and keeping a watchful eye on the village. Are they discussing politics? Is that the reason for the excitement? A younger man, probably in his mid-thirties, with long black hair formed into nonchalant waves, wearing a spotless white shirt and dark formal trousers, comes towards her.

"Bienvenida Senorita! Me llamo Silvio! Excuse me, I speak a little English." He nods politely. "Just like you, I am visiting my great-grandfather for the Christmas festivities," he gestures, with a certain amount of reverence, towards old Pablo who is regarding them with dark watchful eyes. "There are some important things to be said, and although I no longer live here, they have asked me to speak to you about problems concerning your grandfather." Their dark unsmilingly faces intimidate her, but her self-confidence returns with Silvio's friendly smile. She is a performer, accustomed to playing in front of an audience. She turns her head politely and listens.

"Your grandfather is a big problem for this village." Silvio lifts a finger, stops to listen to an old man still making his point, and nods in agreement before continuing. "He has bought some land from people in Madrid, who have inherited property in this village. This land, beyond the hill over there," he points towards the hillside and the olive trees, "is the source of a spring which has been used for hundreds of years by the villagers for watering crops," there's a short silence while he emphasises the next point, "*and the olive trees*. Until last year, when your grandfather purchased the land, many families had earned their living from the olive oil which is famed for its excellence." Here again the emphasis with the stretched finger. "Since your grandfather has refused to allow the pipe to run over his land, and even worse," Silvio raises the finger once more, "diverts the water into his swimming pool, crops have suffered badly; the olives are shrivelled; they're not even worth picking."

"C-C-Can't you speak to him and explain the problem," she stutters, feeling decidedly out of her depth. What do they expect her to do?

Silvio turns to the group of men who have been listening impatiently and then regards her intensely. "I'll tell you what they are saying, with all due respect for your present condition," he bows, with a hesitant gesture towards her expanding abdomen. "They are saying that the devil came with your grandfather when he entered this village! Yes! We have tried to speak, but he ignores us. He is rude and arrogant and has rich friends! But he is not breaking the law. I know, because I am a policeman. My hands are tied. There is nothing I can do to protect my family against your grandfather's rich friends, who will chop down the olive trees, pull out the vineyards and destroy their crops. It is because of these beautiful views," here he gestures widely towards the coastline, "that they will pull down the houses, replace them with hotels and apartments and build a luxurious sanatorium. The climate up here in the hills is ideal for convalescence, especially for diseases of the lungs." While Silvio stops to listen to the men, she stands aside, searching her mind for some logical reason to get up and go. He turns towards her, meaningfully rubbing a finger and thumb. "They have bribed the prefect and the village committee to support their building plans, knowing that they must sell their land and leave the village, if they cannot irrigate their land. It is a scandal!"

"Oh! I'm so sorry. I wish I could do something!"

"Oh, but you can!"

"I can? What do you mean?"

"Allow me to explain further, Senorita. This evening, the whole village will be in the church – not only to celebrate the Blessed Night, but for the tradition of 'The Request'. This year we shall be praying to the Holy Mother to help save our village. You also will be mentioned in our prayers. We shall pray that you may be given the strength to influence your grandfather against selling the land for speculation, and save our water-rights, which are vital to the irrigation of our crops and our livelihood."

Influence her grandfather? Save their village? She, Miss Flummi, the circus clown who would rather make people laugh? But can she ignore their wishes? Expectant eyes are focusing upon her, waiting for the magical wave of the wand. *I'm a clown for fools*, she yearns to shout out loud. *I'd rather cross the village square on my hands than change the ways of a stubborn old man. You need a hero to save your village; not an artiste from the secluded world of a circus, with no ear for the problems of others.*

But wait! They need a hero? She is brave and aren't brave people heroes? The idea is appealing. Heroes are greatly admired. She has seen monuments dedicated to heroes in village squares and parks, outside public building in many of the towns they have been. She will turn her attention to becoming a hero. "I shall help! You can count on me!" she assures the expanding crowd of hopeful villagers. "Ooooooooh!" she puts back her head and coos into the night. "Eeeeeeeh!" She unties the oversized bow on her strange looking sack and pulls out an assortment of indefinable articles one after another; examines them in mock surprise, holding them up for everyone to see, the strange assortment of knickers and oversized socks she carries with her. A clown will do what he pleases, blind to worry and anger. The crowd applauds, and waits for the big moment.

Silvio suddenly sees her as a clown in the ridiculous clothes, the bright orange hair and red nose, dancing through the crowd in her oversized shoes. When she blows her whistle, children squeal with delight as water spouts from her ears. Who is this strange woman, dressed as a clown?

"Cuidado! Cuidado!" More water squirts from her ears, "Cuidado! Cuidado! Usted será mojado!" They clap their hands at her walk-on-act, and roar with laughter at the baggy striped trousers disguising her bulging stomach. The guitars begin to play. A ball appears from Miss Flummi's sleeve; another from her mouth. How did it get there? Can she juggle? Of course she can juggle. She runs about in circles, tripping over her oversized feet but always regaining her balance; shouting and cooing as she kicks the balls, one after the other, into the crowd as Zasto had done.

She won't think about Zasto. It will spoil all the fun and change her mood into despondency, which is not fitting for a clown whose duty it is to make people laugh, especially when they are unhappy.

Miss Flummi dances her way through the delighted crowd. They stand aside and applaud, allowing her a path to the road. "Don't worry, all will be well!" the clown reassures them because there's nothing she wants to believe more, than that.

Dark eyes follow the funny ghost, until she has disappeared at the end of the empty cobbled street. She removes her ridiculous clothes and stuffs them into her funny sack with the oversized bow, leaving a clown's world for the ugly aspects of urban development.

...

Is giving birth the great point of contact between women? She doesn't remember contacting anybody, in the midwife's delivery-room, dreading the next sharp spasms of pain, growing longer, splitting her apart so it seems, when all she wants is to get it over and continue being a clown.

Is she enjoying this overrated experience of giving birth? Certainly not! She is mindlessly terrified and in no mood for heroics. "Don't be afraid," says Conchita, her face drawing closer, equally tortured by having to translate the midwife's instructions.

Don't be afraid? She'll rather leap over a hundred rings of fire than go through this again. And then the all-relieving cry after endless hours of torture, telling her it is over; finally over. She has rid herself of this annoying bundle which has stolen part of her life, keeping her from the ménage; preventing her from making people laugh.

She can't have it polluting her room: neither will she allow this screaming pink bundle to deter her from working the tight-rope, fixed over the swimming-pool by Antonio who does the garden, ready and waiting for her to commence practising her routine. These days, Conchita looks bewildered and distressed. Grandfather roars his displeasure at being neglected – who is more important – he or the baby? But someone must look after the baby while the mother is practising. The midwife's word carries weight, but her attempts at making the girl see sense about looking after her baby are in vain. Nothing will persuade Sally to sleep with the baby; her room is too small, too stuffy, too noisy and even too dirty if she is catching up on valuable practice instead of cleaning her room from the demons that still haunt her. What kind of a mother is she? Has the midwife experienced the likes of it before? Never! The word spreads through the village. People tip their foreheads; some shrug their shoulders, saying 'The apple always falls near the tree'.

The village midwife has said she will look after the baby and Conchita looks secretive when she brings Gloria from her room for a feed, because until now, there has been no milk from an unwilling mother for a tiny girl with dark shiny hair, almond-shaped eyes and in a beautiful white dress embroidered with flowers.

Gloria, oh Gloria! Gloria is so beautiful!

...

Gloria hasn't changed one single bit. She listens to Sally who tells her about the circus and hardly talks about anything else. "Isn't it wonderful, Gloria? My dream has finally come true (do you remember the 'photo-album Gloria?) and now my name is Miss Flummi. Miss Flummi is a real live circus-clown – and guess what, Gloria!

Nothing can stop Miss Flummi from being 'Top of the Bill!'" Later, after spending an hour on the tight-rope, she comes inside and speaks to Gloria once more. "Oh Gloria! Alfonso will collect us and take us home on an aeroplane. And where shall we live? Have patience, Gloria! It won't be long before we are rich! We shall live in a posh caravan with all the trimmings, just like the Moroccans with their fancy curtains, expensive furniture, and glittering lights - and there'll be a car to pull it all, just wait and see!" Now she is leaning over the sleeping baby. "Have patience, Gloria! Because there are a few arrangements to be made before we can leave. Conchita has kept her promise and eased her conscience, by threatening to leave if he doesn't give me the money. Tomorrow is the big day. You will stay with Conchita and I shall drive Grandfather into town. We shall go to the bank and attend to the money."

...

Grandfather in a wheelchair is difficult to manoeuvre from an uneven sidewalk into a revolving door, proving that perfect timing is not only essential in the ménage. On entering the bank, he commands immediate attention, demanding to speak to the manager about this young lady, his granddaughter.

The manager with the glossy hair and handsome face bows over her hand. Such reverence! Such overwhelming respect! He escorts her to a seat, clicks his fingers and coffee is served. She eats the chocolate biscuit wrapped in silver paper thinking if that's how the rich are treated, she'll profit from the power and influence that money creates, or her name isn't Sally Foss.

"Ten thousand pounds sterling to be transferred into your granddaughter's account," repeats the bank-manager. "When? Not yet?" The manager looks puzzled.

"She'll have to earn it! Oh yes! She'll have to earn the money before re-joining the circus," her grandfather grins slyly and continues, "so you'd better start working out how many pesetas it will be, because I've no idea and if a bank doesn't know who the hell does?" He begins a lengthy complaint about awkward procedures of financial transfers, enjoying the attention he receives. "How am I supposed to pay my bills?", he demands to know, "when it takes the whole day to get here from the village where I have the misfortune to live, amid a hoard of inbred idiots – up and down that bloody hill, at my age and state of bad health."

The bank manager speaks only Spanish. A young accountant translates the problem, omitting the insults. The manager's face breaks into an indulgent smile. After a few words, the accountant disappears into an office and reappears with a cheque book. No problems Senor! Just fill out a cheque and send it by post. Here also are bank-forms for transferring money into your granddaughter's account. He smiles benevolently at Sally, who wonders what price she will have to pay, in exchange for a brand new caravan and a vehicle to pull it.

...

Conchita must leave to return to her village, in a bustle of sadness and drama. Oh, the drama of it all! It's a mystery to Sally, why one should mourn an old and feeble mother with such intensity. Nevertheless, a mother is a mother and must be mourned with all the trimmings of a stately funeral, so it seems.

"And who shall look after Gloria?" enquires Conchita between tears, in the back of the car on her way to the bus-station. It is all getting a bit much! She doesn't understand when Sally talks about Gloria having been in her room for the past fifteen years. How does that work out? How can a newly born baby have been in Sally's room for the past fifteen years? Is her English getting worse? She kisses Gloria in the carry-cot, strapped into the seat next to her, and happily sucking her dummy.

"Of course she'll sleep in my room," answers Sally decisively, as if there could be no doubt about it. She turns the car into the bus-station. "Gloria has been sleeping in my room for years, propped between the white lace cushions. They've always been her throne during the day and her bed at night." As she parks the car, she suddenly realises that feeding and nappy changing has never been a problem until now although there has been too much time wasted, removing the aftermaths of unclean activities, the nappies from her room, when she should have been practising on the rope over the pool.

Conchita silently offers her thanks to The Holy Mother. The midwife is a regular and fearless visitor who won't be intimidated by an old man, or anyone else, for that matter.

…

A less formal approach seems to have softened the old man's temper and the icy atmosphere has disappeared, since Conchita's departure. Memories have been recalled and past triumphs dwelled upon.

A stock answer serves an old man's curiosity when he enquires after her parents.

"No! I haven't seen them lately. Yes! They're still doing fine."

Today, his mood is gracious. He nods his head understandingly. "That's how it is with the circus! Here today and gone tomorrow. Pah!" He pushes away the half-eaten dish of soup in disgust, as though suddenly reminded of his unsettled life. "They're in it together," he tells her, "the acrobats and tight-rope artists, sword-swallowers and fire-eaters – one big family! – one for all and all for one. That's how it is and that's how it should be!" With unaccustomed vigour, his bony hand bangs on the table.

"Hey, Granddad!" She prefers to call him Granddad when they're alone, and they have been alone for the past couple of days, since Conchita's departure. The moment has come! The moment for posing the question she has been longing to ask.

"Hey, Granddad!" she repeats in order to gain his undivided attention. "How did grandmother die? Was she ill? Did she have an accident? Mum never told me!"

He sips at the water, puts down the glass and looks at her, straight in the eye. "She took poison. Suicide!"

"She took poison?" the girl repeats slowly. "Why on earth would she do a thing like that?" He's lying, of course. She knows he is lying. There's a newspaper cutting to prove he is lying! Her eyes wander over his face, in search of the truth.

"Her performing days were over. She'd become unsteady. Your mother was to replace her." His voice grows bitter. "A stubborn woman was your grandmother. Too stubborn to consult a doctor, until the headaches had become unbearable and were impairing her vision. By then it was too late." He shrugs his shoulders, "Such a long time ago; who cares, anyway? So she took poison…" his voice trails away.

With an impatient snort, he signals to be taken outside and she pushes him onto the patio. "And how did your accident happen, Granddad?"

There is no reply when an old man is sleeping.

…

"Do you remember that doll you once sent me for Christmas?" she asks him after he has finished drinking his tea accompanied by the usual oatmeal biscuit. "Her name was Gloria and I am so happy she has come back to life. She is still sitting on my pillow like a princess on a throne in my bedroom, wearing that beautiful dress with lace and frills and embroidered flowers."

"I remember!" he says, interrupting her sharply. Is his hearing at fault? The doll is alive...? He won't get involved! "You can thank Conchita for the doll," he mumbles, fixing his hearing-aid.

What an old crap he is! Where is the doting grandfather; the loving granddaughter? If he won't accept her affection she'll carry out the plan. The plan is evil, she has to admit, but brilliant all the same! It has been going through her mind since Conchita left, and put into action a thousand times already.

"Yes, Conchita! Conchita sent the doll. I had nothing to do with it, do you hear?" His mouth curls sarcastically and he leans over the table, enjoying her obvious discomfort. "That woman knows she's indispensable; keeps forcing me into doing things I don't want; threatens to leave an old man to his fate," he adds bitterly. "I'll tell you something! Come here!" he beckons her closer. Unwillingly, she moves towards him, sensing his bitterness. "Don't get yourself depending on people. They'll turn you inside out and have your pockets cleaned before you know it!" Ignoring her presence he turns away. "How many times has Conchita threatened to leave me?" he rants and mutters and she listens intently. "If I don't transfer the money into my granddaughter's account, I'll have to do penance, eh? Penance for her death, eh? That's what she calls it – doing penance! Who the hell does she think she is? If your grandmother had gone to see that goddamned doctor instead of going into the ring, there wouldn't have been any accident. That's what I say, and that's how it was!" He bangs a bony fist on the arm of his chair, reliving the past, mumbling into the wind, recalling half-forgotten memories.

The girl strains her ears, attempting to understand his muddled words "...money from the insurance ... a new partner to keep the act going with Charmaine's share of the money.... ungrateful bitch ...awkward damned girl, refused to take the role of her mother...leaving the circus and marrying that good-for-nothing guy who's your father..." He stops his mumbling and turns to face her. "I didn't give your mother her share of the money and she hasn't spoken to me since," he admits flatly, with no trace of emotion in his voice.

She feels the heat of blood rushing to her face, boiling with anger and hatred. But she must think clearly. Here is the chance to carry out her plan. Money generates respect. Wealthy people have friends. They live in beautiful houses. That is what she wants more than anything else; to make people laugh and be rich. She gazes intensely at her grandfather, who will provide her with everything she needs. As though reading her thoughts, the old man's face takes on a scornful gloat. "I've told you the money will be transferred into your account before you leave, but there's still time to cancel the transaction if you're not willing to please me."

"What do you mean, Granddad?" she enquires hesitantly.

"Conchita is an old woman. Ha!" he laughs without humour. "I haven't seen a young woman's body for years," he announces, sitting back in his chair and chuckling wickedly. "If you want the money, take off your clothes!"

Now she knows the price he wants her to pay; but he won't see her naked – not for all the money in the world!

His gaze wanders over her body, forever destroying the vision of the benevolent grandfather. Should she be afraid of a cripple, inhibited, tied to a wheelchair, either evil or mentally depraved – or perhaps both? He can do her no harm. Her plan is ready and she'll reap the reward when he's gone!

The princess on a tight-rope enters her mind. Here she is, smiling through the years at the strong handsome man, gesturing towards the blur of heads and ignoring her misery. The audience applauds, while the tiny star on the fickle rope of fame concentrates on keeping her balance. Now she can see her father sitting at the kitchen table in front of his take-home meal, lifting the plastic plate divided into sections, separating the rice from the chicken. "Want some, love?" He offers her the plate, always eager to please.

"Where's my dinner?" Her grandfather's voice brings her back, to the distressing situation she'll have to endure to reap her reward. His sudden change of mood never fails to surprise.

"I'll get it," she replies, relieved that the conversation has taken a turn, but suspecting her relief will be premature. Uneasy disgust and oncoming nausea accompanies the hustle and bustle of preparing the table; serving food under his watchful eye. He rolls his chair closer and touches her body and she wonders how Conchita has put up with him for so many years. Does some kind of agreement exist? Perhaps financial? The preposterous idea of Conchita inheriting his money hasn't occurred to her until now. She can't allow it to happen. There are ways and means! She has done it before. When the devils come out to play, she'll do it again.

The old man watches in silence, enjoying her movements as she runs backwards and forwards, preparing the meal.

"The Last Supper, Granddad!" She smothers a hysterical laugh because the simile, in this case, couldn't be less fitting. Having followed Conchita's instructions and taken it out of the freezer in time, she fills the table with Conchita's cooking.

"Don't spill! Put my plate right at the front and push me up! That's right! Now! Give me some turkey breast and not so much sauce. I love breasts – you must know that! Would you like a man to caress your breasts?"

She allows his bony hands to caress her breasts while considering her movements in slow-motion. Then she adds a spoonful of beans to his plate, her mind intent upon the reward she will reap.

"Cut it up and give me my fork. Then answer my question!"

Sally follows his command in silence, aware of the deep breathing, thinking he'll soon be going where the others have gone, down traitor's road which has already been travelled upon, twice before. Meanwhile, it will be fun to provoke. "They say you won't allow pipes to run over your property. You are preventing the villagers from watering their olives," she announces without further introduction and quite out of the blue. She carries on. "You are ruining this village. Soon, it will be empty after everything has died. Do you understand?" Enough is enough! She speaks slowly, pointedly, thrusting her words as though questioning a retard.

His face blackens with fury. "The blatant impudence," He thrusts himself from the table. "This ignorant bunch of goddamned peasants!" he spits, "... these impudent... pah!"

"They're not ignorant or impudent, Granddad! There's a guy called Silvio who is anything but ignorant."

"He's a bloody communist – his grandfather was a terrorist!"

"Actually, I find him extremely pleasant – and attractive," she adds, lowering her voice and smiling sweetly, enjoying his jealous discomfort. "They were all extremely polite and friendly. I must admit; their concern about water being diverted and causing a drought, is quite understandable, don't you agree?"

With surprising vigour, he sweeps the plate of roast turkey from the table. The girl covers her ears as it crashes onto the tiles. In her mind, she sees the huge bag of shopping and the tin of smoked salmon rolling in circles on the kitchen floor as her mother, shaking with exasperation, flings on her coat and rushes out of the house.

Food splashes across the table; sauce trickles down cupboard doors and drops into a thick brown pool on the tiles. "Take me onto the patio and then clean up this mess," he demands, and turns his chair towards the door.

She must overcome her loathing of the monster on the sideboard. She must make those vital telephone-calls and ignore the silent man who has returned, who never speaks when she answers. She remembers punishing Gloria. Gloria had allowed him to enter the house and steal her mother, which was unforgiveable because nobody should be allowed to steal someone's mother. Now Gloria has returned! She has been given a second chance!

Sally lifts the receiver. Her hands are shaking because she hasn't touched a telephone for years and would rather be handling a snake. Telephones are cold and dead, which is more than can be said for the snake she'd once watched, winding itself around 'The Snake-Woman's' body in an unsuccessful attempt at joining the circus, because Alfonso had decided against performing with wild-animals. If she can touch a snake, she can pick up the receiver and dial Alfonso's number. She puts a finger in one of the holes on the disc and dials a number. Then she dials another number, and another. She carries on dialling and then waits, listening to the distant rhythm in an unknown place, ignoring the rapidly expanding bubble in her head, and the silent alien entering the room.

"Si!"

She hesitates for a moment, curbing a strong inclination to replace the receiver and return to her room.

"Si! Si!" repeats the woman's voice impatiently – a younger voice, not Clementina's husky tones, which might have had a calming effect on her nerves.

"Here is Sally. Can – can I speak to Alfonso, please?" Her voice grows bolder as she speaks.

"Sí, un momento, por favor."

"Sally, my darling!" he begins without much announcement. "How is the baby? Good? Clementina is crocheting a dress and matching bootees," she hears a voice in the background and Alfonso continues, "We are so looking forward to seeing the baby." Sally is impatient for him to finish cooing about the baby. "I intended to 'phone you this evening anyhow." There's a short pause; she holds her breath and he continues, "We're planning to return to London on Tuesday! The flight leaves at four, so I'll be collecting you at mid-day, Sally! Sally! Can you hear me? Do you understand?"

"Understand? "You'll pick me up about lunch time? Perfect! Alfonso, you are so kind! Thank you so much!"

The telephone is no longer a fearful monster. She'll use it to inform Conchita that Alfonso will be collecting her on Tuesday. "Of course, Granddad is fine," she reassures Conchita. "Certainly, he'll manage lunch on his own. There's still plenty of food – cold meat and salad in the 'fridge. All he needs to do is put it on the table and later, he'll fall asleep on the veranda and you'll be here when he wakes-up. Of course, I shall miss you Conchita. And thank you so much for your help!"

Perfect!

She disconnects the 'phone, reminding herself to reconnect it before she leaves. There's still plenty of time to practise his signature beneath the fifty-thousand-pound cheque. Later, she puts it in an envelope and takes it to the letter-box outside the village store. When it arrives at the bank, he'll be dead!

...

The old man is glad to be rid of her and mumbles incoherently as she leaves the house with Alfonso and her baby. He is tired of it all; tired of a bunch of strangers hovering around his door; the midwife, unnecessarily fussing the baby and this blasé circus director who blows out his chest like he's continually announcing a new act. More than anything else, he's tired of waiting for Conchita. She'll be back later this afternoon and this will be the last time he takes his afternoon nap in the wheelchair, since his granddaughter has refused to help him into bed – and that's another good reason for him to refuse her the money.

He can hear them in the courtyard. They'll be gone in a minute. Their voices grow fainter; he is almost asleep and can't be bothered with the footsteps on the kitchen tiles. Somebody has forgotten something, no doubt!

Suddenly, his head bumps against the back of the wheelchair; such is the force behind the thrust which sets it in motion, over the edge of the patio. He senses someone breathing down the back of his neck, and then another strong thrust. The chair gathers speed down the slope. There's no point in losing valuable seconds by turning his head. He has already sensed her presence and is aware she will kill him; aware that his granddaughter is as evil as he! The pool is coming closer. He'll stop this helter-skelter by holding the wheels. *God! Is this painful! God! How it's burning my hands! I can't hold the wheels any longer!*

His feeble cry goes unheard at the front of the house where Alfonso is securing Gloria into the back seat of the car and the midwife is still fussing. Nobody has noticed Sally's sudden disappearance inside the house, locking the door less one of them should follow. Who could imagine her at this moment, watching, with dark empty eyes, her grandfather's feeble attempts at avoiding the inevitable tragedy; watching him grabbing the side of the pool, but in vain? The wheelchair capsizes, pulling him down into an empty white-tiled world. He opens his mouth but no-one hears the handsome hero, the star of the circus, as he leaves the ménage and goes to his death.

...

Chapter 16

During the second curtain-call, Nickbone experiences the fulfilment of having done a good job with Merriman the butler; highlighting the witty arrogance of this Oscar Wilde character. The play has been such an overwhelming success that they'd extended the season for a few guest performances, as well as a couple of charity do's, to repair to the church roof and send senior citizens on a bus-trip to Bridlington.

Having stretched his vocal cords to the limit, he wouldn't mind taking a pint of 'bitter' in the 'White Horse Inn', but will have to make do with tea and muffins in the church hall instead. It is packed with people, laughing and joking at nothing in particular; such is the atmosphere in the centre of local activity.

His wife is surrounded by ardent members of the 'Mother's Gymnastic Group', with free tickets for the final performance. Young mothers on low budgets deserve two hours of freedom from family commitments – and no-one had argued against that! Patricia catches his eye and waves in his direction, but indulging in small talk is hard work for a man who'll come straight to the point, unless a crumb of information is passing his way; the missing piece of a puzzle worth following up – and that won't be found in a church hall! Later, he'll wonder how mistaken he was.

Somebody taps him on the shoulder and he experiences the fleeting sensation of déjà-vu. Wasn't it about a year ago? The same man, standing in exactly the same place next to the cloakroom; the same raised eyebrows and timid expression. And hadn't he felt the same urge to reassure him? – 'come on old chap, I won't bite!'

"Last time, you were a king, now you're a butler!" Matthew Foss overcomes his own devil in a broad Yorkshire accent, "Aye lad! This evening's performance was as good as any other I've seen! You wouldn't believe it would yer? – am a great Oscar Wilde fan myself – enjoy a bit of high-brow stuff now an' again!" he adds, clearing his throat apologetically.

"My dear fellow..."replies Nickbone in his best Oscar Wilde manner, wiping an imaginary crumb from the corner of his mouth with the tip of a finger as he gathers his thoughts. "It's always the same! Once you've got into the play, you have to get out of it again, and start something new. My wife says, it's like walking-in a pair of shoes, when you've got used to them, they're through!" Actually, Patricia has never said anything of the sort, but Nickbone fancies the simile. "By the way, how's your wife?"

The shy man shrugs. "Not so good!" Nickbone remains silent, having no intention of relieving Matthew from explaining his present predicament, although it is blatantly obvious he is struggling. "She's in 'Nethersted'."

"Oh, sorry to hear that! Is she ill?"

Without answering directly, Matthew continues, "... during the week. She comes home at weekends when I'm not working."

"Back to the grindstone, are you?"

"At 'Whitey's Gears," he says, and laughs apologetically. "We need the money, you see!" He rolls his thumb and forefinger, smiling the helpless smile of Don Quixote fighting against windmills.

"Sorry to hear it, old chap! But she's in good hands at Nethersted." Nickbone sips his tea and bites into the second chocolate muffin. "I've been up there a couple of times doing some reading – you'd be surprised how much they still appreciate a well turned sentence. I've also agreed to help with their centenary celebrations the first week in June, along with a group of theatre company members." He winks offhandedly to someone in the crowd and then guides Matthew into the cloakroom, exactly as he had done the previous year. The coincidence is mysterious; circumstances one might imagine in the scene of a play rather than in real life. He has the uncanny notion something unusual will happen.

"My wife was fond of Sally; such a talented girl, Patricia always says. How is she is getting along in the circus? No doubt you've heard from her since that enjoyable evening we spent at your house. Hang on! I'll just get hold of her!" Nickbone disappears into the crowd and reappears almost immediately with his wife, bewildered and irritated at the unceremonious interruption of an interesting conversation about bee-keeping, and thinking if it's nothing important she'll give him a piece of her mind!

"Such a lovely evening we spent at your house, Matthew," Patricia continues after the usual greetings have calmed her down. "A year ago, how time flies! How is Sally? We often wonder, don't we, Nick?"

Nickbone nods and waits.

"It's difficult getting in touch with a travelling circus." There's an undertone of embarrassment in Matthew's voice. "The last time we spoke to Sally, it was shortly after the accident."

"Accident?"

"Her grandfather and his housekeeper – drowned! Found floating in't swimming-pool an' as dead as door-nails!" Matthew speaks rapidly, unwilling to dwell on the subject, wishing he could wash his hands of it all. "I spoke to her a couple of months ago. She said she was in a hurry and on her way out to purchase a brand new caravan with the money."

"Ah! She has inherited? How nice!"

Matthew Foss has strong aversion to discussing private problems and reckons he has said enough, although there's plenty more on the tip of his tongue; the letter from the bank, for instance, reminding him of the overdraft. Overdraft? Badly in debt, he'd called it. Could have done with a 'windfall', and what had that bastard of a father-in-law left them in his will? Bugger-all! Nowt! He'd rather keep it a secret that he's well and truly up the shit and can hardly afford a pint with the lads!

Alcohol addiction can be the cause of dementia, the doctor had explained. Could anything be worse than that? Not even the milkman banging on the door and looking uppish about unpunctual payments had troubled him more. Mind you, that bloke from the council who'd appeared on his doorstep had been helpful about getting Charmaine into 'Nethersted Nursing Home', enabling him to start work again and settle their debts. He'd even started going to the factory on his bike again, after selling the car to pay for the accident she'd caused while going through the red lights, and if that hadn't been enough, she'd told the cop he was an ignorant bogtrotter and as blind as a bat. Now things are looking up since the postcard arrived, quite unexpectedly, showing Blackpool illuminations where Circus Poppi has started the season before moving on. 'We open on Black's Field the first two weeks in June, see you then!' she had written. Now that *is* something to look-forward to!

If it wasn't for this useless pile of junk in the garage! His father-in-law's effects, still packed in the crate, and he can't make head or tail of the documents that go with it either. Is he supposed to speak Spanish? Better donate it all to a charity shop – or ask Nickbone. That's the idea! A retired cop knows how to get rid of dead people's togs. When Sally comes home, she can look after the rest. He'll ask!

"No problem, old chap! Let me buy you a beer and we can talk it over. See you in ten minutes, in the "White Horse'. It's still another hour 'till closing time!"

...

In a corner of the local pub, Nickbone decides there's no sense in competing with this raucous rugby team, yelling and bawling at each other, celebrating their victory over some local rival. There's no arguing with these red-faced hunks telling them to shut it or else; even worse, request a little peace and get laughed at. They're a formidable bunch of all brawn and no brain, broad shoulders and matching biceps. He whispers to the barman there'll be a round for the team as soon as they've got their butts on the seats outside on the lawn. After the cheering and the back-slapping, the bar-room quietens down. Matthew is relieved, able to share his troubles. Patricia reappears from the 'Ladies'.

"Cheers!" Nickbone lifts his glass, takes a long pull of beer and with a satisfied sigh wipes the froth from his mouth with the back of his hand. Patricia gives him the look for forgetting his manners, then lifts her glass and says there's a lot to be said for a glass of dry sherry.

Is it possible to ask questions without sounding like a policeman? Nickbone waits for his cue. "I was just wondering if Sally was still visiting her grandfather when he drowned in the swimming-pool."

"She'd just left – with Alfonso Poppi the circus director, to catch the four-o'clock flight to London. A Spanish lawyer sent us a copy of the will, translated into English. He left everything to his housekeeper, Conchita Whatshername – I can't pronounce these foreign names. She was the one who drowned with him! Don't ask me how that happened and Sally doesn't know either! Suppose she fell into the pool while trying to pull him out. In the letter, it says the housekeeper's next of kin will inherit the house if the will isn't contested. That's Charmaine's business 'cos I can't do it for her; wouldn't know where to begin!"

"Quite!" mutters Nickbone, feeling sorry for the fellow. "But the money will make life easier for Sally. It's a hard life with a travelling circus, when you're penniless!"

Penniless...? He won't have his daughter thought penniless! These people have no idea what it's like, living on a narrow budget and supporting a wife who has forgotten her name. "Sally has never been penniless and never will be, as long as I live!" announces Matthew stubbornly.

"Oh! I'm so sorry! I thought...!"

"Whatever you thought, you're wrong!" he thrusts out a petulant lower-lip. "Her grandfather transferred money into her savings account every year at Christmas. According to bank statement copies sent to my wife as next of kin – and they might have been written in Chinese for all she understood – he'd transferred money into Sally's account just a couple of days before his death, making her fifty grand richer." Having found the suitable moment for the important announcement, he continues, "She's coming home the first two weeks in June. That's when Circus Poppi is coming our way and my Sally is topping the bill! Now then, what d'ya say about that, eh?" His eyes gleam with pleasurable pride.

"How wonderful! You have every right to be proud!" Patricia lifts her glass, having remained silent until now.

"By the way," Nickbone enquires in a casual manner, "does Sally speak Spanish?"

"As far as I know, the housekeeper spoke English. She looked after my father-in-law after his accident – he fell from the trapeze and landed in a wheelchair. Only God knows how she put up with the old bugger – pardon me madam," he says, nodding towards Patricia, already into her second dry sherry. "I remember him as an unpleasant bugger – always changing his moods! One minute the dance-floor gigolo and the next minute he'd be at you like a dog with a rag!"

"Was his housekeeper also a circus artiste?"

"Aye she was, although I don't know much about her. Charmaine never talks much about her childhood."

...

It took a while for Nickbone to get hold of the verdict, there being little cause for interest in a fatal drowning accident in a secluded Spanish village, involving an old man who had long since renounced his British nationality. Donald Libella and his housekeeper had both been Spanish citizens.

"Clocks tick slowly in Spain," said Detective Inspector Jack Douglas. He hadn't refused his retired senior officer the favour and had already sent a note to the Consulate, even though Nickbone's inexplicable behaviour was irritating and he'd decided there'd be no more support in this case. "You'll get the post mortem translated into English with a bit of luck! How's that, old chap?"

Patricia watches him in silence as he examines the verdict of accidental death by drowning in the case of Donald Libella and his housekeeper, Conchita Fernandos. At least he might do me the favour of reading it out loud, she reflects, and straightens her shoulders in preparation of the storm that will surely come. "Are you satisfied?" she asks drily.

Nickbone ignores the sarcasm and glances at her over the page. "It says their bodies were discovered in the swimming pool of Senor Libella's house by Antonio Ferres, while delivering gardening items. Senor Ferres testified there had been an object floating on the surface of the pool and he suspected it might be a dead animal. On taking a closer look, he had recognised the body of Donald Libella strapped to his wheelchair and immediately informed Silvio Silento of the Policia Municipal, responsible for village affairs. Together with Antonio Ferres, they had pulled the wheelchair out of the water and discovered the previously submerged body of Concita Fernandos, trapped between the wheels."

"Aha!" remarks Patricia with growing interest.

Nickbone reads on. "On further examination of the wheelchair, the manual braking system was found to be rusty and therefore defect. Due to the sloping terrain of the patio, it has been determined that the wheelchair had slowly rolled into the swimming pool while the deceased slept in the chair. It has also been determined that, on returning to Mr. Libella's house after visiting her family, Conchita Fernandos immediately discovered the accident (she was still wearing her coat). The approximate time of M/s Fernandos death was estimated at 16.30 hours, which according to witnesses, corresponds with the time of her return. Due to the position of the body beneath the wheelchair, it has been assumed that her unsuccessful attempts to rescue Donald Libella, and the fact that she was a non-swimmer, contributed towards a fatal heart attack."

"Oh dear, how sad!" remarks Patricia, obviously troubled.

Nickbone nods in agreement at a case of tragic death that had once been a routine part of his life. He carries on reading. "It is known that Mr. Libella's granddaughter, Sally Foss, left her grandfather's house at 12.15 hours, to be taken to the airport. This has been confirmed by two villagers, Ronaldo Brizuela and Amaralis De Caxias, as witnesses; also her employer, the circus director Senor Alfonso Poppi, who collected Miss Foss and the 'recién nacido' from the house in his car. Mr. Poppi informed us he did not speak to Mr. Libella, but saw him on the patio in his wheelchair, presumably asleep. Mr. Libella often slept in his wheelchair, on the patio, according to Miss Foss."

Nickbone clears his throat. "Any idea what 'recién nacido' means? No? Probably the Spanish word for 'luggage'." He folds the paper and, with an eye on Patricia, returns it to the drawer because her heaving breast suggests trouble.

"You're being over-dramatic! Why all this fuss about an accident; the tragic death of an old man drowned in a swimming-pool and the faithful housekeeper losing her life trying to save him? You should be ashamed of yourself!"

Her words overflow like a shaken bottle of fizz. His silence not only heightens her annoyance, but deepens her concern. He must be suffering from some kind of delusion – might be going mad for all she can tell! The next thing he'll come up with … she'll lay a bet on it! …a sudden trip to Spain!

"Awful, this weather!" Nickbone remarks and looks through the window at the cold, damp greyness of disappointing spring weather. "Why do we put up with it? Why don't we go on holiday instead? I've been thinking about a warm-temperate region with a Mediterranean climate – like Andalusia, for example."

There's a moment of silence before she explodes.

"That's it! That's definitely it! I'll tell you something, Nicholas…" with an outstretched forefinger in the 'schoolmistress-manner' he finds distinctly annoying, she continues, "you're in danger of making a fool of yourself! At your age, you should be concentrating on your 'Literature Evenings', and Amateur Dramatics, instead of suspecting innocent girls of fictitious crimes. As if the poor girl hasn't suffered enough! Not only do you suspect her of murdering her grandfather and his housekeeper, but of murdering the clown, and on top of that, her mother's boyfriend. Ha! It's preposterous!" She laughs suddenly, imagining him dressed in checked tweeds, a deerstalker hat and holding a magnifying-glass. He's the typical mad Englishman, snuffling around the house, inspecting the swimming-pool, the garden and between the bushes (she supposes there are some bushes), in search of some clue to prove that Sally Foss had pushed her granddaddy into the swimming pool, and his housekeeper to follow.

Enough is enough! It's bad enough *she'd* made a fool of herself concerning the girl's talent; had misjudged her introverted character, taken her from one vital competition to the next and dreamt about training her for the Olympics, despite sardonic remarks in the school staff-room. Now Nickbone is threatening to make himself look equally silly. What it is about the girl? Why are their lives being ruled by a phantom?

"But my dear..!" Nickbone stands up and straightens his pullover. "Women!" he mutters under his breath and stares at the neat rows of wooden spoons on the wall opposite his desk, allowing his thoughts to sum up the case. Being an 'old-age-pensioner' (Patricia delights upon reminding him of the fact), one must conserve one's strength and there are more subtle methods of finding the truth about Sally Foss.

He continues staring at his wooden spoons, still gathering his thoughts. *She has murdered four people and disguised them as accidents. Now that really does afford some ingenuity! I can't imagine myself giving such a brilliant performance, although I enjoy acting, and can lose myself in the role I am playing. These days, I'm just the retired policeman relying on my sixth-sense.*

There's a devious plan forming in his mind – but it's only an idea, he tells himself; a dangerous idea that shouldn't be carried out, but there again…! He is uncertain. His plan demands to know more about those accident victims, or victims of murder. *What did they look like, and how did they dress? There'll be a recent 'photo of Donald Libella and his housekeeper among the effects stored in Matthew's garage, or my name isn't Nicholas Lightbone!*

He picks up the 'phone and after the (superficial) greeting, comes to the point. "I'd like to get back to the issue of disposing your father-in-law's clothes and think I've found a solution. Our theatre producer mentioned needing old togs for the prop-box, which reminds me of the clothes in your garage. Might that be the answer to at least one of your problems? Quite! Glad you agree!"

There is a moment of thoughtful silence before his face relaxes and breaks into a smile. "Any time? Not sure when you'll be home from work? Having to work overtime? Yes, I understand – extra money at times like this! I know what you mean; I'm on a tight schedule too, organizing an afternoon carnival the first week in June, for the nursing home's centenary celebrations. Told you about that, didn't I? Yes! I'm sure Charmaine will enjoy it too." There's another long pause as Nickbone listens, with growing enthusiasm, to Matthew's suggestion. "Well now, old chap! That's very decent of you letting me into your garage like that… key under the geranium pot at the far end… appreciate your trust! See you later!"

…

Chapter 17

Circus Poppi comes to town!

Colourful posters in strategic places advertise 'Miss Flummi the Flying Clown' as the unchallenged star of the circus ménage. Her mop of bright orange hair seems electrified. Her eyes are whitened and the huge red mouth opens wide as she flies through the air, defying the force of gravity, supported, it seems, by sprawling limbs, feet first, from the trampoline to the trapeze, against the laws of nature. Who cares? There is an aura of magic about her. She has arrived where she belongs and worked like a berserker to get there.

Sally removes the half-empty cup of coffee from the empire-style table matching the exquisitely furnished interior of her caravan; fitted cupboards in egg-shell and gold, ornately patterned walls and the dark red Axminster carpet which puts her in mind of a previous life, the luxurious house she'd once visited. Memories are no longer awesome for the circus star.

While attending to her clown's face, she'll watch them from behind the lace-curtained window, pouring out of the tent like a swarm of bees, spreading about the field; children in the direction of the miniature zoo where there are goats and a couple of Shetland-ponies to be fed with handfuls of straw. Two miniature pigs belong to 'Fearless Fred the Fire-eater,' who will tell parents that pigs are house-trained and can be kept like a dog, which makes it difficult to explain why they can't have one too. The good-natured llama and the donkey are great buddies. The old horse is being saddled, ready to plod backwards and forwards across the field, led by the young stable-hand who'll charge for a ride.

When it's time to collect Gloria, her beautiful Gloria with the nappies that need changing, the baby girl smiles, and sometimes cries; it means she is hungry, which is strange. Is she no longer the undemanding friend with the permanent smile?

Alfonso and Clementina are her godparents and what they say, goes. Clementina won't put up with the strange idea of treating the child like a doll. "Why does she have to sleep on an embroidered pillow?" she demands to know. "Has she been fed? Give her to me and get on with the show!"

…

The man wanders about the field like a lost piece of luggage, searching for someone who no longer exists. Sally Foss is no longer Sally Foss; she is Miss Flummi the clown and waiting behind the curtain.

"You'll be missing the show if you don't get inside this very minute," says Annie the knife-throwing-target as she makes her way across the field for the cowboy-show, which is better than throwing knives in front of an audience of children. "Do you happen to be looking for someone?"

"I'm looking for my daughter!"

"And who would your daughter be, might I ask?"

"Sally Foss – she's a clown!"

Annie stares in surprise and takes a deep breath. "Now who would believe it, for heaven's sake? You are Sally's father – and if you're Sally's father, you are likely to be Gloria's grandfather, are you not?"

There's a moment of silence as Annie patiently waits for this mild mannered man whose face has suddenly turned a light shade of grey, to find his tongue. "Gloria's grandfather? What do you mean, Gloria's grandfather? Gloria was her doll! This is ridiculous – she can't have come alive," replies Matthew and wonders about the sanity of circus folk, mistaking a lost doll for a baby.

"Alive an' kickin' – an' what is the world coming to when a man doesn't even know he's a grandfather. Welcome to the circus, Matthew Foss!"

Being told he's a grandfather, and in the middle of a circus field, is the last thing Matthew has expected.

"Come inside and watch Miss Flummi entertaining the children and later, you can look after Gloria because Clementina has enough on her plate selling tickets for the evening performance – and look at the queue! Oh my goodness there's no shedding tears in this circus, so wipe your eyes, straighten your tongue and follow me!"

The children love her. The mini-clowns chase her around the trampoline and bunches of flowers appear in their ears. What a surprise! Where do they come from? In the afternoon matinee, the tiny clowns toss the flowers to the audience of children, who yell with delight while Miss Flummi sits in her armchair reading the newspaper, ignoring the activities around her. Suddenly, the armchair springs to life. Higher it goes, up and down on the trampoline. She cups an ear and tries to listen. What are they yelling? She'd better watch out or she'll fall from the chair? The chair has sprung to life. It is performing a somersault on its own. Very mysterious!

Miss Flummi returns to earth. She'll catch that tiny clown with the giant sunflower on his head and stop him squirting the water. How dare he? It is time he was taught a lesson! She'll put him in the box and take him away! (The box is a popular commodity among clowns). But the tiny clown escapes through the bottom and is chasing around the circus ring once more, encouraging the audience to scream even louder while Miss Flummi conjures up a new box. More boxes appear; one for each clown.

The ringmaster has had enough. Off with this wild bunch (two of his grandchildren). He collects the five (lightwood) boxes each containing a clown, and removes Miss Flummi's hat before carefully balancing them on her head. She circles the ring and leaves the ménage walking as stiff as a scarecrow, with the pile of boxes still on her head.

When the 'one-wheel-juggler' makes his entrance, the naughty clowns are forgiven and forgotten. He whizzes into the ring, takes a call on his 'one wheel', rides backwards and forwards, circles the ménage and surprise, surprise – juggles the balls that have dropped from his sleeve.

...

Gloria is asleep on the embroidered pillow when father and daughter, having gone through the dispassionate process of reunification, leave the circus. Sally feels uncomfortable. She would rather be cleaning; ridding her father's filth from her beautiful new caravan home, than visiting her mother in a nursing home.

Matthew has overcome the initial surprise, but feels the sorrow of ignorance and regret, having discovered, too late, that he is the grandfather of this beautiful child, now sleeping peacefully, having been fed. He secures her in the cot, in the back seat of the car, and opens the passenger-seat door. "How time flies!" he remarks for wont of something to say because the atmosphere is still strained, despite Gloria being the centre of attention. "Yes Dad! How time flies!" mutters his daughter, unenthusiastically.

"How long has it been?" he asks without waiting for an answer. "Two years? God Almighty, so much has happened in such a short time. But don't expect much from your mother – keeps going off, if you see what I mean, 'though I've told her you're coming. She won't be dressing up for the carnival – 'Bowling Park Amateur Dramatics' have organized a carnival this afternoon. She's beyond that now," he adds sadly.

Should he tell her about his good pal Nickbone, and his wife, Patricia, who'd once been her trainer? He doesn't think so! He might as well speak to the wall for all the attention she is paying. The girl in the passenger-seat is a stranger. Her lack of interest in what had once been her home, pains him.

On their arrival at the nursing-home, the carnival is in full swing: the music – the three-tact rhythm of a waltz, then the banging of drums and a man's voice announcing another attraction, spreads through an open door. Matthew parks the car in front of the four-storey building, surrounded by a park garden with colourful beds of early spring-heather among bright yellow daffodils. Sally looks around, as though searching for some means of escape, while Matthew unfastens the car-seat.

The lift is blocked by a group of old-age revellers wearing paper crowns pulled from crackers, reminding them of long-gone birthday-parties they'd celebrated as children. "Ah! Here's a baby," they coo over the cot, which Matthew and Sally are carrying between them. There's many a pause to admire a sleeping child as they journey down barren corridors. Babies are rare at the end of their lives. "Come and look at the sweet little mite on the embroidered cushion and wearing a beautiful white dress. Doesn't she look like a doll?"

Matthew and Sally climb the final flight of stairs, still carrying the cot between them, past yellow walls decorated with prints of landscapes and forest glades, until they reach a locked door. "Before your mother came here," Matthew speaks in a whisper, "she'd walked to the other side of town to visit your Grandma Foss; your Grandma Foss," he repeats in a cracked voice, "has been dead for twelve years. Charmaine had forgotten..!" His voice almost breaks and he attempts to hold back the tears.

His display of emotion triggers unpleasant memories and she would rather take Gloria and leave him alone. There's a voice somewhere in her mind, telling her to leave right away. But too late! A nurse opens the door and with the forced cheerfulness of having come to terms with misfortune, allows them to enter.

"Sorry to have kept you waiting. We're a bit short-staffed today. Most of them have been taken downstairs to watch the carnival, so I'll leave the door on a latch to save time when you leave."

"Thank you," Matthew says, and bows politely. "How is she today?"

"Same as usual," replies the disappearing nurse.

Where is the beautiful head-turning woman, the accountant who they had relied on for their business success, and the distant mother and wife? She is now pitifully thin, sitting motionless in the armchair, a crumpled puppet with loosened strings; her rich brown hair has turned grey, wavy tresses once resting on her shoulders have been cut to form around a pudding basin, so it seems. Charmaine stares empty-eyed at the mail-order-catalogue and Sally is surprised to feel her own tears, welling up at the back of her eyes.

"Hello, Mum! It's me, Sally, and I've brought Gloria! Do you remember Gloria, my doll?"

"Hello!" Charmaine replies, looking at Matthew in bewilderment.

"It's our Sally!" Matthew reminds her, but something troubles him about his daughter. Why is she confusing her baby with a doll?

Charmaine's face suddenly lightens and she looks at Sally in pleasurable surprise. "Aaah! Sally! How nice to see you. Could you do me a favour?" she whispers with a touch of conspiracy in her voice.

"Yes, of course!"

"Order something for me?"

"From the catalogue, Mum?"

"From this catalogue," she repeats and with a great deal of effort, lifts the heavy catalogue and shows her the page. "I would like to purchase this rocking horse for my daughter. I promised her one for Christmas."

"Yes!" Sally answers uncertainly. Don't you mean your granddaughter?"

"Don't be silly!" Charmaine frowns. "There's some money in that drawer; take it and bring me the change."

Sally will continue conversation, no matter how ridiculous, with this woman who had once been her mother; who she no longer fears or finds it necessary to please, in an attempt at keeping her happy. And the alien: who cares about the man, her mother's lover? Who cares about Zasto, the father of her child? And who cares about her grandfather, the tyrant, or even his housekeeper? She has forgiven them all. She has reached the zenith.

"Such beautiful toys, Mum! Look at this doll! Gorgeous – just like Gloria!"

Charmaine nods her head slowly. "Isn't she just beautiful? Got eyes just like Gloria; definitely eyes like Gloria. Where has Gloria come from?"

Sally doesn't answer and continues turning the pages.

"Do you know..." Charmaine raises her head and scrutinizes her daughter, "...a strange young woman has just been here, speaking to me in such a presumptuous and familiar manner, that I'm extremely glad she has gone. If you happen to meet her, please tell her not to return. I don't want to see her again."

"Don't take any notice," whispers Matthew, looking alarmed as the girl suddenly collects her bag and is about to pick up the cot. "Where are you going? Stay here! She'll be alright in a minute!"

"Don't worry!" Her mouth is tight, her lips pressed together as she turns before leaving the room. "If I don't come back, I'll be downstairs joining in with the party."

"Then leave Gloria with me and I'll bring her to the car when I've finished talking to your mother." Hadn't he warned her? Hadn't he told her about the state her mother is in?

Charmaine, now oblivious to her surroundings, carries on turning catalogue pages as he follows his daughter outside. The ward door is ajar. Soon, she'll return, having got over the shock. He puts the cot with the sleeping baby out of Charmaine's reach and on a sudden impulse takes her limp hand and kisses it passionately, wishing he could turn back the clock.

...

"Awwwl together now! Everybody clap your hands to 'Knees up Mother Brown'!"

"Come and sit down over here, Edith," somebody calls across the room. Edith hops in a sprightly manner towards the offered chair. The unexpected attention has made her the star of the moment and she won't be pushed into the background until she's ready. "Play my favourite song, will you?" Now Edith is flirting again, head to one side and winking at Nickbone through thinning eyelashes.

"I certainly will, my darling!" Nickbone bends down to listen. "There's an old bridge by the stream, Nelly Dean," he promises and in a wavering soprano, she sings the first line as he holds the microphone under her nose. Her voice grows faint as the microphone wavers and an ice-cold shiver runs down Nickbone's spine as he looks through the window and watches Matthew entering the building, carrying a baby in a cot. He drops the microphone. Edith looks insulted, bends down slowly to pick it up and continues singing while Nickbone freezes with horror. The young woman accompanying Matthew can be no other than Sally and they're carrying a baby – her baby? – it must be her baby – into the building. The truth suddenly dawns on him. What was the Spanish word he'd thought meant luggage? *Senor Alfonso Poppi, had collected Miss Foss and the 'recién nacido' from the house in his car.*

To Nickbone, it's inconceivable she should remain unpunished for her crimes – and there's no doubt in his mind that she has murdered, for some incomprehensible reason which has been of little importance to him, whose life has been devoted to the administration of the law. It has troubled him more than anything, this last, unsuccessful case in a long career and his failure to bring this woman to justice; this woman concealed behind the mask of a clown. What a case! And what a finale! It had needed only a little persuasion, a well-meant suggestion, for Matthew to coincide the girl's visit to her mother with the day of the carnival.

But now he's not sure if he can go through with it all. Is it too late? In a far corner of the hall where the parade will begin, members of The Bowling Green Amateur Dramatic Society are awaiting their cue, having carefully rehearsed their parts: Charmaine's lover, the hobby cyclist, is dressed in racing gear and has been brought back to life by the young amateur actor who is a postman. Next to him is Zasto, a primary teacher, now the clown reincarnated and biding his time. The grandfather, the old man in a wheelchair wearing a Panama hat, is not as old as he looks. Cheryl, the souffleuse and make-up artist has done a good job on Benjamin Sykes the sheep farmer, with the scraggy wig covering the blond hair, bushy eyebrows and wrinkles disguising the healthy taint of a man working outdoors. Behind the old man, is Conchita his housekeeper, the olive-skinned member of the group who'll be dancing the Tarantella before very long. Nickbone has congratulated himself over and over again for attaining the old couple's original clothes which have been donated to the theatre by the unsuspecting Matthew. They'll all play their parts according to his directions, however strange it may seem.

Ready to circle the room on his bike when the music begins, the cyclist sweats profusely beneath the light brown wig which Nickbone has insisted he wears beneath the helm. Old people love a clown. They can't resist Zasto's red nose; the tiny bright green hat balancing on a mop of black hair, his thick white mouth smiling a big smile and the ball which plops from his sleeve. They can't wait for the music to begin.

"Stop it all! Stop it all!" Nickbone's pleading and begging goes unheard as the music begins. The marching music booms through the hall – tarum-ta-ta, tarum-ta-ta, and nobody listens to Nickbone.

Just as before, in an earlier life, Sally runs down the stairs two at a time to the frenzied applause of the imaginary audience, the fanfare of trumpets, rolling of drums and clashing of cymbals. The ringmaster, magnificent in red and gold is waiting for his cue behind the dining-room curtains. "Ladies and Gentlemen..!" she remembers him saying as he enters the ménage. Flourishing his top hat and with a ceremonious bow he announces, "It is my very great pleasure to introduce the one and only...," here, another roll of drums to raise the excitement, "...Miss Flummi, the world's greatest clown!"

The clown follows the sound of joviality. The racing cyclist almost knocks her down as she enters the room. Double-doors are now wide open, allowing the waiting crowd to pour inside and watch them parade around the hall. They step to one side as they march into the corridor and out through the door. Zasto is looking amused. Zasto, Zasto, is it Zasto? He thrusts his face towards her, showing dark teeth against thick white lips. His eyes are cold; his smile is humourless and vicious. The cyclist follows, glares at her accusingly. "Get out of the way if you don't want to be trampled upon," he threatens, already in a bad temper and sweating beneath his wig. Grandfather glares at her through bushy eyebrows and the woman behind him stares accusingly, telling her she's an ungrateful bitch for sending a helpless old man and a well-meaning housekeeper to their graves.

A sudden scream echoes throughout the room. People turn their heads. Such a horrendous scream! Could it be one of those 'problem patients' on the third floor?

The ghosts are watching with cold, evil eyes. They follow her as she flees up the stairs, higher and higher. Will she find protection in the arms of her mother?

The arms of her mother are cold and motionless, like the rest of the woman. There's no help to be got from the limp and lifeless man, standing in the corner and holding the doll she wants to take with her. He won't let it go.

She must fly without Gloria! When she flies, she is safe; nothing will harm her. The bed is her trampoline and she is almost there, gaining height, higher and higher, what a wonderful feeling. Who would have thought she could reach such a height?

Up and down, up and down, gaining height, almost reaching the window. The window is open. It is the door to freedom. Why is the trampoline creaking? Trampolines don't creak!

Figures around the bed; she can hear them yelling and howling. Why the noise? Up and down, up and down…does it matter that they are shouting when she is gaining more height? Up and down, higher and higher. At last! One more jump and she has reached the ultimate goal. The ultimate goal is the swing. Nothing! – not even the devil can reach her when she floats through the air on her swing.

She pulls herself up, balances on the crossbar, eager to acknowledge the applause. If they weren't behind her, she'd be taking a call. *Open the window as wide as you can. Isn't it a wonderful experience, flying through the air like a bird?*

There are people below, the cyclist and the clown, the old man in a wheelchair and his housekeeper behind. She can see their faces turned up towards her and waiting. She won't disappoint them; she will fly when the hand lets go of her ankles. The man with the microphone is vaguely familiar. Hands grab her clothes like claws – horrible ghostly hands. She tears them away; she is strong and powerful; they can't hold her back. They won't be allowed to pull her inside!

How funny they look! She laughs hysterically as their faces draw closer; the alien cyclist in red and black stripes; Zasto the clown with the red nose and silly green hat. Behind the shabby old man in the wheelchair is Conchita wearing the floral patterned apron. They have come to meet her and she won't disappoint them. Their faces are rushing towards her, getting larger and larger as she flies through the air. She sees the sudden flash signalling the end of her flight and feels the agonizing pain spreading through her body. A wall of blackness surrounds her. It is taking her away, further and further…

****

Other books written by Susan Duxbury.

Also published by BoD.

'Up The Gum Tree': The adventures of young pioneers in the Australian outback.

'Buschleben': translation of 'Up The Gum Tree' in the German language.

'Spooky Tales' A short book of funny short stories.

Appearing shortly -

"Little Germany' – a history of Bradford's Germans.'

A history of German settlers in Bradford during the 19th-century until World War 1.

Published by Amberley Publishing plc, Stroud.

Available approx September, 2015.